ROUGH RIDE

ROUGH RIDE

PAULLA HUNTER

CAVEL
PRESS

Kenmore, WA

A Camel Press book published by Epicenter Press

Epicenter Press
6524 NE 181st St.
Suite 2
Kenmore, WA 98028

For more information go to:
www.Camelpress.com
www.Coffeetownpress.com
www.Epicenterpress.com
www.paullahunternovels.com

This is a work of fiction. Names, characters, places, brands, media, and incidents are either the product of the author's imagination or are used fictitiously.

Cover design by Scott Book
Design by Melissa Vail Coffman

Rough Ride
Copyright © 2022 by Paulla Hunter

ISBN: 978-1-94207-864-7 (Trade Paper)
ISBN: 978-1-94207-865-4 (eBook)

Printed in the United States of America

*I would like to dedicate this book to God, St. Philomena,
My Husband Roger Schreiner, and My Daughter Stacie Keiter
all of whom have been on my fan bench for decades.*

ACKNOWLEDGMENTS

IF NO MAN IS AN ISLAND that goes double for a book. To all of my Beta readers over the years for all their suggestions, to my two critique groups who all have eagle eyes and kind hearts, to my husband whose knowledge of rodeo was invaluable, and to all my family and friends who never lost faith. And finally I'd like to thank Jennifer McCord, Executive Editor & Associate Publisher Epicenter-Coffeetown-Camel Press for being so patient with me since this was my first rodeo.

CHAPTER 1

Darcy Moreland parked at the dusty north end of the Cheyenne Rodeo Days midway and got out of her well-used baby blue Audi 2000. The hot July sun slipped toward the western skyline. She had been in Cheyenne less than a week and her apartment looked like a disorganized warehouse with open cartons of clothes, books, and other essentials for herself and her dog Mac spilling onto the floor.

It didn't seem possible that she was back home again in Cheyenne, Wyoming. The small city was the capital of Wyoming, filled with whole blocks of government buildings. It was over a mile high and inserted on an unremarkable rolling prairie in between two mountain ranges the Rockies to the south, and the Snowy Range to the west. Originally, it was a supply town for the Union Pacific Railroad and dubbed "Hell On Wheels" because it had more saloons than railroad workers. A slight exaggeration, but the drinking culture still flourished especially during Cheyenne Rodeo Days.

She had lived here all her life except when she left to go to the University of Wyoming in Laramie and took her first job at a Kansas City, Kansas TV station. She had liked the work and was delighted when her boss moved her from doing the weather reporting to investigative reporting which she loved. Coming back home and working for the one, small, TV station seemed like a step back.

She mentally ticked off the usual reasons for returning home, romantic failures, loss of job, though technically she quit. In her four years at the Kansas station she still didn't feel like part of a community. She tried. She really tried. But Kansas wasn't Wyoming.

When she called her old college friend Zach Horton to tell him she was leaving Kansas he asked her to come work for him at KCWY TV News. The annual rodeo was gearing up and he knew she had cut her teeth on Cheyenne Rodeo Days. Her dad, a retired Electrical Engineer, had been a rodeo volunteer for over thirty years and worked his way up to being the Rodeo Chairman, one of the ten major committees that oversaw the 2,400 volunteers each year. The rodeo was almost 125 years old and still a favorite for cowboys looking for a high pay day and raising their chances of going to the National Finals Rodeo in Las Vegas.

She took a moment to gaze at the brilliant sunset trailing gold and pink streamers across the endless horizon. When she used to live here, she took for granted the multicolored, pastel, or brilliant gold, red, and purple sunrises, and sunsets.

She smiled, took off her new straw cowboy hat and put on her laminated press pass which dangled from a lanyard, and replaced her hat. "Good to go," she said aloud.

Beyond the gate, she spotted the videographer she had heard of but not yet met. Bill Netters slouched against a post, cell phone plastered to his ear, and camera bracketed between his feet. Seconds after he saw her, he jammed his phone into his back pocket.

"Is the glare going to be permanent every time we work together?" Darcy asked when she reached him.

"As long as you keep screwing up my time off." He bent down to jerk up his camera.

Darcy took a deep breath. "Netters, I requested you because I heard you're the best. It's as simple as that. I'm new at the station and I want to show them what I can do. I didn't know you had a date tonight or I wouldn't have asked for you." She waited for some cooperative sign. She needed to have a good work relationship with this guy.

Netters shrugged and shouldered the unwieldy camera. "Let's get this done."

Relieved, Darcy smiled. "How 'bout we shoot a sweeping wide shot focused up the midway to catch all the lights and the crowd and a medium close-up for my spiel?"

"Okie-dokie."

She caught the not-so-subtle sarcasm. "Is that code for, 'Bite me, Darcy Moreland? That's a lame-ass, cliché shot?'" she smiled. "I can take constructive criticism you know."

Netters shrugged, but his mouth twitched into a grin.

"Dazzle me, Mr. Videographer. What would you suggest?"

"A short master of the crowds and lights, then a subjective, traveling shot as we near the Ferris wheel. The 'You Are There' feel. I'd do a Dutch angle to make the wheel look even higher than it is."

Darcy's gaze slid to the wheel. She arched her head back, held onto her hat, and took in in the sheer height of the 30-foot ride. "You'd have to lie on the ground to do that, wouldn't you?"

"Yeah. So?" Netters cleaned his lens, then stuck the soft cloth into his back pocket.

Darcy braced her hands on her hips. "So, I thought you had a date. You don't want to get all gunked up just for a fancy shot, do you?"

"Is 'gunked up' a professional term?" Netters sighted in the angle.

"You know what I mean."

He barked a short laugh. "Don't worry about my non-existent love life. I was just talking to Cheryl when you walked up. She said she'd meet me downtown."

"That's good, isn't it?" Darcy ambled along beside him as he got in position.

"No. It means 'catch me if you can.'" Netters looked down at her from his gangly six-foot height. "How long has it been since you've been downtown during Rodeo Days?"

"A while." Darcy realized she hadn't been home the last four years for Rodeo Days. At first, Darcy was the newbie at the Kansas station and hesitated to ask for an extra week of vacation. Later, she got buried in her work and didn't vacation at all. She couldn't count the number of times her parents had asked her to come to Cheyenne in the summer or to their winter home in Prescot, but something always came up.

"Let's just say, a little 'gunk' isn't going to be a problem."

Netters sauntered farther up the midway switching his grubby Bronco's cap, so the bill rested on his back and neck He turned around and walked backward for a couple of steps, gauging the distance.

Darcy watched Netters and admired his focus. The sounds and the bright lights of the carnival midway did not distract him as he looked through his camera to set up the frame.

He lowered the camera, motioned her out of the shot, and strode toward the Ferris wheel. People dodged out of his way; the bright light mounted on his camera clearing the path.

"Now, you." He waved the end of the camera at her as if it were an assault rifle. Darcy stepped in center shot, and Netters moved close enough to count her fillings.

"Back off!" Darcy squirmed. "Medium close-up, not microscopic surgery."

He laughed but hauled the camera back.

"Levels?" She placed the mic at chin level.

"Yeah. Say something sweet."

"'Candy is dandy, but liquor is quicker.' Dorothy Parker. How's that?"

"Fine. Whenever you're ready."

She raised the microphone and began her narrative:

"The carnival takes on a unique look and ambience at night. The lights sparkle, and the noises fade to a low hum. There are still a few children out with parents in tow, but the average age of the crowd on the midway has increased and the smell of cotton candy, corndogs, and spilled beer, is stronger, which almost mask the slight barnyard stench from behind the arena and the rough stock pens.

"Muffled strains of the Night Show in the arena clash with the raucous bells and jangling of the carnival attractions.

"Excited shrieks pierce the summer night from riders on the Zipper and the Hammer, raised a counterpoint to the overall melody of celebration."

She slashed the flat of her hand under her chin. "Okay . . . cut. How was that?"

"Poetry."

Darcy shot him a full-watt grin. "Yeah, wasn't it?"

"I'm going to lie down now. Make sure no one steps on me. Think you can handle it?"

She opened her sherry-colored eyes Kewpie-Doll wide and simpered, "Maybe we should call Zach and have him send out some of those big gaffer guys who work at the station."

Netters ignored her sarcasm and dragged his foot in short arcs at the base of the Ferris wheel and cleaned a patch of asphalt. Satisfied, he handed over his camera, got down on his back, and motioned for her to pass it back.

"Face the other way, so you can stop some drunk from crashing into me." Netters ignored her irreverent three fingered Girl Scout salute.

The crowd eddied around them as if they were rocks in a stream. She prodded a large man wearing a *Cowboys Can Ride All Night* T-shirt to the side It was a charmed summer night on the carnival midway.

Her mind wandered and even the strident music, whirs, and bells could not dampen her spirit. It was good to be home.

Kansas had been great for her first job out of college. She liked the station she worked for, but she couldn't get used to the tornadoes and the heavy humidity. Kansas ranked second nationally for the number of tornadoes per year. Whenever she hovered in the apartment building's basement with Kevin, her longtime boyfriend, and co-worker, she'd remind him that the worst that ever happened in Cheyenne was a blizzard or a hailstorm. All you had to do was have food on hand and wait until they cleared the streets. Darcy knew it was a total fantasy, but perversely she liked predictability.

Meanwhile, Kevin had accepted a job to produce the news at a Tampa Bay station, and insisted she move with him. Annoyance turned to clarity, when she realized she didn't love him as deeply as she should have. They parted as friends and assured each other they would keep in touch, but Darcy had no illusions about a long distance romance.

If she moved anywhere, she wanted to move home. Darcy missed her mom and dad who would come in soon from their winter home in Arizona.

She missed the crisp air, the bright blue clear sky, and the incredible view of the Rocky Mountains just a short drive out of town.

Once she decided to move back home, things moved rapidly. She transferred from a larger market TV station to a much smaller market station with no trouble. She barely had time to call her folks and tell them she had arrived safely, and already had a job as an investigative reporter and expert on all things about Cheyenne Rodeo Days at the local TV station. And yes, she had an apartment, but thanks for the offer for the basement guest room.

A thud from behind her punctuated by a loud, "Oh, shit!" from Netters and screams from the crush of people who pushed close, jolted her from her trance.

She spun around. "Oh, my God!" she gasped. High-pitched shouts for help burst from the crowd.

Netters lurched to his feet, his face ashen. He scrambled about three yards toward the ground by the Ferris wheel.

The crumpled body lay face up at the foot of the Ferris wheel. A pale hand rested in stark contrast to the black asphalt, arms outstretched, as if trying to fly. With a lurch, Darcy thought at first it was a small child.

Netters crouched low and peered at the body. It was a teenaged girl, her face turned to the side, her long light brown hair straggled behind her.

Darcy couldn't look away, transfixed by the blood pooled like a small, black lake under the girl's head, the moist, metallic smell of blood in the soft summer air made her gag.

"A fall . . . from the Ferris wheel . . . two minutes ago." Netters shouted into his phone.

Two minutes? Had it been that long? Darcy's stomach lurched, and her knees went weak. *Don't throw up!* She told herself. *Don't throw up!*

The girl looked about sixteen or seventeen. She wore a pair of putty-colored jeans, a boldly-patterned pink shirt, and a pair of cordovan boots barely scuffed on the soles.

Darcy forced herself to squat. She snaked her unsteady hand under the girl's shoulder-length hair. She tried to find a pulse in the girl's small neck, glanced up at Netters and shook her head.

"No pulse," he said into the phone. "That's right, south end of the midway. Bill Netters . . . yeah. I'll stay." Netters stuffed his phone into his back pocket.

The alarmed crowd swelled to four or five people deep and pushed closer.

"Stand back, folks. Give us some room. Clear a path for the ambulance."

Darcy's head snapped up. A large man, at least six feet, with massive shoulders and a belly that spoke of excess, rushed toward them, his bulk blocked the glare of the garish lights.

"What happened? Did you see what happened?"

He frowned past Darcy and the girl on the ground and spoke to Netters.

"She fell from the Ferris wheel." Netters glanced up.

The man squinted, staring at the now motionless Ferris wheel. The ride had stopped, trapping passengers. "Get those people off that damned thing!" he shouted at the carney in charge of the ride, then turned back to Netters.

"Are you sure? Could you be mistaken?" The large man had a muddy-beige-tinged face with all the color leached out. Darcy noticed the greasy sheen of sweat on his forehead.

"I saw her fall." Netters's stood and his voice shook a little, but he tensed as if prepared for a fight.

By now, two patrolmen on park assignment began to clear the perimeter. They separated all the people who disembarked from the Ferris wheel to interrogate.

The shrill yowl of sirens interrupted the exchange and an

ambulance pulled up, paramedics jumped out, stooped to check vital signs, then covered the body out of respect, and waited for the Medical Examiner and the crime scene investigators. Darcy backed out of the way and pulled Netters with her.

Two police cars flanking the ambulance and one black F150 Ford pickup pulled onto the midway. The big guy's face turned red. His eyes darted from the crowd, to the body, and then to the cops. He stared at the camera Netters had tucked under his arm.

"Um, listen. My name is Tom Hayes, and I own and operate this carnival. I'd appreciate a look at that video." He smiled, but it was not sociable.

"Sure thing." Netter's lips thinned to a slash. "Tune in to the ten o'clock news tonight."

Hayes's jaw turned white. He took a deep breath and forced his voice to sound reasonable. "I'd like to see it before it hits the news. Any chance of that?"

"I'm more concerned we get that girl out of here." Netters looked at the assembled crowd and back at Hayes. "Has the Medical Examiner been called?"

"I'm guessing they ME was called right after you notified the police." Darcy said

"Does anyone recognize this girl? Was she with anyone?" Darcy asked, shouting over the crowd noises.

"It's Bridget Emerson . . ."

Darcy spun around and noticed a skinny, teenaged girl, trembling so hard her bones almost rattled.

The name tugged at the edges of Darcy's memory. In another time, she had known a little girl named Bridget Emerson, with deep brown eyes and a cap of bouncing curls. This couldn't be her.

Darcy seized the girl's arm. "Not Doc Emerson's kid?"

The young girl swiped at the fat tears on her cheeks with the back of her hand and nodded.

Darcy watched the police take photos, place markers, place the body with care into a black bag. After the Medical Examiner called time of death, they lifted her onto a gurney and pushed her into the back of the Medical Examiner's vehicle to transport her to the County Morgue. Darcy gazed at the taillights as it pulled away.

"Damn it to hell!"

The girl flinched. Darcy softened her voice. "Sorry, sorry. I used to babysit Bridget a long time ago." Darcy glanced again at the ambulance. How could this happen? She shook her head to clear it and turned back to the girl. "What's your name?"

"Stacie Rogers."

"Stacie, what happened?" Darcy slipped her arm around the horrified girl. The girl's face looked yellowish-green, like an old bruise. Darcy worried the girl would slip into shock once she realized Bridget was dead.

She led Stacie away from the center of the confusion over by the back of one of the merchandizing tents.

"Stay here," Darcy told the weeping girl. "I'll see if I can get you some water." Stacie nodded and Darcy scanned the midway for a close-by source. She was so focused she almost collided with a brick wall of a man. He was dressed in a black t-shirt and black jeans, and had a toothpick dangling from his lips. He did not step back, just grabbed her upper arms to keep her from falling.

He looked down at her. "Are you all right?"

"Yes, I'm fine." Darcy said. "I'm just trying to find some water for that young girl. She was a friend of the girl who fell, Are you with the police or something?"

"Detective Hank Nelson," he said, and pointed to a leather-backed badge at his waist.

Darcy noticed his dark hair curled from beneath a faded black cap with some indistinct insignia on it. His blue eyes stared into hers with mild curiosity. "And you are?"

She held up her laminated press badge from around her neck "Darcy Moreland KCWY News. This is Bill Netters, my videographer."

Detective Nelson pulled a small notebook out of his back pocket and wrote their names and the station's number.

"You two watched her fall?" He shifted the toothpick to the other side of his mouth.

Darcy shook her head. "No, I didn't. Netters did. He was on the ground." She gestured toward the camera clutched in Netters's hand.

"You don't have it on video, do you?" Nelson's attention shifted back to Netters.

"Sure do."

"Now wait a minute!" Tom Hayes pushed himself between Netters and the detective. "I need to see that video."

"He's official," Netters clarified for Hayes and turned to the detective. "You can look at a playback from the camera, or we can hook it up to a video source."

"That would be a big help. We'll have to take custody of the tape until we can make a copy, but can you meet us at the station? I'll give them a head's up." Detective Nelson pulled out his phone. "I'll meet you down there."

"Sure," Netters said and looked at Darcy. "Would you square this with Zach?"

Darcy gaped at him. Was he crazy? They needed to get this on the air . . . unless the police asked them not to. She grimaced. "This should go over well."

Detective Nelson glanced at her, cocked his head. Annoyed, Darcy faced Netters. "I've at least got to give him some kind of timeline."

Nelson continued to jot notes. "Tell him about an hour."

Darcy raised her phone. Wendy, the station's receptionist, patched her through. She glanced around the area secured with yellow police tape. Darcy bought a bottle of water at a vendor. She looked for Stacie. The girl huddled on the edge of the crowd. Darcy walked toward her but stopped when Zach Horton yelled in her ear.

"Where the hell are you guys? This was a simple assignment." Zach made no effort to hide his irritation.

"A teenage girl fell from the Ferris wheel. Doc Emerson's kid, but that hasn't been confirmed," Darcy blurted and tried not to focus on the gruesome reality of the statement.

"Shit!" There was a slight pause. "Do we have video?"

"Yes, but the police want to watch it first, notify next of kin etc. Netters is meeting them downtown."

"When do I get the story?"

"I'll make preliminary notes, and the detective said Netters would be done in about an hour. I'll do the lead-in in the studio."

Zach sighed. "Definitely not CNN. We will break it on the 10 o'clock. Um . . . Darcy . . .?"

"Yeah?"

"You okay?"

"Yeah, wobbly, but I'll make it. Damn it, Zach. I used to babysit her." She snapped her mouth shut, to block a sob. She had forgotten for a moment she was talking to Zach-the-station manager, not Zach-her-long-time-friend. This was not the time to blubber. "Bye."

Darcy continued toward Stacie. A uniformed officer had finished questioning her and walked away.

Between the back end of The Hat and Tack tent and another that sold western wear, Stacie huddled with her arms wrapped around her slim body as if trying to comfort herself.

Darcy opened her arms. The sobbing girl staggered into them and collapsed against her. She stroked Stacie's back and murmured phrases like "It's okay." when it clearly was not. Darcy handed Stacie the water.

She fought to keep her own tears at bay. Stacie leaned back and wiped her eyes on her sleeve, looking down at the ground embarrassed.

"It's a horrible tragedy." Darcy passed Stacie a tattered, but clean tissue from her jean's pocket and looked around. "Did you come out here with friends?"

"Yeah, but they're all in the Expo Hall. I don't want to go find them. The police offered to give me a ride, but my folks would have a heart attack if I came home in a cop car."

Darcy glanced at her watch. "I have a little time before I have to get back to the station. I could give you a ride home."

Stacie looked up, relieved, and gave her a wobbly smile.

"Let's go." Darcy slipped her arm around Stacie's shoulders and they hiked through the crowd. While Darcy clicked the remote to unlock the car doors, she looked across the roof at Stacie. "Won't your friends wonder where you are?"

"I'll text Jason that I'm going home."

Stacie tapped in a text. She didn't mention Bridget's death, Darcy assumed. Not news you'd want to leave on a text, Darcy thought.

"He didn't pick up," Stacie explained, "but he checks his phone a lot."

Darcy drove Stacie to her home in The Hills, a small neighborhood north of the park. "Had you known Bridget long?" Darcy negotiated the sharp right turn onto a main road.

"Yeah, since we were little." Stacie stared out the open side window. A small moan escaped, and tears splashed onto the front of her shirt. "We don't hang out together much anymore."

"Why?" Darcy prodded. "Did you stop being friends?"

"Bridget was busy. School, new boyfriend, CRD Riders." Stacie sniffled and wiped her eyes again.

"Little Bridget Emerson was a Rider?"

The Riders were an equestrian group of high-school-aged girls who tried out every year to represent Cheyenne Rodeo Days. Darcy was a decent rider, but she had never been tempted to try out.

"Yeah. The last two years. It took a lot of time." Stacie pointed. "Right here. We're the second house from the corner."

"Is someone home?" Darcy made the turn onto the wide driveway.

"Yeah. My mom and dad never go anywhere. I'll be okay. Thanks." Stacie slid out of the car.

Darcy watched her run to the door of a ranch style house draped with luxurious purple clematis.

Stacie waved goodbye after she opened the unlocked door, and Darcy backed her car down the driveway and headed for the studio.

Bridget's un-scuffed boots and new clothes made sense now, knowing she was in Riders. Riders got several new outfits each season.

Gripping the wheel until her knuckles whitened, Darcy sped around a dawdling slate-blue Cadillac.

She did some mental calculations. Bridget was six when Darcy had watched her. Darcy had been fourteen at the time and thought she was pretty grown up with her first job. Two years later, distracted by boys and volleyball, Darcy stopped babysitting.

Bridget pestered Darcy at the Rodeo Committee picnic every year. Darcy remembered being annoyed and winced now at the memory. Hot tears flooded her eyes. She blinked, to clear them. Bridget was too young to have died in an instant like that.

How could such a bright and vibrant young girl just fall from a Ferris wheel? Didn't they have safety regulations or something? Who was responsible?

She remembered Tom Hayes and how determined he was to look at the video before the police did. Probably behind on his safety inspections and terrified of liability and litigation.

She swerved around an SUV slowing down to take a corner.

The questions kept swirling. Why was Bridget alone? Didn't she have any friends with her? Stacie was the only person who'd admit knowing her, and she said they hadn't been together tonight. Bridget's death was distressing and dramatic, surrounded with silence on all sides.

Darcy remembered a quote by broadcaster Amy Goodman about journalism. "Go to where the silence is and say something…"

The raw image of the small, broken body oozing dark blood, and surrounded with the refuse of a carnival midway, turned Darcy's stomach.

Strewn amid the empty beer cans, the discarded hot dogs, and the crumpled paper was all that remained left of a once beautiful child.

Darcy vowed to go to where the silence was and say something.

CHAPTER 2

THE DRIVE BACK TO THE STATION was too brief to sort out her feelings. Darcy never imagined she would miss those long metro-commutes she'd endured in Kansas City, but tonight she did.

She pulled into the KCWY parking lot, turned off the engine and sat there for a minute, resting her forehead on the steering wheel.

When she thought she was calmer, she opened her car door, took a deep bracing breath, walked the few steps to the building, and pushed through the wide glass doors of the studio. Zach stood at the reception desk, chomping on a large unlit stogie.

"Nice look, Zach. Your Sicilian ancestors must be proud." She smiled at him.

Zach's handsome face split in a toothy grin. "My ancestors are always proud. Arrogance is my birthright." His smile faded as he took in Darcy's strained face.

"Com'ere." Zach grabbed her arm and steered her into his dingy corner office, kicking the door closed with his foot. He deposited Darcy into the nearest chair.

Edging his hip onto his littered desktop, he leaned into her. "I know you've had a rough night," he said softly. "You need to gut it out a little longer. I got a call from Netters, and he'll meet us here in about fifteen minutes. Can you hang on that long?"

"Absolutely," she said with more confidence than she felt. "I'll go touch up my smeary mascara, fluff up my hat-hair, and meet you back here to shoot the lead-in. Okay?"

"That would be great." Zach patted her on the shoulder.

Darcy stood. "Zach?"

"Yeah?"

"Thanks."

"Sure, all part of the job."

Zach gave her a short peck on the cheek, and she suddenly felt much better.

"I thought you had to sell your soul to be a station manager," she teased.

"You'd think so, wouldn't you? Turns out even Satan has standards."

Darcy laughed. Not a belly-shaker, but a laugh, nonetheless. It felt oddly healing.

THERE OUGHT TO BE A LAW *that you don't have to look in a mirror for at least twenty-four hours after you've experienced an emotional trauma.* She sat and stared at her reflection in the merciless glare of the makeup mirror. She tried to clean off the brown smears of mascara and replenish her lipstick and liner.

It felt therapeutic to go through the motions of the habitual activity. It implied control . . . obviously a fiction of the most awful kind.

Darcy finished her primping and went to find Netters and Zach holed up in one of the editing rooms. They didn't turn around when she entered.

The police had kept the original but allowed Netters to make a copy. The first shot opened on the monitor, the walk through, and the stand up where Darcy gushed about the delights of the midway—then the change of angle. Holding her breath, she knew what was coming, but she couldn't look away.

The Ferris wheel climbed higher and higher, rising into the sky. The camera panned up, and there it was—the horrifying picture of Bridget beginning her free fall from the top of the Wheel. Darcy gasped as Bridget bounced off an empty basket on her way down. The girl didn't flail or kick, and if she screamed, it was lost in the general noise of the carnival.

Darcy's hands covered her mouth to keep from screaming as Bridget's little body hit, her back on the asphalt, did one thuddy little bounce, and sprawled in a motionless heap. The view changed to a confusion of leg shots and wild angles. Netters had left the camera live as he rushed to Bridget's side.

"The police asked that we only show a brief shot the Ferris wheel and not show the fall," Netters said. "They kept the original of the video to analyze. They think there might be a shadow of a figure in the basket she fell from."

"You mean she wasn't alone up there?" Darcy could barely choke it out. "That would mean . . ."

"At the very least it would mean that someone knows how she happened to fall," Zach said.

"At the very worst . . . someone might have pushed her," Netters added.

The door clattered open, and the tall young man swaggered into the room. He resembled a sulky, preppy brat with his spiked blond hair and his mouthful of perfect teeth covered at the moment with whitening strips.

Three heads swiveled toward him. Netters smacked the pause button on the console and dimmed the screen completely.

"Hi, guys," he greeted them with forced joviality.

"What are you doing in here, Adkins?" Zach asked, talking around his still unlit cigar.

It was telling that Zach was being so abrupt. She was still trying to work out the people and the pecking order at her new job.

"Um, I got a tip from my police source—"

"You mean the receptionist you're sleeping with down there?" Zach interrupted.

Adkins' face flushed, and his jaw tightened, but his voice remained calm. "My *source* told me there was an accident on the carnival midway, and it might have been the result of 'foul play' as they say."

"Adkins try not to be any more of a jerk than you absolutely have to be, okay?" Zach said.

That answers my question about Adkins.

"You don't have to be insulting, Zach. I was just offering my investigative services."

Zach finally removed the cigar from his mouth and used it to poke in Adkins's general direction. "Darcy Moreland, this is Bryce Adkins. He fancies himself a young Mike Wallace. You know, run-and-gun journalism, tabloid-trash reporting."

She tried to squeeze a smile out, but her cheeks froze.

Adkins rewarded her effort at social pleasantries with a dismissive wave of his hand. "Yeah . . . yeah. I know. The new girl from Kansas."

"Did he just call me a girl?" She stood.

Zach grasped her arm before she reached Adkins. "The *boy* has trouble with the English language, Darcy." Zach tugged her back into her chair. "He meant to say the new investigative journalist this station hired, right, Adkins?"

"Right, yeah. Whatever. Whatever. Whatever. I thought if you needed me to poke around on this . . . Adkins perched on the desk in front of Zach.

"What I need, Adkins, is for you to cover what I assign you to cover, without pissing everyone off. I got a call from Gary Romero, the rodeo chairman."

"What was he whining about?"

"He wants you to stay out of the cowboy ready-area unless you've been cleared. Is that simple enough for you?"

"This local-yokel-cow-fest has too many stupid rules."

"Follow the damn rules of this *cow-fest,* or Romero will have you banned from the park."

"He can't do that."

"Of course, he can—and will. It's private property. If you lose your press credentials, you're of no use to me." Zach let the implied threat linger.

Adkins grunted and scooted off the desk. He almost slammed out of the editing bay but caught himself in time.

Zach watched him leave. "Guy's an idiot. I wouldn't tolerate him on staff except . . ."

"He has a concerned, connected relative who wants to get the kid some broadcasting experience, right?" Netters supplied.

"Got it in one." Zach continued to gnaw on the now soggy end of his cigar.

The three of them turned back to watch the video again, mesmerized by the gruesome sight of Bridget falling passively through the air.

"I don't think I heard her scream, did you?" Darcy turned to Netters who was resetting to the beginning one more time.

He stopped what he was doing and looked up at her, startled. "No, come to think of it, I didn't hear anything except the generic noises of the carnival until her body landed. Certainly not the panicked shriek you'd expect from someone hurtling to the ground like that. Hang on; let me see if I can zoom in a little closer."

"Poor Bridget. She was a sweet little girl." Darcy shivered. "Doesn't this feel ghoulish to you? Zooming in . . . and . . . and watching it over and over again?"

"Yeah, a little," Netters answered as he adjusted his playback board. "But now I'm curious. It happened so fast, I wonder if I hadn't been filming at that particular moment, anyone would have noticed her fall in all the confusion."

"My God." Darcy wrapped her arms around her waist and curled into a slouch. She felt sick to her stomach. "Not much of a crowd even gathered until you and I knelt down by her."

"Yeah. The owner yelling at people to clear the way for the ambulance, only made more people push in to see what had happened. Let's see what shows up on the video."

He played it again. The three of them were silent. Netters found the first track once more and played it again. The click of the controls sounded as loud as artillery fire. They stared at the screen. Bridget fell. Her mouth didn't even open. She could have been a bag of garbage flung off the porch. The video showed no human reaction, no arms spinning, no legs kicking, just gravity pulling her tiny body inexorably to her death. Maybe she was already dead.

Netters rewound to the beginning of the segment he needed to cut for the story. He handed the thumb drive to Zach.

"By the way, boss. I'm going to grab a couple of beers at the brewery. I won't be back tonight."

"See ya tomorrow."

Zach nodded then draped his arm around Darcy's shoulder. "Can I buy you a beer after you do your report?"

"It might work better if I had the beer first."

"Probably not." He chuckled as he gave her half a hug.

"Seriously, I want to do this report and go home, and watch it on the news like everyone else. Maybe it will seem a little less real that way. Does that sound crazy?"

"No—but don't take my word for it. I'm not all that sane myself."

Darcy laughed. "Give Kelly and the boys my love," she said over her shoulder.

Darcy sleepwalked out of the building after a short taping session in front of a blue screen. Blessedly, no one tried to talk to her. The soft summer night air wrapped around her like a blanket. She stood by her car door and forced herself to breathe deeply.

It took her about five minutes to get to The Algonquin Apartments. She had rented an apartment in this somewhat archaic building that she had always loved. It was right downtown and had the added bonus of being the home of her former English teacher, Abby McNeil, who turned out to be a wonderful dog sitter. Darcy climbed the front steps wearily and tried to put on a happy face for Abby, and Mac, her Cairn Terrier. It was comforting to have someone waiting.

Her finger poised to ring the bell when the door flew open.

"I was getting worried, and—" Abby said. She looked at Darcy intently. "What happened? You look awful."

Mac scampered around her feet. Darcy leaned down and picked him up and hugged him tightly. He licked her cheek, and she petted his rough coat. Dutiful greetings completed, she put him down, and he trotted off to play with his toys.

Darcy sank into the welcoming embrace of a Chesterfield armchair and let out a large sigh. "Didn't turn out to be an easy shoot," she said.

"I can see that. Before you tell me, what happened, let me get you some hot cocoa."

"Thanks, Abby, but I think this is a little beyond cocoa."

"Not the way I make it." She smiled and left the room. "Go ahead and take those boots off. Nobody in this building will still be up after the ten o'clock news to see you pad to your apartment in your stocking feet."

"I'd need a boot jack to get these off."

Abby poked her blonde head around the wall that separated the kitchen from the rest of the apartment. "In my youth I preferred some guy with his cute butt facing me while he pulled off my boots, but sadly those days are gone. You'll find a boot jack under the sofa."

Darcy got down on all fours and peered under the sofa and sure enough . . . a bootjack. "I wouldn't have taken you for someone who wore cowboy boots regularly enough to keep a bootjack handy."

Darcy cocked her heel into the jack and slid her foot out easily. She repeated with the other boot, then leaned back contentedly, and wiggled her toes.

"Old habit . . . a hangover from my errant youth." Abby smiled as she came in with a tray with two steaming mugs frothed over with whipped cream.

"You had an errant youth? Tell, tell." Darcy took a mug and a spoon.

"Not right now. Too long a story and too brief a night." Abby settled into the corner of her overstuffed sofa and picked up her own mug.

Darcy blew over the top to cool it down and took a hearty sip. Darcy's eyes popped open in surprise. "Why Ms. Abigail McNeil, you've spiked my cocoa."

"Just a whisper of Bailey's Irish Cream. What do you think?"

"Tasty."

"Well, now that the preliminaries are over, what happened?"

Closing her eyes, Darcy leaned her head back for a moment and tried to form the exact right words in her mind, but she was too tired. She gave up and just started.

"A teenaged girl fell from the Ferris wheel and died."

Abby didn't even gasp. Darcy opened her eyes to see if she was still in the room. She was. She sat quietly holding her mug carefully in her hands, waiting for Darcy to say something more.

"I didn't see the fall, but Netters got it on video, and I watched it at the station. It was vile. She was so young. Oh, Abby! I used to babysit her. Her dad and my dad were friends, and I took care of her."

"Did you see her body?"

"Netters and I were the first to reach her. I felt for a pulse, but she was already dead."

"Sometimes reporting the news isn't pretty, but it is necessary. Chroniclers have always been important to civilization," Abby said in her her her best teacher voice while she patted Darcy's knee.

"It didn't feel important. It felt horrible and sad."

Mac must have heard the change in her voice, because he left his toys, a huge sacrifice, and sidled over to plop at her feet. The combination of Mac's loyalty, Abby's support, and the lovely, spiked cocoa was working well. She felt her kite string begin to unwind.

"Will the report be on tonight?" Abby sounded concerned.

"Just a shortened piece. The police want to go over our video and see if they can piece together the whys and hows."

"Are there mysteries? Well, of course there are. What a silly question for me to ask."

"Not silly at all. One of the temptations of this job is trying to put stories into cubbyholes, to sort them and solve any inconsistencies—like lining up all your shoes in the closet. Trouble is people and events don't always sort well."

"But when they do, it must be satisfying. More cocoa, dear?"

"No, I'd better not. I'm melting already."

"Don't sit up and watch the news with me. You've had a long, trying day. Why don't you scoot off to bed?"

Darcy extracted her now boneless body from the recesses of Abby's comfortable chair. "I think I will. Tomorrow's likely to be hectic." She knelt down to start to pick up Mac's toys.

"Leave them, dear. I assume he'll be visiting tomorrow as well?"

"He'd be thrilled, but don't you want to be alone? You haven't had much time to yourself since I moved in."

"Nonsense. I enjoy his company. He's no trouble at all."

"Okay, but I want you to think of some way I can repay you."

"Not necessary."

"It is for me. If you can't come up with something, I can't bring Mac here." Darcy's jaw tightened in a stubborn line.

"Well, all right, dear." Abby began to gather the cocoa mugs and head to the kitchen. "Don't worry about waking me in the morning. I rarely sleep past six."

"Great," she said as she scooped Mac up under her arm and picked up her boots. "We'll see you tomorrow."

"Uh-huh," Abby grunted assent over the sound of running water.

She let herself out. Darcy climbed the steps to the second floor. Mac didn't weigh as much as a bag of sugar, but she put him on his feet as soon as they got to the top of the stairs. She wasn't sure she could hold herself up, let alone carry Mac.

Compared to Abby's apartment with its homey smells and overstuffed furniture, her apartment felt bleak. Boxes still littered the floor and furniture was scattered about with no plan.

"Well, no place looks its best at night," she muttered. Blatantly untrue as that statement was, she felt reassured. "At least we have our bed, Mac old boy."

She led the way to the bedroom and began to get ready for a long numbing sleep. She had barely pulled her cell from her pocket and put it on the dresser top when it rang. Startled, Darcy almost dropped it.

"Hello?"

"Hi. This is Hank Nelson at the police station . . ."

"Yes?"

"I'm sorry to call so late, but I didn't know what your schedule tomorrow would be . . ."

"How did you get my cell number? I only gave you my office number at the scene." An irrational fear crawled up the back of her neck. When she had lived in Kansas, she had learned to be suspicious of inventive strangers.

"Um, Netters gave it to me when he dropped off the copy of the video. Is that a problem?"

"I'd prefer that he not hand out my cell number."

"It's okay. I'm a cop. You know, one of the good guys."

"Don't patronize me, Nelson." She was tired, she was stressed, and she felt totally wrung out.

"Detective."

"What?"

"Detective Nelson is what you call me. After we know each other better, you can call me Hank."

She sighed and tried to dial down her snark level. "I guess I deserved that. I apologize. So . . .?"

"So . . . I would like to talk to you tomorrow if you could come down to the station."

"Why?"

"Because you were at the scene and . . ."

"Netters saw it, not me. I can't tell you anything."

"Do you have a phobia about police stations?"

"I don't want to waste your time." Darcy ambled to the bed and flopped on her back.

"Thanks for your consideration, but a lot of times people at the scene see something or remember something that helps. They just don't connect it to the crime."

She sat straight up. Her stomach rolled over. "Crime? As in murder?"

"We're not sure yet. Someone rode with her in the basket, and the fact that they didn't come forward is at least suspicious, at most criminal. So, can you help?"

"Of course. I'll try. What time?"

"If you want to come in early, say 7:30 or 8, I'll buy you a cup of coffee. Okay?"

"Sure."

"Thanks. See you tomorrow."

"Bye." She waited for a response, but he'd hung up.

Murdered? Little Bridget—murdered. She was just a baby. What had she done in her short life that would lead to such a horrible death?

Shimmying out of her jeans and into her favorite old University of Wyoming T-shirt and panties, she scrambled into bed.

She felt exposed without any curtains up and made a mental note to do something about that soon. There was not much privacy facing a well-used street even on a second floor and especially with the population exploded for Cheyenne Rodeo Days.

Maybe it was some stranger on the Ferris wheel with Bridget. Young girls made bad choices all the time, looking for excitement. Rodeo Days appealed to tourists from all over—some looking for more than just a good rodeo. Darcy punched her pillow in frustration.

Mac stood on his hind legs and braced himself on the edge of the bed. He could have easily jumped on the bed by himself.

He might just be lazy, but she liked to believe he was being chivalrous . . . not jumping into a lady's bed without an invitation. She knew some two-legged males who could learn a lot from Mac.

Darcy pulled him up, gave him a quick cuddle, and rolled over, determined to sleep. On no account was she going to think about Bridget. She most assuredly wouldn't think about Hank Nelson either. Both subjects were distressing in different ways.

CHAPTER 3

DARCY WOKE WITH A CRICK IN HER NECK. She had slept hard and dreamlessly thanks to Abigail McNeil's sovereign cure. She rubbed the sleep out of her eyes and lunged off the bed. Mac was doing his let's get out of here dance.

"Okay, Mac my man," she said as she reached for a pair of wrinkled sweatpants to wear with her UW t-shirt. "I'll race you."

Grabbing his leash, she opened the apartment door and Mac flew past her, down the hallway, and headlong down the stairs. For a second, she was sure he was going to miss his footing and tumble like a small fur ball, bouncing down every step.

Luckily, there was a separate door to the outside, or she would never have caught him.

Darcy was not suited to exuberant movement or anything else in the morning. Her idea of a good way to start the day was to sit somewhere quiet and sip strong coffee; Mac's was going for a romp.

Mac sat and waited for her to click his leash on and trotted out the door. They walked east on 18th, over to Celebration Park just a few blocks east of her apartment. The dog sniffed and squirted as much as Darcy would let him.

"Enough. If they don't know there's a new dog in town by now, they never will."

She reveled in the lack of people in around this morning. It was like having the park all to herself. She saw a couple of runners zip by with a friendly nod, which required no human contact from her other than a responsive smile.

Darcy took the leash off Mac and let him run free for a while. She kept him in sight, ready to pick up any calling cards he might leave. Mac romped around the park, sniffing the trees, and dashing back to her as if to invite her to join in his fun. His eager little face made her laugh. After about twenty minutes, Darcy clipped the leash on Mac who obediently turned toward the way they had come.

Showered and dressed in her black Roper boots, black Wrangler jeans, a long-sleeved shirt in dusty teal, and her new straw hat. Darcy knocked on Abby's door.

"Good morning." Abby greeted her with the enthusiasm of an early riser. "I am so thrilled to have the company." Abby laughed as Mac cavorted around her legs until she stooped to pick him up.

"Here's my cell number if you need anything. I'm not sure what today will bring, but I'll try to call you."

"Now don't let them overwork you. You had quite a day yesterday." Abby juggled Mac in a one-armed hold.

"I have to go meet with Detective Nelson first thing this morning."

"What does he want?"

"Heaven knows. I told him I didn't see anything, but he insisted that sometimes people who are on the scene remember helpful details they happen think about before. I doubt if I have useful detail tucked away in my subconscious, particularly since I *am* subconscious in the morning, but I'm willing to try."

"I'm sure you will be a big help, dear."

"I gotta go. You be good for Abby, mutt." Darcy scratched Mac behind his ears.

"Remember dear, today is a parade day. You'll want to park as soon as you can."

"Thanks. I forgot. Does it still go down Capitol and up Carey?"

"Yes. The marching bands and floats line up on the Capitol lawn and the carriages and horses still come down the wrong way on Carey, then turn onto Capitol to load the riders. I think if you can manage to get down to the police station before they fire the gun to start the parade, you'll be okay."

"Great. The police station is right in the middle of that mess. Even if I can find a place to park, I'll be stuck there until the end of the parade. This is shaping up to be a fine day." She opened the door.

"Bye-bye," Abby said as she made Mac wave goodbye. Darcy always hated that when other people did it, but from Abby and Mac, it was almost cute. *Oh, God. I'm turning precious.*

Slamming into her little car, she jacked up the stereo, and drove into downtown. She circled the block that held the police station. Volunteers wearing their identical Parade Committee shirts were setting up barricades and she couldn't park anywhere.

On the second go-around, she spotted Detective Nelson getting out of a black Ford 150 truck in the reserved lot. Swerving in and stopping scant inches from an empty patrol car, she zipped down the window.

"What does a girl have to do to get a parking spot around here?" Darcy hollered out at him.

At first the Detective looked startled. He glanced at her Kansas plates. Only after he leaned in her open window did he recognize her.

"Oh, hi."

"I didn't get here early enough start for parade day," Darcy said.

"I am sorry. I totally forgot about it being parade day. Why don't we drive somewhere more off the beaten path?" Nelson smiled.

"I'm with you."

"Let's go to The Bakery on 19th Street."

"The Bakery? Is that the name?"

"Yup. What else do you need to know?" His smile was blindingly white against his tanned skin. Darcy felt a tingle but dismissed it as caffeine deprivation.

"There's a thought . . . but how do you distinguish it from other bakeries in town?"

"By the quality of their muffins." Detective Nelson sauntered back to his truck. Darcy couldn't help but notice that the detective had a nice butt. Again, a little tingle. Ok she said to herself, he's handsome.

She followed him to a small brick building squatting on a shady corner in an older residential neighborhood.

Nelson held the door for her, and the smell of fresh bread wafted toward her.

"Dang, I love baked goods more than sex."

Nelson raised an eyebrow in her direction. "Duly noted."

A young guy who looked as clean-cut as an escapee from the Disney Channel came up and smiled.

"What can I do for you this morning?"

"We'll need a couple of coffees . . ." Nelson glanced to make sure. Darcy nodded. "I'd like one of your blueberry scones, and the lady will have . . ."

"I would kill to have some of everything." Darcy grinned unapologetically. "Probably not the right thing to say to a detective. Okay, I guess I'll try a scone too."

"Blueberry, Peach, Strawberry, Honey-Cinnamon . . .?" the young man with the impossibly red hair asked.

"Whoa. I have a weak heart." She held up her hand in surrender. "Peach would be fine."

Taking the coffees to a small round table, Nelson left her to bring the scones. "Here okay?"

"Sure." Darcy pushed his scone, resting on the square of white paper toward him. "Did you not change your clothes from yesterday?" she asked.

"I did, but I always wear the same thing. I don't like to wear a lot of color," he answered. "Speeds up getting ready in the morning."

"I couldn't stand wearing the same thing day after day."

"I think most women would agree, but it works for me."

It certainly does, Darcy thought. His well developed tan arms, flat stomach and cute butt worked very well for him."

Detective Nelson stirred sugar into his coffee while she poured a couple of tubs of half and half into hers. Neither of them spoke, both reluctant to ruin a perfectly good morning with talk of death.

Finally, Nelson looked at her removed the toothpick from his mouth and chuckled. "You know, I'm going to have to ask you some questions, or I can't write this breakfast off."

"Yeah, I know, but let me savor the first bite at least, okay?"

"Sure." A bemused smirk played around his mouth, but to his credit, he didn't laugh.

Darcy bit into the scone through the crunchy, rough exterior into a pillow of soft peach and butter richness. She compressed her lips as if the flavor would jump out of her mouth.

"I've never seen anyone enjoy a scone more."

"I'm a firm believer that you should savor whatever the pastry gods deign to deliver to you." Darcy bit off another chunk.

Smiling at her, Detective Nelson pushed back from the small bistro table as if by moving he could make this more official. "When did you get to the park last night?"

"Didn't Netters tell you?" Darcy took a sip of exceptional coffee.

"Yes." He stared at her and waited. He was good at this.

"About 7:30 or 8:00 o'clock. I wanted some night shots for the feature I was doing on the Carnival."

"You were standing by the Ferris wheel when the girl fell?"

"Not exactly. Netters was on the ground shooting up—you can tell from the video, and my job was to make sure no one stepped on him. I had my back to Netters and the ride. I didn't even know something terrible had happened until I heard Netters cuss."

"You didn't hear the girl scream," Nelson prompted.

"No, but with all the midway noise I'm not sure anyone could've heard her. I watched the video several times last night at the station and she didn't seem to be screaming. She also didn't thrash around like you'd expect from a person who fell accidentally. Why didn't she? I mean was she dead before she fell, or did she die from the impact?" She could feel her journalistic juices start to flow.

"We don't know yet what the cause of death was, but we think she died from the impact." Detective Nelson took a bite from his scone and chewed. His bright blue eyes fastened on Darcy.

"Bridget didn't look alive on the video. She didn't even react when she bounced off that empty basket on the way down. Was she drugged?"

"We won't know that until we get the toxicology report back from the lab." The Detective looked at his notes again. "Did you happen to notice her getting on the ride? Standing in line?"

"No. I was focused on keeping Netters from being trampled. But she wouldn't have gone on the ride alone, would she?"

"What makes you think so?" Nelson's eyebrow raised.

"Because when you're a teenager there are only two reasons to go on the Ferris wheel. Either you go with a guy you like so you can make out, or to go with your girls to scope out the midway for hot guys."

"You sound experienced." A glimmer of a smile crossed his face as he sipped his coffee.

"I had my moments." Darcy felt vaguely embarrassed. She shifted into offense. "Who do you think she was with? Could you enhance the video Netters gave you last night?"

"Nothing definitive. We're fairly sure she wasn't alone, but we didn't have much luck finding anyone who saw her get on or who would admit to being with her."

"What about the guy who was running the ride?"

"By all accounts, he was replaced for the evening after he started the ride and is at present recovering from a marathon drunk. He's on our list. Can you think of anything?"

"No. I wish to hell I could. I knew Bridget Emerson when she was a little kid. I used to babysit for Doc Emerson and his wife when I was a teenager."

Darcy was enjoying spending time with this good looking police detective with his deep blue eyes and focused attention engendering a feeling of trust, and just a little flicker of lust.

"Ms. Moreland," the detective broke the spell.

"Yes?" Darcy felt confused for moment. Recovering quickly, she asked, "Was there something else you want to ask me about?"

"Can you tell me anything more about the kid?"

"Bridget."

"Bridget," he corrected. "I'm sorry, I know this is personal for you, but this is an ongoing investigation, so I can't share any information I might have. Here's my card. Call me if you remember anything." He stood and looked down at her. "And Darcy, please don't even think of snooping around on your own."

"That would be Ms. Moreland to you—Detective." She stood facing him. "After we've gotten to know each other better, you can call me Darcy." Using his own phrasing from the night before, she was gratified to see him smile and replace the toothpick. She liked a man with a sense of humor.

She had always relished mysteries. She could not help herself. She blamed her Aunt Barbara who got her hooked on the Nancy Drew's series when she was incredibly young and impressionable. Tenacious and talented, Darcy wanted to be just like Nancy. Investigative reporting became her calling. She knew herself well enough to know she couldn't or wouldn't just drop it.

SHE HAD TRIED TO CALL DOC EMERSON several times, but it went to voicemail. He was probably devastated and didn't want to talk to anybody. Darcy's journalistic sixth sense kicked in on the five-minute drive to the station. Detective Nelson hadn't confirmed Bridget had been murdered, but he hadn't denied either. She slammed through the station's door and stormed through the outer office at Mach speed. People stared at her and got out of her way.

Zach intercepted her before she reached her cubbyhole office. "What happened? It isn't even 9 o'clock yet."

"Bridget was murdered," Darcy blurted without preamble. "She was likely pushed out of that basket on the top of the Ferris wheel and fell to her death."

"Are you sure?"

"I just had scones and coffee with Detective Nelson. He gave the typical non-denial denial that all cops use when they don't know anything except that there's something suspicious."

Zach pushed her into her office and closed the door.

"I want you to listen to me, Darcy. This is a small town . . ."

"Close to 60,000 plus people makes it more than a small town . . ."

"Regardless of demographics, this is a small town in all that is important—and you need to be careful about interfering in a police investigation."

"So Detective Nelson told me."

"It is essential that you establish professional relationships. The police will be your sources, or not, depending on how trustworthy you are with the information they give you."

Darcy looked at her old friend Zach. He didn't look friendly.

"You got it, boss," she executed a jaunty little salute.

"I'm serious."

"I know. I'll be careful not to step on any toes."

"Good. Now I want you to take Netters and do some kind of rodeo story."

"Why not the parade?"

"We've got that covered. I didn't know when you'd be in, so I scheduled you for a later shot after lunch. Go sit in the park. Take that mongrel dog of yours for a walk."

"Mongrel? Mac's a purebred . . ."

"Yeah, yeah Cairn Terrier. I know. See if he can dig up your sense of humor."

"In my defense, I'm not used to bodies falling from the sky. Especially bodies of young girls I used to know. It makes me cranky."

"I know it's been stressful, but you'll rally."

"I sure hope you're right," she said, but wasn't convinced.

DARCY MADE A QUICK STOP at the grocery store, determined to shake off her blue funk. She bought Mac's favorite treats, some deli meats to share, and a box of fried chicken to nibble on. She rounded the selection off with a loaf of sourdough bread, fruits, and a variety of bottled juices.

She was smiling as she knocked on Abby's door. Abby opened the door wearing a light pink track suit and a big smile.

"Hi Abby. I came to take you and Mac for a picnic at Celebration Park."

"Oh, I don't think so. You go ahead and take Mac. I'll putter around here."

"No. I want you to come. I've got goodies in the car . . . oh, except napkins and . . ."

"I have all that stuff, but . . ."

"No buts. Let's go."

Darcy dashed into the kitchen, grabbed some paper towels, and stooped to seize Mac and tuck him under her arm.

"I try to avoid the Rodeo Days crowds if I can help it." Abby looked tempted in spite of herself.

"We will. Everyone will be at the rodeo arena or downtown at the parade. Look, Mac wants you to go." Darcy was not above using blatant manipulation if needed.

Abby capitulated easily. Darcy drove down to the park, and they effortlessly found a shaded area to let Mac run free. He was good about staying close.

"Zach said I needed a break. He was probably right." Darcy took a swig of bottled water.

"Why did he say that?"

"He just knows I am still upset," she nibbled at a potato chip.

"Well, I think that's sensible. You've had quite a shock." Abby said as she reached for a piece of chicken.

"It's not wholly empathetic on Zach's part. He knows Detective Nelson told me not to go snooping around—that it was an ongoing investigation."

Abby opened her mouth to comment, but Darcy held up her hand to forestall her.

"I know. I know. But damn it, Abby. I have to do something." Darcy picked up a Granny Smith apple and gnawed it down to the core.

"What do your instincts tell you?" she prodded gently.

"That she was murdered by someone pushing her out of the Ferris wheel basket. But who would do that? The police can't find anyone who'd admit to even being with her earlier."

"Do you have any leads? That is what they call them, isn't it?" Abby brushed some crumbs from her lap.

"I drove Stacie Rogers home last night. She said she was a friend of Bridget's. I think I'll start with her. I'll be right back. I need to get her number."

She ran to her car and found the Cheyenne phone book she always kept stashed in her back seat. It was a few years out of date, but it would work. She had to unearth it from the rubble of hamburger wrappers and doggie treat bags.

When Darcy returned to the blanket, Mac was curled up by

Abby's side and she was feeding him little scraps of thinly sliced roast beef.

"Should I be nervous about my dog's loyalty?"

"No," Abby laughed. "I'm turning into a doggie grandma. Heaven help me."

Darcy skimmed through the Rogers, looking for the address. "Bingo."

"Find it?"

"Yup." She punched in the number and waited a moment for someone to pick up.

"Hello Stacie? This is Darcy Moreland. I was wondering if you could answer a couple of questions for me?"

"I guess so," Stacie sounded cautious.

"Great. You said Bridget had a new boyfriend. Do you happen to know who he is?"

"He's Sam Carson—um—a bulldoger."

"Is he older than Bridget or about the same age?"

"Older. She'd brag that when he came to town on weekends, he'd buy her beer and stuff."

"When he came into town? Where's he from?"

"Um . . . Greeley. What is this all about?"

Greeley was a town across the Colorado/Wyoming border about fifty miles down the road.

"Just getting some background information for a follow up story. Did she see him every weekend?"

"No. Bridget was a Rider. They travel a lot—and he did too. You know, because of the rodeoing."

"Well thanks, Stacie. That helps."

Darcy made a mental note to pump the secretary at the rodeo office, who just happened to be her old high school keyboarding teacher. Damn little got past that lady.

She slipped her phone into her back pocket and stared into space for a minute, gnawing on a drumstick. The boyfriend or the husband was often the first and best suspect; probably for good reason, she thought.

After everyone had eaten their fill, and the food was packed up,

Darcy dropped the bags and Mac off with Abby and promised to call her and let her know when she'd likely be able to break away.

Driving into CRD Park, she was passed through security on her press pass and found a space by the Rodeo Committee cabin. She enjoyed her AC while she dialed Netters's number.

"Hi, Netters. I'm on the park by the Rodeo Committee Office. Where are you?"

"Eating lunch, thanks."

"On the park or . . .?"

"At Subway—and I'm going to finish my sandwich if it's all the same to you."

"I don't even have a plan yet. How 'bout we meet over by Chute 9?"

"The roping chutes? Sure. When?"

"Will forty-five minutes give you enough time?"

"Yup. Meet you there."

The line went dead.

Needs work on his people skills, she thought. Forty-five minutes to poke around. Darcy smiled.

Walking into the Rodeo Office, she glanced around, looking for Maggie Miller. Maggie had been the volunteer secretary for the Rodeo Committee forever.

Darcy used to hang out at the Rodeo Office when her dad was a volunteer and later when he was one of the committee chairmen. Maggie worked for CRD during the summer and for the school district during the winter. If anyone would level with her, it would be Maggie.

She was on the edge of hot and dusty, and the cool air conditioning felt wonderful. A couple of guys waved and headed out the door to the arena if their red and white vests were any indication. They were running the boards. Their job was to stand by the judges during the rough stock riding. The possible danger to life and limb from a cantankerous animal added to the thrill.

"Look who the cat drug in."

Darcy whirled around. Maggie gave her a warm hug and then pushed her to arm's length.

"Let me look at you. I'll bet your dad's busting his buttons with pride."

"He's thrilled I'm educated and employed."

"What are you doing? Visiting?"

"No, actually working. I'm working as an investigative reporter at KCWY. Don't you watch the local news?"

"Not generally, but if you're doing it, I will." Maggie draped her arm around her shoulders, walked her the main office area.

"I'm doing mostly features for now, but I did a short report about Bridget Emerson who fell from the Ferris wheel last night."

"I heard about that. What a tragedy. Her dad's been a volunteer vet on the park for years Nice guy. Poor Frank. I gathered he was devastated."

"Yeah. I tried calling him several times, but it went to voicemail. I don't really know what I would say to him if he did pick up. 'Sorry for your loss' doesn't quite cover the death of your only child."

Maggie hugged her. "Sometimes just letting folks know you're thinking about them and care is about all you can do." She put an arm around Darcy's shoulder and led her into her office.

"Yeah. I suppose you're right. I just feel so helpless." Darcy sat on a folding chair and Maggie moved back at her computer. Maggie was the official fire extiquisher. If anything went wrong during the rodeo, she was first to know, and the first to find someone to fix it.

Darcy squirmed a little in her seat. She didn't know how ethical it was to pump Maggie for information, but she'd give it a try. "By the way, one of Bridget's friends said she had a boyfriend who was a bulldoger from Greeley. Do you happen to know him? Stacie told me his name was Sam Carson."

"Bridget was a Rider, wasn't she?" Maggie began tippy-tapping on her computer keyboard.

"Yeah. I don't know for how long—two years, maybe."

"Okay. That would make her 16 or 17, right? I remember her boyfriend now. I think she came in with him when he registered. He's um . . ." Maggie punched in some code. "He's entered in the first go-round in steer wrestling. Should be competing today."

"Thanks, Maggie. By the way, do you know how old he is?"

"As a matter of fact, I do. He's 23. I remember telling him to be careful around Bridget. Jailbait you know. Some of these cowboys don't have the sense God gave petunias." Maggie frowned. "He was a real piece of work. Tried to get special stable privileges for his horse."

"Because he's so special, right?" Standing up, Darcy bent to hug her. "Thanks again, Maggie. You've been a big help."

"You didn't hear any of this from me."

Darcy walked into the glaring sunlight and wandered south, grateful for her straw cowboy hat and hoped it would keep her from getting sunstroke. Reviewing the new information in her head, she trudged down the dusty path.

What would a twenty-three-year-old man want with a seventeen-year-old girl except for the obvious statutory reason? Was he with her the night she died? And why would anyone kill someone that young? Maybe he was the shadow in the basket. Darcy shivered.

Rather than take the route through the midway past the Farris Wheel, she took a wide sweep by the Indian Village and came up on the back side of the arena where the roping chutes were, flashing her press badge at security.

Five guys were sitting on top of their horses, watching the first run of bull riders.

"Any of you guys seen Sam Carson today?" she shouted up to them.

"Nope," said the cowboy closest to her, sitting on large dun horse. The other cowboys shook their heads.

"If you see him would you tell him that Darcy Moreland from KCWY TV would like to talk to him?"

"Sure," the cowboy answered again.

"He didn't cancel his go, did he? "she asked.

"Not that I know of. Why would he?"

"Well, his girlfriend died in an accident last night," Darcy said.

"Which one?"

CHAPTER 4

DRIFTING OVER TO THE WOODEN STEPS that led up to the Chute 9 timed-event booth, Darcy sat in the shade. She needed the cool-down. She decided to touch base with her high school BFF Liz. Liz knew practically everyone in town and could update her fast. For a minute, she was afraid she was going to get Liz's voice mail, but she finally picked up.

"Darcy. I watched the news last night. Are you okay? I was going to wait to call because I didn't want to wake you."

"Yeah, I'm fine. It shook me up some. I used to babysit for Bridget back in high school."

"OMG! That's brutal."

"There was so much blood . . . and the poor kid turned out to be only seventeen." Darcy tipped her hat back and dabbed at the sheen of sweat on her forehead with the back of her sleeve

"Yeah, I know. I already got a call this morning from Frank Emerson's lawyer. He's filing a claim against Tom Hayes, the owner-operator of Hayes Shows Inc., as well as the CRD General Committee and the Board of Directors for wrongful death."

"How can he do that? The police can't even determine what caused the fall."

"Doc Emerson is shattered and lashing out at anyone he can hold responsible—tragic, but understandable."

"Liz, do you underwrite some of CRD's insurance?"

"Yup, sure do. This must be my lucky year. First, a rained-out concert in Laramie, and now this. If this keeps up, I'll have to volunteer with the Girl Scout's Jamboree to get a summer vacation."

"Is it really going to put you in a bind?"

"It might. We'll have to see."

"I'd better go," Darcy said. "I need to come up with a feature story idea on the rodeo."

"I'll talk to you soon, okay? Oh, and Darcy, remember to get some time off on Wednesday."

"Yeah, I remember . . . Cheyenne Day . . . gotcha."

Darcy remembered Cheyenne Day, when many Cheyenne businesses gave their employees the afternoon off to enjoy Rodeo Days. It almost guaranteed you would see everyone you knew and meet several you would like to know. It was just a reason for a big booze up, but it was doubtful if she'd be up for it this year.

She had barely stuffed her phone away when she had to scoot over on the steps to let Butch Reynolds, the chute boss CRD hired every year to run the timed events, get by.

"Don't worry. I won't step on ya, lil' lady." He smiled his Texan-dazzler smile. "Say, aren't you Ed Moreland's little girl? Um, Debby?"

"Darcy." She stood and stuck out her hand. "I'm flattered you remember me."

"Well, I sure do like your dad. Is he in town yet?"

"No. They're running behind schedule this year, but he'll be here. You know Dad."

"Yeah. It wouldn't seem like Rodeo Days without him."

"I'll tell him you said that. Mr. Reynolds. May I ask you a question?"

"Sure."

"Do you know a bulldoger named Sam Carson from Greeley?"

"Tall, barrel-chested guy?"

Darcy laughed. "Aren't they all?"

"Got a point there. Let me think. Oh, yeah, now I got him. Sandy blond hair has a puny patch of fuzz on his chin and is sure he's irresistible to women. That the one? I wouldn't recommend him, Darcy."

"Why not?"

"Can't trust him."

"In what way? Maggie at the Rodeo Office said there he had some trouble about the stall he'd been assigned, but other than that . . ."

Darcy chose not to mention the implication that he had several girlfriends. It had been her experience that a lot of men thought that it a plus rather than a minus.

"He's a whiner. Challenges the times he gets, the draw, or the condition of the arena. If he gets a good time, it's 'cuz he's terrific; if not, it's 'cuz it's someone else's fault."

To be called a whiner damned a cowboy among his peers. Rodeo didn't tolerate diva attitudes. The one area of intolerance that was universal in the sport.

"Well, thanks for the information, Mr. Reynolds. You haven't seen him yet this morning, have you?"

Reynolds squinted into the sun as his eyes swept the holding area.

"Yup. He's over there." He pointed at a large cowboy sitting atop a sorrel horse with a white blaze on its forehead. "Be careful."

Darcy flashed him a large smile. "Sure will. Thanks."

"Say hi to your dad when he gets in. Tell him to come up for some Mare's Milk sometime, okay?"

Darcy knew about Mare's Milk, a unique alcoholic concoction prized by the timed-events crew to get the blood stirring during the early morning slack completion. Only the foolish or careless drank more than one shot. It was rumored to make grown men blind.

She waved goodbye and clomped down the steps in search of the whiner.

Gazing up into the hot July sun, Darcy had a hard time finding Carson. By the time she got to the front of his horse, he had seen her coming. Looking at his self-satisfied smile, she knew he thought she was a buckle bunny—rodeo groupies who hit on cowboys.

"Hello. You looking for me?"

"Are you Sam Carson?" Darcy had to hold onto her new hat when she looked up at him.

"Guilty." He reseated himself in his saddle. He almost preened as he leaned forward across the saddle horn. "And who are you? You aren't that little gal from the Lariat Bar last night?"

"No, I'm not." Darcy could hardly hide her disgust. "Would you get down for a minute, Mr. Carson? I have a few questions I'd like to ask you."

"Sure thing." He swung out of the saddle like John Wayne. "What do you want to know?" He tipped his hat back on his head and flashed a practiced smile.

"My name is Darcy Moreland and I work for KCWY TV."

"Yeah?" His eyes darted around to see if the other cowboys were listening.

"What can you tell me about Bridget Emerson?"

He looked uneasy for the first time. "Um. I don't know. Nice kid." He continued to look past her shoulder, and over his shoulder, but never in her eyes. "Sad about what happened," he said as an afterthought.

Darcy felt her jaw tighten. It always did that when she was trying hard not to bust someone's chops. "I heard you'd been dating her."

He stuffed his hands in his back pockets and shifted. "Not really. I'd take her to the movies or something if I was in town."

"Were you in town often?"

His eyes narrowed, and he looked down from his six-foot-plus height. "What's it to you?" he finally answered.

"I'm doing a piece on her and we're trying to put together a report about her accident."

Carson bobbed his head once to answer her.

"You didn't happen to be with her last night, did you?" Darcy couldn't get a read on him. He seemed indifferent, but not necessarily guilty.

Carson glanced around as if he were trying to decide how to answer the question. "Yeah. I guess. For a little while."

"How little?"

Carson didn't answer. He mounted up again as if the added height would give him courage. He glared down at her. "I bought her a corn dog, and we talked . . ."

"And a beer?" Darcy pushed because he was obviously uncomfortable, and she wanted to know why.

He leaned over his saddle horn and skewered her with a defiant stare. "Lady, what are you asking? Did I contribute to the delinquency of a minor?"

"So, you knew she was a minor?"

"She was turning 18 in a couple of weeks. Plenty old enough to . . ." His eyes widened like he knew he'd stepped in it. "I'm done answering questions. I got work to do." He kicked his horse forward and melted into the small batch of bulldoggers waiting for their run.

Darcy wandered over to the fence to watch. He was the third out in the section. His hazer galloped his horse along the right side to "shape" the steer, to keep it running straight. Carson's horse galloped on the other side and he jumped for the steer as soon as he pulled alongside. He missed his hold and literally bit the dust.

Darcy smiled at his "no time" score. His horse continued to run. Carson had a long dusty trudge toward his horse who was now at the far end of the arena. His hazer didn't bother to catch Carson's horse and bring him back. Few of the other contestants talked to him. Usually, cowboys are supportive of each other, but Carson didn't seem to have many friends in town.

Darcy wondered what Bridget had seen in the arrogant punk. He certainly hadn't valued Bridget much. She tried to remember back when an older man seemed exciting and dangerous. The illegal beer and the cowboy mystique would be potent for a young, impressionable girl. She remembered catching the same cowboy flu, pining for cute bull rider. Her face grew hot as she remembered how she had followed him around. When he left after the rodeo, she regained her sanity even if her dignity had been dented.

It was about time to meet Netters and she was grateful to have something to do. She needed a distraction. Maybe it would wash the bad taste out of her mouth Carson had left. Darcy watched as Netters shambled over to her.

"Hi." She smiled at him. "Are you Cowboy Bill?" Netter dressed western; blue jeans, and a long-sleeve shirt required of anyone who might need to go behind the chutes. Except for the Copenhagen ball cap and his black cross trainers, he looked legit.

"You're thinking of Buffalo Bill, Calamity Jane." He smiled.

"Love to trade quips with you, but we need to get a story. Any ideas?"

"You're the talent. I'm the grunt." He put the camera down on the ground, flanked by his Nikes, and waited.

"You worked for the station last year."

"Yeah, so?"

"So, I don't want to do what's been done before. Give me a clue, Netters. Please?"

"You might interview the guys in the booth. Some of them have been here for years."

Darcy looked up the steps. "Like Butch Reynolds?"

"Actually, I was thinking of the volunteers. Reynolds is colorful, but not a volunteer."

"Good point. Let's wander up and see who we can find, okay?"

"Whatever you say, Calamity."

She let it pass. From his point-of-view, it was fairly descriptive of her disaster-based-career so far at KCWY: screwing up Netter's date, witnessing a girl's death, semi-annoying Detective Nelson, and Zach, not to mention Sam Carson—yup. Not much positive in that list.

From the top of Chute 9 she got a sprawling view of the arena, the carnival, and the Indian Village. It was a favorite place to bring VIP's. Darcy spotted the yellow police tape still stretched around the Ferris wheel and looked away.

In the timed-event judge's room, they found Butch Reynolds seated front and center at an open window that looked down over the starting pens. Two volunteers flanked him keeping the tallies and entering them into the computers.

The first section had run and there was a lull in the action. Darcy pounced on the first guy she recognized.

"Don McLeod. Hi." She gave him a big hug. Darcy had known Don for years. He volunteered with her dad and went on to be a Rodeo Committee Chairman like her dad had. Now he was back as a regular volunteer.

"Why little Darcy Moreland. I heard you grew up . . . but I didn't believe it. Where's your dad?"

"En-route. Late start this year. Just between us, I think Dad stalled so Mom couldn't buy any more stuff at the Western Art Show. She got carried away last year."

"Well, it's good to see you. What are you doing?"

"I'm working for KCWY TV and I want to interview you."

"Naw. Interview someone less craggy-faced," he said, but he smiled.

"I want the crags. They make you look trustworthy. I want you to talk about the volunteers. I also want you to talk about the timed events. Please?"

"How long?"

"Easy short piece. I'll ask you questions, and you answer them, okay?"

"Well, let's get to it before the steer roping starts."

"Okay." She turned to include Netters. "This is Bill Netters from the station." The men shook hands and Darcy tried to frame the shot. "Netters, would it work if we shot so we can have the rodeo and stands behind him?"

"I can get both of you and the action behind you."

"Great. Oh, thanks." Darcy said as the other volunteer gave up his seat for her.

"Darcy, this is Jack Johnson. Darcy's Ed Moreland's girl."

"Nice to meet you. I am going to grab a Coke. You guys want anything?"

They shook their heads and set up to do the story. Netters checked the levels, and they began:

"I'm talking to Don McLeod, a fixture at Cheyenne Rodeo Days. He's one of over two thousand volunteers here the park. Have you always worked the timed events, Don?

"No. When I started on the Rodeo Committee, I was about twenty. The first jobs I got were cleaning stalls and painting fence.

Darcy laughed. "And yet you still came back."

"It doesn't take much to get rodeo fever. Besides back then it was a great place to meet girls."

"So since you first began, you've worked all over the park. Is that right?"

"Pretty much, but working the rodeo is my first love. Now I just work the timed events."

"What exactly are the timed events?"

"Steer wrestling, steer roping, tie down, and team roping. All of the events have their own rules, but basically the cowboy has to control his animal in the shortest period of time."

"So the score depends on time?"

"And technique. Lots of technique."

"Well, thank you, Don. Cheyenne Rodeo Days has something for everyone. If you like old-fashioned, rough-and-tumble rodeo this is the place to come. This is Darcy Moreland reporting from Cheyenne Rodeo Days for KCWY TV."

"Cut." She said to Netters, then shifted back to Don while Netters packed away the camera and mic. "Good job! You're a natural at this."

"No problem. Now get out of here. Say hi to your folks for me."

"Okay." Darcy waved for Netters to follow her. She didn't talk to him until they were on the ground, walking toward the Indian Village.

"I talked to Bridget Emerson's boyfriend before you got here."

Netters shrugged. "So . . . ?"

"Oh, don't pull that disinterested act with me. I watched you replay the scene over and over. You're as curious and appalled as I am about what happened last night."

"What'd the boyfriend say?"

"That he barely knew her."

"Maybe he was telling the truth."

They wound their way, single file, around the crowds of people who strolled in and out of the old-fashioned storefronts collectively labeled Cheyenne Junction.

The replica of an old western town full of crafts and demonstrations pulled in the tourists. They passed the blacksmith's in time to see him douse a red-hot horseshoe into a water bath filling the air with the metallic steam. The water hissed and the cluster of kids surrounding him oohed and aahed. Darcy smiled in spite of herself.

"Seriously," she continued when she finally walked beside Netters again. "Maggie at the Rodeo Office said they were a 'thing' and that she'd warned Carson that Bridget was a minor."

"So?"

"So, when I asked, he acted like they were casual friends."

"Maybe they were."

"You don't get it, do you? If Maggie warned Carson, she must have seen some fairly explicit PDA . . ."

"What?"

"Public display of affection . . . it was what they called swapping spit when I went to high school. Anyway, Maggie must have seen something like that for her to comment. She's not easily shocked after all her years of teaching high school and working with cowboys."

"Okay, they were hot-and-heavy. What does that prove?" Netters barely dodged a young kid racing the other way.

"When I walked over to talk to him, he thought I was some vapid buckle-bunny he'd met at the Lariat."

"So the guy gets around. It's not a crime, Darcy."

"He said he bought Bridget a corn dog, and they talked. And then he shut down the conversation. I'm dying to know when he was at the Lariat. He acted like Bridget's death was a piece of uninteresting gossip."

"I think all this prying is the police's job. You want to be stirring everything up based on how coldhearted her boyfriend was?"

"Just like a man. Women are as expendable as Kleenex. Use them, wad them up, and toss them away."

Netters's eyebrows shot up. "Are we still talking about Bridget Emerson?"

"Okay, so I got a little carried away. But I still want to know where Sam Carson was last night."

"Leave it alone, Darcy. You don't want to mess with Detective Nelson. If he finds out you've been questioning people behind his back, he'll arrest you for obstruction."

"I'm exercising my first amendment rights as an investigative journalist. It's my job."

Netters snorted, but they dropped the conversation. By now, they were back to the Rodeo Office where she had parked her car.

"Why don't you take the equipment back and I'll meet you there. Tell Zach I have a small errand to run."

"An errand? What? Wait. No, I take it back. I don't want to know. This has 'Calamity' written all over it. See you back at the station." He swerved off to find his car.

Darcy got in and drove directly back to the Rodeo Office. Maggie was busy. Darcy strolled into the break room and grabbed a Coke from the refrigerator, like she had done a hundred times as a kid. She had grown up hanging out at the Rodeo Office. She held the can to her forehead and then the back of her neck.

"People usually drink those rather than use them as an ice pack."

She spun around. A tall handsome man dressed as a Chairman stood there.

"Hi. Darcy Moreland from KCWY." She stuck her hand out.

"Gary Romero, Rodeo Chairman. Please tell me you're the replacement reporter from the station."

Darcy remembered now that Bryce Adkins had had a run-in with Romero earlier.

"Sort of. I signed on to cover Rodeo Days for the station." She didn't want to try to defend Adkins to this man.

"What are you doing here?" He narrowed his eyes at her. Darcy saw the hint of doubt slip across his face.

"Um . . . I wanted to get some information from Maggie, but I'll wait."

"About what?" Romero slid his butt on the table edge as if he could wait forever.

"I'm doing a report on bulldoggers, you know uh steer wrestlers," Darcy lied, "and I wanted to get some contestant's pictures."

"Why don't you take some yourself?" Now he looked at her with open suspicion.

"I forgot my good camera and I want to make sure I put the right stats and name to the right face. It's okay, isn't it?"

Romero looked at her closely for a second. "I guess, but don't tie her up too long. We're in the middle of a rodeo."

Darcy flashed him a smile. "Thanks for reminding me. I probably would have missed that."

Romero laughed and walked out the back, letting the screen door slam behind him.

Maggie was easy after Romero. Darcy told her she was doing some further checking on Carson and Maggie copied off the PRCA Media Guide photo.

"You be careful, Darcy," she said. "Don't take any unnecessary chances."

"I won't and thanks, Maggie." Darcy ran out to her car and drove from the park towards downtown.

During the rodeo, the traffic was still hectic but not horrible. She swerved around to the covered parking garage and punched the machine for a ticket. There were still lots of spaces and The Lariat Saloon was right across the street.

Inside it was cool and dark. Several people perched on stools along the bar as well as a few tucked in at small tables scattered around. It wasn't packed yet, but by evening Darcy knew you wouldn't be able to walk through here without knowing how much change a guy had in his pocket or if he was happy to see you.

She swung her leg over the stool but had to jump up to sit on it. A woman bartender with blonde-streaked hair and white-capped-toothy smile slapped a napkin in front of her.

"What'll it be?"

"A Bud Lite and some information."

"The beer's easy."

While the bartender left to get the beer, Darcy pulled Sam Carson's picture from her back pocket and smoothed it out on the top of the bar.

"Boyfriend?" the bartender asked as she placed the beer and a frosty glass in front of her.

"Nope. I'm trying to get information about him."

"Are you a cop?"

Darcy laughed as she imagined Hank Nelson's face if he'd been there. He would have a coronary.

"Nope. I'm a TV journalist. I'm doing a story about cowboys

and their lifestyle."

Darcy flashed her press pass. The bartender squinted at the laminated card hanging from a lanyard around Darcy's neck and nodded slightly.

"Do you know him?"

"Looks familiar." She picked up the picture and tried to slant it in better light. "What's his name?"

"Sam Carson from Greeley. He's a bulldoger."

"Oh, yeah. Now I remember him. Cocky little shit. Always trolling for girls." She tossed Carson's picture back on the bar.

"Sounds like him. Was he here last night around 7?"

"No, he was here, but I remember it was later than that. The band had already started its first set, and he was bitching about the music they were playing. I think he'd had a lot to drink."

"About what time was that?" Darcy tried to sound merely curious.

"Hmm, I'd guess it about 9 or later. He picked up some girl and left before the band's first break."

"When do they take their break?"

"About 10."

"Thanks. You've been a big help." Darcy left some money on the bar and attempted to slip from the stool without landing on her butt.

"Hey. Don't you want the beer? You didn't even touch it."

"No thanks. You keep it."

The bartender leaned across the bar. "Just between us, you could find a better example of a cowboy than that slimy S.O.B."

"Yeah, I know," Darcy said over her shoulder.

CHAPTER 5

B Y THE TIME DARCY GOT BACK TO HER CAR, she was sweating again. It was particularly hot on this day in July. She let the AC run on high and tried to sort out her thoughts. Carson must have had something to do with Bridget's death. Bridget fell a little after 8 p.m. and he didn't get to The Lariat until around 9 p.m.

So what? That meant nothing on the surface of it. Circumstantial evidence. He could have just talked to her and left. But why would he leave her? Darcy continued to argue with herself. Bridget sounded like she'd be a sure thing for Carson. Maybe they fought about something and he left her. He definitely got prickly talking about her.

She put her car in gear and wended her way around the corners to exit the parking garage. She drove east and pulled into the lot by the station. Netters's truck was already there.

There were few people in the outer office and Darcy battled the urge to plop down in one of the empty chairs in front of the ancient air conditioner wheezing in a small window. Instead, she strolled back to the production offices.

Zach leaned over a copywriter's desk, micro-editing a piece for the 5:30 news. He nodded companionably in her general direction and went back to blue-penciling. Must not be too worried about her not getting here with Netters, she thought.

Darcy found Netters in the editing room, running the CF card that had the McCloud interview at Chute 9.

"Thanks for showing up, Calamity." He grinned, but it did not soften the implied criticism. "Did you find out what you wanted to know?"

"Yes and no," she said as she inched her hip onto a corner of the table facing Netters' back as he hunched over the computer. "Carson was at the bar last night, but he got there around 9. That would give him plenty of time to talk to Bridget and leave before she took the header. Or he could've been with her and left the park when the cops appeared."

"You're right. That *is* definitive," Netters muttered.

"Well if you're so smart, what do you think happened?"

"I think that a young girl tragically fell to her death. All the rest is just details." Netters never looked away from the monitor.

"You don't fool me. You're as curious about this as I am."

Finally, Netters twisted around to stare at her. "Yeah, I'm curious, just not obsessed. If that makes me callous . . .so be it." He swung back to the monitor.

"Our conversation over?" She paused a second, but Netters did not respond. "Well that's clear," she said, and left the editing room.

She stood with her back braced against the editing room door, arms folded, and stared into space. She wondered if Netters was ticked because she had left him to polish the piece alone, or if he was more upset about Bridget's death than he wanted to admit.

Zach, coming down the hall in his usual tear, pushed his face in front of hers. "You have some story for me?"

Darcy blinked. "And a happy afternoon to you too."

"Do you?" Zach did not look like he wanted to play, which made her even more determined to pound a dent into his anal-retentive attitude.

She pushed away from the door and stood in front of him. "Yes, sir. Mr. Netters is editing it as we speak. It is an innocuous little piece. Not so sassy as it is informative. Hope it will please."

"You know Darcy, sometimes you're a real pain in the ass."

"As if that is a surprise. How many years have we known each other?" Darcy flashed a bright smile. When he didn't smile back, she asked seriously, "Okay boss, what can I do for you?"

"I left you a memo on a story I want you to cover tonight on a live feed."

"I can hardly wait."

"You might want to check your cheeky attitude at the door, Ms. Moreland. I know it sticks in your craw, but I *am* your boss."

"Yes sir, boss." Darcy turned toward her office and waved goodbye airily behind her back. She grinned at the thought of Zach gnashing his teeth behind her. He had never been a big fan of sarcasm.

Slipping into her small office, Darcy turned on her banker's style lamp rather than endure the fluorescent blue haze of the overhead lights and settled into her 1950's-style green vinyl chair.

A yellow sticky-note stuck haphazardly on the green glass shade of her lamp as if it would otherwise be lost among the snippets of paper littering the surface of her desk caught her eye.

She yanked the note off and held it in the golden pool of light. It was Zach's memo. He wanted her to do a live remote about the merchants on the midway and the exhibition hall. *The excitement just kept on coming.*

Darcy dragged her legal pad forward and began to jot some notes. She remembered the man who had steamed her new hat. He would make a good subject for an interview. She should probably highlight the jewelry vendors who were a large part of the shopping experience for tourists and locals alike.

She dialed the office manager's desk. It rang three times and Wendy picked up. In her mid-twenties, Wendy was friendly and efficient, a rare combination, often mutually exclusive in office managers.

"Hi, Wendy. This is Darcy Moreland. Zach scheduled me for a live feed for this evening during the 10 o'clock broadcast. Did he happen to write down the videographer assignment?"

"Yeah. He's assigned Netters to work with you."

Darcy chewed on the eraser of her pencil. "Are you sure? I've been crosswise on that bull before."

"I heard." Wendy chuckled on the other end. "No. No mistake. Either Zach likes you as a team, or Netters has asked for more night assignments. Either way, you're together again. Isn't there a song like that?"

"Very funny. Will you tell Netters I'll meet him around 8:30 by the east entrance of Exposition Hall to do some preliminary setups."

"You got it."

"Thanks, Wendy." Darcy said and clicked off. The assignment would come better from Wendy. Netters was probably still not speaking to her.

She leaned back in her chair and plopped her dust-covered boots on the desktop. Her mind spun like a blender, swirling disparate thoughts around and around in vivid color . . .mostly blood red.

Images of Bridget sprawled on the ground kept replaying in her mind. She could have fallen all by herself, but that didn't jibe with Bridget being both agile and athletic. Darcy didn't think suicide was likely either. According to statistics, girls who commit suicide either took drugs or cut themselves. Guys were more likely to jump or use a gun. It just didn't fit.

She thought about Bridget and Sam Carson. Darcy didn't like him. He made her skin crawl, but that didn't make him responsible for Bridget's death. Being an arrogant creep wasn't against the law yet, more's the pity.

His response had been cold-hearted and shifty, but not so defensive as to imply guilt over some really heinous act. He was guilty of something all right. He was a low-life bottom feeder, but Darcy didn't think he had enough balls to do anything as gritty as murder. She could be wrong, she argued with herself. After all, he was a bulldogger, a recklessly aggressive sport. *Yeah, but he wasn't particularly good at it.*

Darcy wondered what, if anything, Hank Nelson had found in his investigation. She didn't think for a moment he'd share anything with her, but Zach had made it plain that she needed to forge a professional relationship with the detective.

Maybe she should call him and—and. She was drawing a blank. Darcy had no idea what she would say to him, "Hi. This is Darcy Moreland." She imagined the hideously awkward silence that would follow. She had to find some way to make it work. Before she talked herself out of it, Darcy dialed Abby's number. Abby answered on the first ring.

"Hi," Darcy said. "I have to do a live feed tonight out at the park, and I was wondering if I could bring home some of that to-die-for barbeque from that trailer guy before I go? Does that sound good to you?"

"You betcha. I love that stuff. It's a shame we can only get it during Rodeo Days. I could make a good dent in some baby-backs."

"You got 'em. Oh, and Abby, would you mind if I asked Hank Nelson to join us?"

"You think it'll help?"

"I'm going to make the effort if it's okay with you. He'll probably refuse the invitation, but it's the thought that counts."

"Okay. I'll set the table for three. Maybe I could say I was your chaperone."

"Amusing. Irritating, but amusing. I'll be there about 6, okay?"

"Okay. See you."

Darcy listened to the click and the dial tone. She dreaded the next call, but she dug his card out and punched the numbers. Darcy was praying she would get a machine or something, but after about the fourth ring he picked up.

"Detective Hank Nelson."

"Um . . .Hi, Detective Nelson. This is Darcy Moreland." He didn't say anything, so she rushed ahead.

"I'm picking up barbeque for my friend Abby and myself. I wondered if you'd care to join us."

Silence again.

"Detective Nelson?" She needed to know he was still there. *Awkward.*

"I think we can call each other by our first names now don't you, Darcy?" She could imagine him smiling on the other end. "Thank you for your gracious offer. Where and what time?"

"Around 6 at the Algonquin. Apartment 101."

"Is that your place?"

"No. Abby's. I live on the second floor, but I haven't had much time to settle in, what with the murder and all." *Oh, damn. What possessed her to say that? And to him of all people?*

Silence and then, "Who told you she was murdered?" he asked

quietly. "I only said it was a suspicious death."

Gone was the lightly teasing tone, replaced by the glacial questioning of the police detective. This time she was silent.

"Darcy?"

Evidently, they were still on a first name basis, barely. "Yes?"

"Are you going to answer my question?"

A good offence is sometimes better than a good defense. "Was Bridget murdered? She sure as hell didn't look like she jumped."

"I'll see you at 6." He hung up.

Darcy sat stunned for a moment trying to process what he'd just told her. She'd theorized murder, but it was a theory, until Hank confirmed it. Her heart pounded, and she had to force herself to inhale deeply.

Grabbing the half-full Styrofoam cup of cold coffee left over from this morning, she gulped down a swallow. It was nasty, but it calmed her. Hank would, she hoped, fill her in on the details over dinner. If not, she'd find out on her own.

She had a report to prep for and based on the premise that work cures most evils, Darcy picked up the phone once more and began to make some calls.

She called CRD Headquarters to get the Concession Chairman's number. Bob Cochran was in charge of the food vendors, the carnival, as well as the exhibitors.

"Hi Mr. Cochran, this is Darcy Moreland from KCWY we are planning to do a live feed from the park tonight and I was wondering if you knew of any particularly interesting exhibitors we might talk to."

"Well, the jewelry concessions are always interesting," he said.

"I'd planned on that along with Charlie Sanders who shaped my new hat, but I thought you might think of some others we could talk to that would capture the feeling of the midway."

"I know this sounds silly, Ms. Moreland, but one of the biggest draws on the midway is the smoked turkey legs concession."

"Great idea. Thanks." Darcy said and meant it.

Darcy assumed she could handle the questions for Charlie and the Turkey fellow, but jewelry was out of her league.

Roughing in some possible questions on her legal pad, she reached for the phone and called her mother's friend, Kari Vickers, who had been buying jewelry at Rodeo Days for years. Kari remembered every piece she had ever bought, where it came from, and how much of a bargain it was. She was an encyclopedia of information and generally all around nice. In a fifteen-minute conversation, she gave Darcy several ideas for questions.

She checked her watch. It was late afternoon, but not late enough to get the ribs. She decided to look at the clip of Bridget's fall again now that she was fairly sure it was murder.

Darcy slipped into the editing bay and hunted through the pile of thumb drives. She found the one she was looking for almost immediately and plugged it into the computer.

Watching closely with the sound off she reset it several times and tried to slow it down to run practically frame by frame. "How does Hank know it was murder?", she whispered as she peered closer to the monitor.

Darcy watched with all the fascination of a rubber-necker at a car wreck, as Bridget tumbled to the black asphalt. Netters had shifted to zoom in on her fall and Darcy could not shake the feeling that Bridget looked like a Raggedy Ann doll flopping, spinning, and landing with a jolt.

After about the third time through, she clicked on what was right behind the Ferris wheel. It was the back of the tent where Charlie Sanders steamed hats. Darcy remembered while he was working on her hat, he had a flap of the tent raised to let in some fresh air.

What were the chances that he had been there or seen something? Since she was going to see him tonight, she didn't see any harm asking a few extra questions.

Darcy wouldn't discuss this with Hank, she decided. She didn't need him getting heavy-handed on her about asking questions. It was her job after all. She put the card back in place, turned off the monitor, and left.

After a short stop at her office to retrieve her backpack, Darcy strolled out the door. She would tell Zach tomorrow how she'd made nice-nice with the cranky police detective. Zach would be stunned that she actually followed his orders. Imagining Zach being stunned made her smile.

THE LONG LINE WAITING FOR BARBEQUE moved quickly and in a short time, she left clutching a greasy brown bag full of baby-backs, tubs of extra sauce, and artery-clogging white bread rolls.

Darcy pulled up in front of the three-storied, red-bricked Algonquin Apartment House. At first glance, the building looked grand and imposing with its matching plantation-like pillars flanking the front entrance. On closer inspection in the half dusk and glimmering streetlights, the building looked like a dowdy maiden Aunt—genteel, but a bit frayed around the edges.

She didn't know if the detective was already there. He struck her as the "fifteen minutes early is like being an hour late" kind of guy. She tried to remember whether she had told him that Abby was her old English teacher in high school.

As she gathered up her things, Darcy played back their conversation in her head. Nope. She was sure she hadn't said anything except Abby was a friend. It made her smile. She was sure Hank was imagining dinner with two young ladies.

Straightening her shoulders, she huffed her way up the porch steps and pushed open the heavy oak door. The cool of the dark foyer was refreshing. The entry way was dimly lit by a couple of inadequate candle sconces with phony amber flames dancing energetically but ineffectually in their tiny, pointed globes. The place had a vague, musty-dusty smell implying decaying wood and too many passing years.

Darcy walked around the corner to Abby's door. She had barely raised her hand to knock when the door swung opened. Hank stood there blocking the way. Mac scampered between his legs and rushed at her.

"I'd like to believe that you missed me," Darcy squatted to scratch Mac's ears, "but I'm fairly sure you smell the barbeque."

Hank relieved her of the bag. She smiled up at him. "Taking up a new career as a doorman, are you?"

"Your friend is busy making a fruit salad to go with the bar-beque." He reached behind her and closed the door.

Darcy headed for the kitchen, and he followed her with the bag of food.

"Whoa, cowboy." Darcy stopped him with her hand on his chest. "There's not enough room in here for all three of us. Four of us. That means you too, Mac. Scat." Mac scurried off. Hank stood there and looked at her hand. Darcy could feel a warm rush of a blush rise from her neck to her cheeks. She pulled it off and tucked it in her back pocket.

Abby looked up and laughed. "Why don't you get the plates and silverware, Darcy? I'll be done in here in a minute. Detective Nelson, you can grab a beer from the refrigerator. Darcy, can you have a beer?"

"No, I'd better not. I have a shoot later tonight." Darcy reached into the cupboard and got the plates. "Do you still have that bottle of diet ginger ale?"

"Get whatever you need and get out of here." Abby continued to slice chunks of apple into a big white bowl.

After she set the plates out, Darcy snatched the green bottle from the door in the refrigerator, poured a healthy splash into a glass, and followed Hank into the living room.

Hank sat on the small settee put his toothpick in his front pocket and twisted off the top of his beer. "You could have warned me."

"What do you mean? Oh, you mean about Abby. I didn't mislead you intentionally. I didn't realize I hadn't told you she's my former teacher until I was almost here, but why should it matter?" Darcy sat in Abby's favorite chair facing him.

"It wouldn't, except I thought for a minute I had the wrong apartment. The thought did cross my mind that you might have planned this to aggravate me." He took a healthy swig and grinned at her.

"Well, you have a lovely opinion of me."

Hank laughed and took another long sip. She hadn't touched her ginger ale yet.

"You're wound too tightly, Darcy."

She smiled. "Really? You think so?"

"I do. You were just a witness at a murder scene and . . ."

"How do you know . . .?"

"I was there . . .remember?" He raised a brow at her and grinned.

"You know what I mean. How do you know she was murdered? I watched the clip again before I picked up the barbeque, and I couldn't see anything except Bridget falling."

Hank put his beer down on the small marble coffee table, and ran his fingers up and down the bottle, catching some of the damp condensation. "This is not for publication," he said, "but the Medical Examiner found evidence of bruising on her upper arms, and a high concentration of rohypynol and alcohol in her system."

"Rohypynol? Isn't that the date-rape drug?" Darcy leaned forward.

"One of them, yes."

"Is that why she didn't flail her arms and legs as she fell? She was out of it, wasn't she? I don't know if that makes me feel better or worse." Darcy flopped back into the soft padding of the chair.

Abby breezed in carrying a large platter of ribs in one hand and the bowl of fruit salad in the other.

"Hope you guys are hungry," she said as she set the food on the table.

CHAPTER 6

Abby took one look at both Darcy slumped in her chair, and Hank with his jaw set like granite, and knew something was not as it should be.

"Honestly, you two. I only left you alone for a minute. You're not enemies you know. Shall we sit in the dining room?"

Darcy and Hank walked to the small round oak table. Hank held a chair for Abby. Darcy picked up the rolls from the ledge in the tiny kitchen. She plucked up her napkin and slid it across her lap. "We're not fighting. Hank simply implied . . ." Darcy paused and looked across at Hank for permission to share the information. He nodded wearily as if bowing to the inevitable.

"You understand that this is an ongoing investigation . . ." she hedged.

"Yeah. Yeah. Get to the good stuff. I won't tell a soul. I promise." Abby held her hand up in like she was testifying in court..

"The investigation indicates Bridget Emerson was murdered. The Medical Examiner found both alcohol and a date rape drug called 'roofies' in her system. She was also pregnant." Hank said, unable to tolerate this torturous dance. "The Medical Examiner's report is going to be made public tomorrow anyway."

"OMG!" Darcy said. It came out sounding sharper than she intended.

"Dear, the age of *The Scarlet Letter* is long since passed.

Regrettably, young people still insist on participating in dubious activities, but it's hardly new, nor something for which she deserved to die." Abby smiled at Darcy to soften the implied rebuke.

"I didn't mean it like that. Don't you see? The pregnancy could be a motive. Maybe it was Sam Carson's baby, and he didn't want her to have it. Maybe he thought it would tangle up his life too much, so he drugged her and pushed her off the top of the Ferris wheel. Bye, bye, Bridget and bye, bye, baby," Darcy slapped her hands against one another as if removing dirt from them.

"What do you know about Sam Carson?" Hank glared at her.

Uh-oh. The Police Detective just entered the room.

"Well . . ." Darcy began slowly, trying to pick her words carefully. "I asked around about him. I guess he saw her the night she died—was murdered, I mean."

Hank's jaw tightened, but when he spoke, he spoke softly. "And you would know that because?"

"I talked to him."

Hank leaned across the table. Darcy thought if Abby hadn't been there, he might have vaulted across it. She raised her hand to stop him from saying something they'd both regret.

"Hang on. I only spoke to him for a moment. He said he'd seen Bridget earlier, but then left her to go downtown."

"You hang on. This is now a murder investigation. You're not prying into allegations of illegal garbage dumping."

The last investigative report Darcy had filed when she worked at the station in Kansas City was about a city council member who was illegally dumping garbage on some land to drive down the resale values. He intended to clear out the surrounding land, buy it for a song, and make a fortune. He was now awaiting trial.

"How did you know about that?" she narrowed her eyes.

He didn't even have the grace to look embarrassed. "You may think we're all a little backward here, but we are familiar with the World Wide Web."

"You investigated me? Well, of course you did." She folded her arms across her chest. "So you undoubtedly found out that my station took a lot of flak because of that story."

"So, they fired you?"

"No. I left for professional reasons."

"Such as?"

"Such as they wouldn't give me any investigation stories anymore. If I wanted to be a feature's reporter, I figured I could do pretty much the same thing here and be close to my friends and my family."

"Pass me your plate Detective and I'll give you some salad," Abby trying to change the subject.

"Call me Hank please, Ms. McNeill."

"Then you must call me Abby. I don't much like being called Ms. McNeill since I've retired." She piled on the salad.

"Who do you think you are?" Darcy finally found her voice.

Hank took a bite of salad and chewed it thoroughly before he responded. "Do you always use your bad temper as an emotional smoke screen?"

"What's that supposed to mean?"

"That you side-stepped the serious point of my statement about this being a murder investigation by getting righteously indignant that I looked you up on the internet." Hank smiled, genuinely amused. "Nice try, but it won't work."

"I don't have any idea what you mean," Darcy lied. *It was one of her favorite tactics; deflect and redirect.*

Hank cocked an arrogant brow in her direction, but he smiled at her. "Yes, you do. Stay out of it. I mean it, or I'll be forced to arrest you for obstruction in a police investigation."

"More ribs anyone?" Abby interrupted.

"How can I possibly obstruct an investigation that isn't happening in the first place?" She smiled back at him.

"Don't you love these white rolls they pack with the ribs? I don't know whether it's the rolls or the honey butter, but they sure are delectable." Abby licked her lips.

Hank and Darcy looked at her, sitting cherubically tearing a small morsel from a roll and slathering it with butter. Her bright blue eyes sparkled as she savored the bread. Hank and Darcy dissolved into laughter.

"Well, they *are* delicious." Abby sounded defensive.

They knew they had just been "handled." Neither of them wanted to reopen the argument, anyway. They both were aware where the other one stood—in direct opposition.

By the time they'd cleaned away the remnants of the meal, it was time for Darcy to pack up and head for the park.

"I'll follow you up," Hank offered. "I have to talk to some people at the park too."

Darcy looked at Abby. She was no help. Abby shrugged her shoulders, but her eyes twinkled. Darcy was wary of Abby when she resembled a naughty two-year-old.

Darcy picked Mac up and scratched his ears. "You be good for Abby, okay boy?" She glanced at Abby. "It is okay if I leave him with you isn't it? I didn't even think to ask."

"No problem. I've long since given up going down to the bars at night during Rodeo Days. Since they don't do street dancing any-more and no one rides their horse into the bars, there's not much I'm interested in. Mac is always welcome. So are you, Hank." She beamed up at him.

"Darcy's always had a stubborn nature, but it's not personal," Abby said to him softly to Hank as he passed.

"With *some* people, it's not personal," Darcy said over her shoulder.

Darcy strode toward the lobby door. Hank got there ahead of her and held it open. Confused by his gallantry, it must have shown on her face. "Simply because you aggravate the hell out of me, doesn't mean I don't like you." He smiled that irritating "gotcha" smile.

"Why thank you, kind sir. And simply because you are officious and arrogant doesn't mean I don't appreciate the courtesy."

Hank laughed.

They went to their respective cars and drove to the park. It was annoying having Hank follow her. She would usually go about five miles faster than the posted limit which a regular patrolman would let slide, but she was fairly sure that Hank would pull her over only to be perverse. She was also concerned that Hank would try to stop her investigating Bridget's death. She couldn't, wouldn't, give it up.

Bridget's father deserved answers, and Darcy would do whatever she had to do to get them.

Entering the park, she flashed her badge at the volunteer security guard, and drove to the PR Office. It was a short walk to the north end of the midway. She checked her rearview mirror to see if Hank was still behind her. She breathed a deep sigh of relief when she saw his pickup veer off to the right toward the Buckin' A Saloon.

Jack Brady, the van man, and Bill Netters were standing outside the van, leaning against it.

"Hi guys. Been waiting long?"

"Nope. Just got here," Brady said.

"Where do you want to set up?" Netters glanced around.

"I want to do a long shot of the midway concessionaires, then shift to an inset shot for each of the interview venues. Let's start with the Turkey Leg guy, add the Mesa Jewelry lady and finish at the south end of the midway with Charlie Sanders the hat steamer. We'll do all the interviews as medium shots and pull back to a long shot and move down the midway. Does that sound okay?"

"Yeah, that's doable. You think they'll let us park the van by the concession trucks?" Brady asked. "We should be able to get a clear signal if I raise the mast up high enough."

"Wait a sec. I'll check." Darcy swiped on her phone and found Bob Cochran, the Concession Chairman's number. They would need his permission.

After a short conversation, Cochran cleared it with Security. Darcy stuffed her phone in her back pocket and hopped into the van. "Let's round 'em up and head 'em out."

"What's with her?" Brady asked Netters.

"Cowboy fever," Netters said. "You know how dudes are. Give 'em a hat and a pair of boots and they try to out 'aw shucks' everyone in sight."

"Everybody's a critic." Darcy laughed.

It didn't take long to find a place to park and raise the mast. Darcy and Netters did some wandering checks to make sure the signal was clear from all three venues. Since this was live, they didn't have the luxury to shoot and edit later. They did a check through with Bryce Adkins at the station. He was anchoring the nightly news.

Darcy took time to set up the people to talk to on camera at each spot. Charlie was shy, but she finally talked him into it. They returned to the starting point by the Turkey Leg Stand.

Netters established the connection with the van, and they waited for the signal to begin. Darcy checked her notes. Live remotes always had the added drama of the possibility of things going terribly wrong.

Moving in, Netters shot a close-up.

"Thanks, Bryce. This is Darcy Moreland on the midway at Cheyenne Rodeo Days. As you can see . . ."

Netters did a long shot, and she kept talking.

". . . a large variety of concessionaires offer a dizzying array of goods and services. Today we're going to visit three different areas. Our first stop is at the Turkey Leg Stand."

Pulling back to a medium two shot, Netters adjusted the focus.

"With me is Ned Luce, the owner/operator of all the food concessions on the park. Mr. Luce, what's special about the Turkey Legs as carnival fare?"

Darcy stuck the mic under his mouth, and he smiled into the camera. He had obviously done this before.

"Well Darcy, I'd have to say that it's good carnie food because it's portable . . ." He held up a giant turkey leg for the camera, "and it has a unique flavor."

"Could you share a little of how that unique flavor is achieved?"

"Sure. You begin with a mixture of lemon lime soda; mix it with pepper sauce, onions, sugar, and hot sauce."

"Wow. That's quite a combination."

"Yeah. The best part is after you boil the legs in this concoction for about forty minutes; then take them out and smoke them slowly. To help create the light brown crust, we drizzle a little honey over them to seal in the juices. Here. Try one."

Darcy hadn't bargained for that, but she took the leg and bit a chunk off. It was good. Rolling her eyes, Darcy smiled covering her mouth. "Certainly worth coming out to the park for," she said as soon as she could swallow. Darcy surreptitiously handed him the leg out of the frame. "Thanks very much." They shook hands and Ned palmed a wet wipe into her sticky hand. She smile at him thanking him for his thoughtfulness.

Netters followed as she wandered down the center of the midway until she stopped at the Mesa Jewelry tent. She turned and faced the camera, still licking the honey-sweet residue of the Turkey Leg from her lips. Using the wet wipe to erase any lingering residue, she smiled brightly at the camera.

"If the food doesn't get you, the jewelry will. Mesa Jewelry is a traditional favorite for both locals and tourists. As you can see . . ." Netters did a quick pan while Darcy continued. ". . . they offer an astonishing variety of jewelry with precious, semi-precious and traditional Southwestern designs. Here to speak with us is Barbara Childers, a longtime veteran concessionaire of Rodeo Days. Thanks for taking the time to talk to us."

"Thanks for having me." She smiled into the camera. Another pro, Darcy thought.

"Can you tell us what the most popular trend in jewelry these days?" Darcy asked.

"Turquoise is always a favorite, but we're seeing it produced in a wider variety of colors now. This . . ." She held up a stunning necklace of silver and a darker blue stone than the light blue shade usually called turquoise. ". . . is called denim turquoise because it's the color of a new pair of jeans."

"Beautiful." Darcy took it and looked at it briefly.

"This is called White Buffalo for obvious reasons." She held out a pendant of a silver trimmed white stone with random flecks of black. Netters came in for a close up.

"There's certainly a huge variety," Darcy gushed.

Ninety percent of a live remote like this was the gushing. She remembered Mr. Roberts in her television production class had told them that "planned enthusiasm" as he called it, could be a real asset. So she enthused all over the place.

"We try to offer our customers the best choice and value we can."

"Thanks so much for giving us a small feel of what's available here at Mesa Jewelry,"

"Almost everyone who comes to Rodeo Days buys a cowboy hat," Darcy said as they were on the move again. "It's part of the fun. There are places all over the midway to buy hats. Here at Hats and Tack, another traditional vendor, you can buy the high roller 40X Stetson or a tourist straw that will last the two weeks but not much beyond." She picked up the planted samples for the camera.

"Whichever you choose, you'd be wise to avail yourself of the services of Charlie Sanders. Mr. Sanders is a hat shaper. Mr. Sanders, what exactly is a hat shaper?"

"Uhm, well. I . . ."

Darcy had to turn Charlie toward the camera. Unlike the previous two, Charlie was decidedly uncomfortable.

"What's this thing for?" She gestured toward the steamer.

"That softens the material of the hat, so I can form it better."

"Does that work for both felt and straw?" Darcy asked. She figured if she kept him focused on the process, he would forget the camera was there.

"Yeah. 'Course the more expensive the hat, the longer the shaping will hold."

"I see. Why should people have you shape their hats for them? I understand it's a free service offered here at Hats and Tack."

"That's right, we don't charge for it. If you're going to buy a hat, even if you only wear it here for the rodeo, it needs to look right. Hats are unloaded from boxes and sometimes one side of the brim is mashed or the curve they put on it at the factory isn't right for your face or the crown or crease is off, so I fix it for you." He smiled at her. "I see you're still wearing the one I shaped for you."

"Yes I am." Darcy smiled back. This guy was hard to resist. He was grandpa-sweet, charming. "I've gotten a lot of compliments on it. By the way, do you ever recommend a particular style of hat? I mean if someone chose a style that was too big or small in scale, would you tell them?"

"Sure. Lots of people don't know what'll look good on them. Sometimes they pick one off the rack that looks like their idea of a cowboy and it's all wrong. I usually ask how long they want to wear it and for what. I check their coloring and the shape of their face. Then I try to shape it according to what they need."

"Thanks for the information, Mr. Sanders. Anything else we should know about hats?"

"The hat and shape you choose says a lot about you, so pick it carefully."

"Or if you're new to the experience, try to find someone like Charlie here who can help you get the best look and fit. Thanks, Charlie."

"Sure." Charlie smiled.

Netters gave Darcy the signal to wind up. "I hope you've enjoyed this small sampling of the vendors here on the midway. We've barely scratched the surface, so come on out and see for yourself. This is Darcy Moreland from, KCWY News Channel 23. Back to you, Bryce."

Netters signaled cut.

"How was it?" Darcy asked.

"You mean content or signal?" Netters began winding up cables.

"Both." Darcy plopped her fists on her hips. What was with all the men around her lately?

"Brady how was it?" Netters said into his headset. "He says it was golden. We done here?"

"Yeah. Why don't you guys take off? I want to talk to Charlie for a minute. If you need me, my cell's on, and thanks."

"Sure thing." Netters smiled at Charlie. "Nice to meet you."

"Same here," Charlie said. "Come back when you want a real hat. "Charlie said to Netters. "Never could understand why anyone'd want to wear a baseball cap with someone else's brand on it and pay good money for the pleasure."

Netters laughed. "You've got a point. He took off his grungy cap and looked at it.

"'Course I can turn this around when I need to shoot video. You can't do that in a cowboy hat."

"True enough." Charlie's wrinkled face curved into a smile.

Netters left, and Darcy turned to Charlie. "You did really well. I knew you would."

"Thanks, but don't ask me to do it again. I don't much like it." Charlie went back to his little alcove behind the counter.

"You got it. Charlie. One more question. Were you working the night that girl fell from the Ferris wheel?" She figured Charlie would appreciate her not wasting his time.

"Yup." He picked up a black open crown hat and held it toward the jet of steam. Darcy watched, fascinated as he gently ran a crease down the center of the crown.

Peering up at the triangular view through the open tent flap, she could observe the whole wheel from here.

"Did you see anything? Did you notice how she fell?" It had not yet been made public that Bridget been murdered, so she was treading carefully here.

"Nope."

"Are you sure? She was a really young kid. Was she standing up in the bucket or something?" Darcy was pushing but it felt important to try and jog his memory.

"I didn't see the little gal till she hit the ground. I heard the thud from here."

Darcy winced, remembering. "So, you didn't witness anything odd?"

"I didn't say that." Charlie continued to shape the crown with the two dimples on either side of the main crease.

Darcy waited, but it was hard. Sometimes with guys like Charlie if you shut up and let them tell you what they knew, you'd get more out of them than if you peppered them with questions.

Charlie began to steam the brim, holding the curl gently until the heat left and the curve stayed. "I did see a young buck jump from one of the cars when it got closer to the ground."

Her heart flip-flopped, but she focused on trying to sound calm. "Can you describe him? How tall?"

"Medium-tall, I guess."

"Build?" she pressed.

He put the hat down on the counter and looked at her like she'd just cussed and spit. "It was dark, and it happened fast. All I can tell you is his hat had a buckaroo telescope crease, with a double loop stampede string."

"What's that?"

"It's the kind of hat Tom Mix wore in those 1920 shoot-em-ups. High crown with a front slanted crease. Got his hat knocked back. That's why I noticed the stampede string."

"Are you sure?"

Charlie looked at her and picked up the hat he was working on.

"Okay. Okay. You're the expert. One more question. Would a bulldoger be likely to wear a hat like that?"

"Not likely. They tend to favor the lower brimmed cattleman's crease, like this." He held up the hat. Less likely to get knocked off by the wind."

"But perhaps for dressing up at night . . .?"

"A man tends to choose his style that announces who and what he is. He's not likely to change the style for nighttime."

Darcy remembered Sam Carson's hat. It was not the least like a Tom Mix style. So who was it that jumped off the back end of the wheel that night?

CHAPTER 7

D ARCY AMBLED DOWN THE MIDWAY, turning over the new details in her mind. Bridget was pregnant. From what Stacie Rogers told her, Sam Carson seemed a reasonable suspect. Darcy wondered why any young girl in this day and age would intentionally get pregnant unless she was trying to trap someone into marrying her. Carson was definitely old enough to know how to avoid that entanglement.

The guy was also a self-centered womanizer who might see Bridget's condition as an "inconvenience" which would justify getting rid of both the girlfriend and the problem.

But if what Charlie Sanders told her was right, maybe it wasn't Carson. Maybe Bridget got depressed or frightened and jumped. No—she was full of roofies and alcohol. Bridget was lucky to even get on the ride, let alone deliberately jump off. Whoever stayed up there with her either murdered her or accidentally caused her death.

She pulled out her phone to call Hank, then slipped it back into her pocket. He had made it crystal clear that he wanted her to stop asking questions. Until she verified the information, it would really be a waste of Hank's time, she rationalized. It might be nothing. The phrase, obstruction of justice, niggled at the edge of her brain.

She glanced around. Early evening brought people out looking for cold beers and hot thrills. Flashing lights and whirring bells of the rides added to the crazy-quilt atmosphere.

From a distance, she heard Garth Brooks singing at the night show, "...I've got friends in low places..." The arena crowd roared.

That was the trouble with cowboys, rodeo cowboys at least. They thought in terms of the next show on down the road. To their sorrow, lots of girls had learned, in terms of priorities, relationships ranked low for most of the young rodeo cowboys, and there weren't too many old rodeo cowboys around the circuit. Once they got older and so banged up it wasn't worth the risk or the life, they quit. Usually they stayed in ranching. Some even became stock contractors for rodeos all over the United States.

That was why she had been so sure Sam Carson had killed Bridget. He was still young enough to think himself too young to be tied down. But if not Sam Carson, who? Could it be another cowboy?

The top of the Ferris wheel dominated the other rides. It was certainly one of the tallest. The yellow police tape had been removed. Amazing how efficiently the crews worked to make sure the "show" went on. Even death didn't slow it down.

She walked over to see if the carnie was back from his drunk. Perhaps he'd remember Bridget or more importantly, the guy she got on the ride with.

The man running the ride looked typically carnie. Late twenties or early thirties, he wore a smudgy gray t-shirt, and torn, faded jeans. He hadn't shaved in at least a day or more. Standing by his side out of the way, Darcy caught a whiff of garlic-tinged sweat.

"Hi. I'm Darcy Moreland."

"No free rides," he barked at her as he pulled open the gate closure and three tweeny girls jumped off and giggled their way down the exit ramp.

"I was wondering if I can talk to you for a second."

"'Bout what?" He eyed her suspiciously and loaded an older couple into the basket then slammed and latched the gate.

"Were you running this ride on the night that young girl fell."

He glared at her while he pulled the lever to bring the next bucket forward to be unloaded and loaded again. "Lady I don't know who you are. You're not a cop. That's for damn sure."

"How do you know?" Darcy bluffed.

"No badge. Cops either wear 'em or flash 'em."

"Oh. Have you had a lot of experience with the police?" She really didn't care about the answer, but she wanted to keep him talking.

"Lady, I'm busy here."

Darcy tried her most soothing voice. "I need to know if you remember anything, like who she was riding with?"

"Some cowboy." He motioned her back and began the ride. He watched with bored detachment as the huge wheel revolved slowly through the summer night air.

"Did you notice anything strange?"

"You mean like did I notice she was falling down drunk? Yeah. None of my business. If her boyfriend wanted to cop a cheap feel on the ride, I say go for it."

"But she fell—"

"Not my problem either. I didn't do nothin' wrong."

"No. I didn't mean to imply that you did. I meant it ultimately became more serious than copping a cheap feel."

"Still, not my problem." He pulled back on the lever and reversed the direction of the ride.

"Didn't you think it was strange that her boyfriend didn't yell for help or something?"

"The cops asked me the same thing. Harry had relieved me for my dinner break. I wasn't running the ride when she swan-dived."

"Can you at least tell me what her date looked like?" Darcy leaned against the gate railing.

"Why should I?" He stuck his grease-stained hands into the front pockets of his equally grimy jeans.

She pulled out a twenty and held it up, so he could get a glimpse of Jackson on the front.

He snatched it out of her fingers and stuffed it into his pocket. "About six-foot, black hair. Didn't look like no real cowboy to me."

"Why?"

"Dunno. Hands was too white and his clothes too new or some-thin'. He had new boots."

"What else?"

"He looked scrawny; you know like a kid who grew too fast. I was kinda like that when I was a kid." He did a slack-jawed chuckle, which afforded Darcy a gooey glimpse of the wad of tobacco stuffed between his lower lip and bottom teeth.

"If you had to guess, how old do you think he was?"

"Not more'n eighteen. I remember he looked real scared when I loaded them. Bet he'd never tried to feel a girl up before." He laughed at his own joke.

"Do you remember anything else?"

"Why do you want to know? Who are you, lady?"

"I'm with KCWY, and I was here the night she, um . . . fell."

"Oh, you was that gal with the camera guy? I saw you down there." For some unfathomable reason that revelation made her questions okay.

"Name's Ken Runnel." Wiping his hand on the back of his butt, he thrust it out. He smiled a yellow-tinged smile

Darcy took his hand. "Darcy Moreland. Nice to meet you." She smiled at the absurdity of this cocktail party exchange happening here on the ramp to the Ferris wheel.

"I only remember one weird thing. I mean besides the fact that she was drunk . . ." He let the sentence hang and began to unload and load passengers from the ride. He returned to Darcy while they waited for the next basket to align.

"What was weird, Ken?" She deliberately used his name.

"She didn't have a wristband on, but he did. Don't ya think it's weird he'd buy a wristband for himself, but not for her?"

The bands were good for the night and sold in color-codes of neon pink, bile green, or bilious blue to designate the day they were good for.

"Maybe she wasn't much of a carnival fan. I mean, possibly the only ride she thought she could stomach was the Ferris wheel. My mother's like that."

He went to open the next basket. "I don't see that happen much, is all. A guy takes a girl to the carnival, and she don't like to ride, he don't usually buy a wrist band for himself."

"Well, you'd be the expert." Darcy smiled at him. "I guess that's all for now, but if you think of anything else, could you call me at the station?" She passed him a generic card with the station's number and logo on it.

"Sure. Darcy—um?"

"Moreland," she supplied. "Thanks."

Pulling out her small notebook, she wrote "wrist band" with three question marks after it and veered down the ramp.

"Well hi, stranger."

She heard the greeting seconds before being enveloped in a huge bear hug that knocked her hat off.

"Hey. Take it easy on my wardrobe." Darcy returned the hug. Her father, Ed Moreland was grinning down at her.

Her father wasn't a big man, but he was solid, and he gave the best hugs. Darcy twisted in her father's arms and greeted her mother standing nearby. Handing Darcy the hat after brushing off the dust, Donna Moreland leaned in for a motherly peck and quick hug.

"I didn't think you were in town yet." Darcy said.

"Just," her mom said. "I was going to call you after I found a quiet corner. Your dad insisted we get to the park ASAP. I haven't even unpacked." Donna linked her arm through her daughter's and began walking forward letting Ed follow behind. "Your father barely let me dump my stuff and change before we came out here," Donna said over her shoulder to make sure Ed could hear. "He's like an old circus horse." Darcy and Donna shared a laugh. Her dad loved everything about Rodeo Days and they both knew it.

"Are you working tonight?" Darcy asked. Her parents always volunteered to work a couple of shifts up at the CRD Club during Rodeo Days.

"Nah. We're not scheduled till tomorrow for the lunch rush," Ed said. "We thought we'd come have a look around. Are you working?"

"Not at the moment. I did a live remote earlier, so I'm off for the rest of the evening."

"Great. Let's all go up and get a drink." Ed started to steer Donna and Darcy toward the exposition hall.

Pushing past the doorway clogged with people they began to climb the green concrete stairs to The Club.

"I thought you guys were going to come later this year," Darcy said as she turned to look down on them below her.

"We are later. We missed the Corn Ball and the first rodeo and first parade." Ed scowled at his wife.

Darcy tried to look shocked. "Oh no. You missed the Coronation Ball? Do you think she'll be a legit Miss Frontier since you weren't here to give her a blessing? Do you think they'll revoke your buckle?"

Her dad playfully swatted her butt and Darcy scampered up the rest of the stairs laughing.

The CRD Club was an organization of former Chairmen and their wives. Darcy referred to the distinctive rectangular buckle that marked a man as a chairman or former chairman.

During the year, The Club met once a month, but during the "show" they worked to provide a quiet air-conditioned place for the volunteers to rest and get a cheap hot dog and beer. It had a nice symmetry to it. Kind of like your former boss coming in to give you a meal and a break.

The security man at the door was a friend of Ed's and after greeting and glad-handing, they passed through.

The first fifteen minutes in the club, her dad worked the room like a politician. Her mom was almost as bad, but the three of them finally strolled to the food line and ordered.

Darcy got an egg salad sandwich which she divvied up for her mom and her. Her dad got a chili-smothered hotdog. Donna shuddered at Ed's choice and he offered to go to the drink line which was separate from the food line. He ordered two Bud Lites, one for him and one for Darcy, and white wine for his wife. Darcy and Donna went to find a table. The night show was still going, so it was easy to find a table by a window overlooking the midway. Darcy deliberately chose not to sit facing the view of the Ferris wheel.

"So, how was your trip?" she asked and licked the residue of gelatinous egg salad from her top lip. "Was there a lot of traffic coming out of Prescot?'

"Pretty uneventful, actually," Donna said. "A little traffic on I25 out of Denver. Every year it gets worse. And then the usual hassle of packing up and dealing with your father's impatience."

"I wasn't impatient. I wanted to get here before the whole two weeks was over." He glared at his wife.

Turning to her daughter for support Donna said, "We had a condo-owner's meeting to go to before we left. They want to expand the pool and they thought it might be best to schedule it for next winter when the temperatures are more reasonable,"

Darcy smiled in sympathy. Her dad had tunnel-vision about Cheyenne Rodeo Days.

"Anyway, the residents were split, and we had to be there to vote."

"Won't make a damn bit of difference. They'll do whatever they want while we're gone," Ed grumbled and took another mouthful of his hot dog.

They ate and got caught up with everyone's news. Darcy assured her folks that she was enjoying working at the local station. When they started to ask what she was covering she got a little evasive. Darcy stood up.

"Just general feature stories right now about rodeo week. Just the usual, you know. Want another a beer, Dad?"

"Yeah. Thanks."

"You finally made it." Ginny Swain, and old friend of the Morelands, swooped in hugging them alternately. "Oh and look at little Darcy. My heavens you've grown into a beautiful young woman."

"I was going to get Dad a beer. Would you like something?"

"Oh yes, dear. Some Hard Lemonade. Thanks."

As Darcy was leaving the table, she heard Ginny begin to relate the gory details about the accident on the midway. She knew it was going to get ugly by the time she got back, so she picked the longest line to stand in and found herself looking at the broad back of Gary Romero, the Rodeo Chairman.

"Well, hello there, Darcy," he said when he turned. "Are you up here alone?" He'd dismissed the old guy with the pot belly and red suspenders who was standing behind her in line.

"I ran into Mom and Dad on the midway." Darcy got a scathingly brilliant idea. If Romero could run interference for her, maybe her dad would stop short of going nuclear. "They're over there. I'm sure they'd like to say hi."

He smiled at her uncertainly. She was babbling, but she couldn't seem to stop.

"Okay," he said, but watched her carefully from under the brim of his hat. He waited politely until Darcy got her order and walked back to the table with her.

"Darcy did you know there was an accident on the midway?" her dad asked as she put the beer in front of him.

"Of course, she did," Ginny said. "That's what I'm trying to tell you, Ed. She reported it on the news, didn't you honey?"

"Yes," she smiled tightly at Ginny. "Mom, Dad, you remember Gary Romero, don't you?"

The blessed reprieve didn't last long. Her dad was nothing if not tenacious.

"You didn't see it happen, did you?" he growled at her.

She winced and braced herself to charge through the explanation. "It was Bridget Emerson. Doc's daughter."

"Damn!"

Darcy rushed on. "I saw the body. We were doing a story on the Ferris wheel and Bill Netters—he's my videographer—was lying on the ground getting the . . . shot, when Bridget fell out from the top of the Ferris wheel, and . . ."

"Damn it, Donna. Didn't I tell you something like this was bound to happen?"

"Almost every waking minute, dear." She patted his hand dismissively, then her face grew serious. "What a tragedy. Go on, Darcy. What happened next?"

"Nothing much. The Medical Examiner took her body, the police came, and I went back to the station. That's it. End of story."

"Not exactly," Gary piped in. He had been watching the group dynamics.

"What do you mean?" Ed asked.

"Well, as I understand it, Darcy's been investigating without a license. She got some information from Maggie about Bridget's boyfriend. I know she practically lived at the Rodeo Office when she was growing up, but she is using her access to get information she shouldn't have."

Ed swiveled to his daughter. "Were you assigned to do a follow-up story or something? Please tell me you don't think the poor girl was pushed."

Romero butted in before she could answer. "Her station manager told me she was supposed to be covering feature stories, nothing else." Romero folded his arms. Darcy watched the look that passed between them, Chairman to Chairman.

"Damn it, Darcy. This is exactly why I didn't want you to go into this field in the first place. You can't leave well enough alone. Never could. This isn't like that story about illegal garbage dumping, young lady, this is serious."

"Not you too." Darcy snapped her mouth shut, knowing she'd already said too much.

"What does that mean; 'not you too'?" her mom asked.

"The detective assigned to the case looked me up on KCTV. com, the Kansas City's station website. Do you know they still have that damn story about the crooked council member loaded? You'd think after all this time . . ."

"Don't change the subject," Ed interrupted. "Are you going off half-cocked again?"

"I never go off half-cocked." She gathered her hat and her trash from the table and stood abruptly. "Gotta go. Bye, Mom, Dad. I'll see you later," kissing them both on the fly; she threaded her way to the back exit.

As she clomped down the steps, she thought about her dad's overprotective reaction. She couldn't blame him. If a young girl like Bridget could die in the middle of Rodeo Days, there was no place safe in this world. At least that would be the way he saw it.

The midway was sparkling as usual. Darcy kept thinking about Bridget's dad. *Doc must be devastated. She made a mental note to try to call him again. She also needed him to call Liz tomorrow and see if he was still intent on suing the carnival. She guessed that once the police announced she'd been murdered; the suit would be dropped.*

Darcy hitched her purse higher on her shoulder and headed toward where she'd parked her car. Someone shouted her name. Turning, she saw Gary Romero.

"Aren't you supposed to be some place official or something, or is there someone else you want to throw under the bus?"

"Nope. I already did the obligatory appearance on the pad, I'm free as a breeze right now."

The pad was a concrete slab in front of the stands where the Chairmen sat for the rodeos and night shows. They usually didn't stay long because they had details to take care of. You could watch the cell phones go off and one or another would leave.

"I just thought your dad ought to know what you're doing, and I wanted to give you an unofficial warning myself." He cocked the brim of his hat back and smiled.

"Don't you like Garth Brooks?" Darcy was still annoyed with him.

"Yeah, I do, but I had to put down a minor insurrection at the Rodeo Office."

Her reporter instinct kicked in. "Really? What?"

"If I tell you, will you forgive me getting you on the wrong side of your dad?"

She couldn't help but smile. "You can tell this has been a long-time argument between him and me. He's terrified something will happen to me, and you just fed his paranoia."

"Yeah, I know. I figured that out when I watched his blood pressure rise. I knew you were snooping around. I have to say, I kind of agree with your dad. This could get really messy before it's over."

"In case you haven't noticed, this is my job. I dig for details."

Gary turned her to face him. "No. You're supposed to be covering the show, not the accident. Zach Horton was clear about that when I talked to him."

"My job is to report the news wherever that takes me." She glared at his hand still on her arm then let her eyes slide up to his face. He let go.

Gary raised his hands in mock surrender. "Okay. Okay. I give." He was laughing.

"Sorry. I'm intense about this. I knew Bridget when she was little. She was young, and her death was senseless. I was half convinced her steer-wrestling boyfriend pushed her off, but that's not falling into place."

"You mean Sam Carson?"

"Yeah. You know him?" Her surprise was legitimate. The rodeo had about 2,000 contestants competing in seven events not counting the barrel racing and the wild horse race. It was unlikely that Gary would know them all.

"I do now," Gary said.

"Why is that?"

"Let me buy you a drink and I'll tell you the whole sordid tale." He paused and riveted her with his soft brown eyes. "Most of this will be off the record. Okay?"

"It's a deal." *If the story was off the record, it was probably juicy.*

"Let's go over to Chute 10. It'll be quiet as long as the concert is still going on."

"I haven't been in Chute 10 since Dad got off the Committee. You're on."

Chute 10 was a private bar staffed by the current committee usually, or by former chairmen and their wives during the show. It was meant to be a place to relax, but also to meet with stock contractors, champion cowboys, representatives from other rodeos, or sponsors. It also served as a meet and greet place for the night show entertainers. It wasn't posh, but it was cool, quiet, and empty when they strolled past the security volunteer at the door.

"Hi, Don," Gary greeted the guy behind the bar. "Can you believe it? This is Ed Moreland's girl, Darcy. Darcy, this is Don Grant. He's a former Security Chairman."

It felt odd to go back to being introduced as Ed's kid. In Kansas City, she was just Darcy Moreland, on-air busybody. "Hi. Nice to meet you." She smiled.

"What'll you have?"

"A Bud Lite, please." Darcy ran her palm across the top of the bar covered with CRD memorabilia embedded under epoxy, trapping the past like a fly in amber.

"Need a glass?"

"Thanks, no."

"Same for me, Don," Gary said.

Don placed the beers on the bar, and they moved down to sit

at the far end. Darcy had barely hooked her heels on the rail of the barstool before she said, "Okay, spill."

Romero laughed. His brown eyes turned the color of a dark whiskey.

"You don't go in much for foreplay, do you?"

"Only if we're talking sex. We aren't talking sex, are we?" Darcy tried to embarrass him, but he looked unfazed.

"Isn't that what talking is, foreplay?" Gary cocked an eyebrow at her.

"Remind me to get you a good how-to book."

"Preferably one with pictures. I like pictures," he smiled then sipped his beer casually.

She gave him points for sheer audacity. "Seriously, what was the brouhaha about at the Rodeo Office?"

He looked at her for a moment as if he were deciding what to tell her. "This is off the record until he's arraigned tomorrow. You understand?"

Darcy jerked to attention. "You mean they've arrested someone for Bridget's murder?"

"No. No. Nothing like that. Do you remember Randy Johnson, the barrel man?"

"That nice old guy with the cute dog? Sure, I do. What about him?"

"Well as I understand the story, Randy came into the barn where he'd settled his donkey and the other animals he uses in his act, in time to see Sam Carson rousting them out of the stall. Randy went up to him and said something like, 'Young feller. That's my livestock you're messing with there.' Carson ignored him and loaded his horse into the now vacant stall. When Randy protested, Carson started to beat him up."

"My God. That's awful. Is Randy all right?" Carson was younger by at least thirty years, heavier and taller than the small rodeo clown.

"Bruised up some. Some of the cowboys found Randy lying on the floor of the barn. Carson was nowhere around. Randy didn't know who Carson was, but one of the boys recognized Carson's horse."

"Carson's being arraigned for assault?" Darcy was stunned. Guys who were big tended to either be intimidating jerks or big teddy bears. Nothing soft and cuddly about Sam Carson evidently.

"Yup. Tomorrow at ten."

"Does he lose his entry fee? You're not going to let him still compete, are you?"

"That's what Nate Myrick asked me. You know Nate, don't you? The General Chairman?"

"Yeah, yeah. And you said . . .?"

"I said the guys would likely handle it." He smiled and sipped his beer. His eyes twinkled at telling the story.

"And? You're not testifying in front of Congress. Spit it out."

"Seems one or two young bucks cornered Carson in the barn. Randy's pretty well liked around the circuit. Keith Simpson, from my committee, asked Sam if he had a picture of himself. Sam said, 'Yeah. Why?' Simpson said, 'So you can remember what your face used to look like.' Then he proceeded to pound him to mush."

Gary and Darcy shared a laugh. She wasn't usually a proponent of fighting, but this one sounded like pure old-time Western justice.

"He doesn't get to compete, right?"

"Wrong. We can't keep him from competing just because he had a fight out of the arena. If we did that, we'd be short a slew of cowboys after Saturday night. He's still slated to go during slack tomorrow.

"Don't you hate having to be fair?" she swigged her beer.

"Lady, you have no idea."

CHAPTER 8

$\mathbf{D}$ARCY WAS ENJOYING HERSELF, BUT GARY said he had to get going. His days began with slack competition every morning at 7:00 a.m.

The early morning roping events called slack, ran timed events like roping, steer wrestling, tie down, and barrel racing. Timed events didn't have an entry limit so slack was used to narrow the field. Rough stock entries, bull, bareback and saddle riding were run during the regular rodeo and held to about 160 entries.

"When the show is over, I'll have time for a real life." He smiled at her as he held the car door open.

"You mean this is your 'pretend' life?"

"'Bout sums it up." He grinned.

"Maybe we can get together after this party's over." She slid in behind the wheel.

"Oh, I'm sure you'll be underfoot for the duration. I'm bound to see you again." He touched the brim of his Stetson in an old-fashioned show of courtesy.

Ignoring his "underfoot" crack, Darcy pulled out of the parking lot and focused on the information Gary had given her.

So, Carson was a bully. Sadly, Darcy knew the type. No matter where you go in this world there are bullies. School bullies are the worst because you're too young to have built up a tough hide. Adult bullies usually used passive aggressive behavior, or if they are real morons you used your fists. By the time she pulled up in front of her apartment building, she was more certain than ever Carson was guilty of Bridget's murder. He may not fit the description of the guy who saw her last, but Carson might have drugged her, which would make him ultimately responsible for her death. What if the other guy was just trying to help her? All she had to do was get the proof.

As she locked her car door, she could hear the faint strains of music drifting up from downtown. It was Saturday night, and the partying was full on. Not for her; she was beat. All she wanted to do was get out of her boots and jeans, chat with Abby, and cuddle with Mac.

Raising her hand to knock, she jumped when the door jerked open.

"Oh, Darcy. Thank God you're here."

"Abby? What's the matter?" Darcy draped her arm across Abby's shoulders and closed the door behind her. Abby was dabbing at her eyes with a handkerchief. Darcy could tell she had been crying.

Darcy attempted to lead her to her chair, but Mac was jumping around trying to get her attention. She finally got Abby seated and scooped up her annoying dog and sat next to Abby.

"What's happened?" Darcy asked.

"Mac was getting restless after you and Hank left, so I decided to take him for a short run in the park before we settled in for the night, and . . ."

"Are you okay?" Darcy took both of Abby's hands in hers.

"Of course, dear. It's just that things like this don't happen here, at least to me."

"What things?" She let go of Abby's hands, Mac jumped off her lap and onto Abby's. "Easy to see where his loyalties lie."

Abby laughed and scratched Mac behind the ears.

Having Mac near calmed her, and she smiled at Darcy. "I'm sorry dear. You must be tired and here I am greeting you at the door with what is probably a silly prank."

"Tell me what happened."

"Well, I let Mac off the leash once we got to the park. He's always such a gentleman . . ."

"Abby." Darcy practically growled at her.

"Okay. This time Mac ran away from me toward the playground. Someone was calling to him; you see . . ."

"Who?"

"That's the point. It was getting dark, and I couldn't see well, but I could hear a voice calling to Mac, saying 'Come here boy, I've got a treat for you.' I ran after him as fast as I could and I made him spit out the doggie treat they'd given him, but whoever it was disappeared by the time I caught up."

"Was it a man or a woman?" Darcy tried to probe gently.

Abby looked like she might break out in tears again any minute.

Darcy had to stand and pace to try to get rid of the adrenaline that started pumping through her.

"I couldn't tell, honey. It was a sort of raspy whisper. It could have been anybody."

Darcy crossed the room and hugged her. "It's okay, Abby. It's probably just someone in the park who likes to feed the dogs."

"I doubt it." Abby shifted her weight in the chair, pulled out a crumpled slip of paper from her pocket, and handed to Darcy.

Darcy looked at Abby's worried face and tried to smooth out the paper on the coffee table. It was one of those notes that looked like it was banged out on a 1930 Underwood—funny—real funny.

```
Listen Bitch. Stop snooping
  or your damn dog will die.
```

Darcy read it through a couple times, but she couldn't process the words. Her mind veered off to the doggy treat they'd given Mac. It could've certainly been poison, but then the warning note would make no sense.

"The note was stuffed under his collar. I'm so sorry. I'd never do anything to put Mac in danger." Abby sat and wrung her hands.

Since Darcy was now sitting at Abby's feet, she rose up to give her another reassuring hug. "Of course not."

Mac tried to insert himself between them, and they let him. A few licks of his rough tongue did the trick. Abby laughed and pushed him back down in her lap.

"I've studied it over and over. I thought maybe I could figure out a syntax clue or something."

"What?" Darcy kept staring at the grubby piece of paper lying on the coffee table. Her mind was whirling. It couldn't be anyone she knew well but they obviously had something to do with Bridget's death. Couldn't be Sam Carson though could it? Maybe it was someone she worked with. Bryce Atkins was a real piece of work, but even he wouldn't stoop this low. She didn't think so anyway. Lost in thought, Darcy almost missed Abby's analysis.

"Well, you know, since English is an ever-evolving language, I thought maybe the language would give us a hint about, you know, age or education or . . ." Abby trailed off.

Tamping down her personal paranoia, Darcy focused on what Abby was saying. "Did you come to any conclusions?"

Darcy probed not only because she was interested, but because she thought Abby would feel better if she could talk.

"Not really. *Bitch* is an epithet for an amoral woman which comes from the Old English *bicce* and used in that derogatory form since the 15th century. Unfortunately, it is one of those words that seems to come down through every generation. Sad thing that."

"Uh-huh," Darcy responded as she held the paper up to the light to see if it had a bond or water mark. No luck. Plain, cheap, white.

"Snoop appeared around 1832, but snoopy and other derivations are a bit more modern, around the early 1920's."

"Mm hmm," Darcy hummed assent but was rubbing the print to see if it was produced by an actual typewriter or a font printed with ink jet. No bumps. Ink jet.

"My conclusions, I'm sorry to say, are sparse. I believe the perpetrator of this disgusting threat is young."

"Really? Why?" Now Abby had her attention.

"The vulgar name they used to address you is all too commonly abused by young people born and raised at the end of the last century. We crossed some linguistic Rubicon after the sixties, and I doubt we'll ever fully return to a humane, gentler use of language."

"You're right. Few people even blink when they hear that used anymore."

"I blame the rappers," Abby said with assurance. Darcy tried not to giggle, and Abby continued.

"I do. That word appears prominently in their music, which brings me to the word snoop. Not a word you often hear now except as it refers to Snoop Dogg, a rapper I might point out. Or it could refer to Snoopy *the* dog, also an image that appeals to the young."

Darcy could not help herself. She had to laugh. "I'm sorry Abby, but this is a little far-fetched even for me."

"I harbored a brief hope that maybe they were trying to be witty, you know, a play on words: Snoop Dogg and dog will die if you snoop, but even I couldn't jump that chasm."

"Well, thank God for that."

Abby arched her eyebrow in quiet disapproval and continued. "No, by its brevity and its threatening tone, I have concluded it was written by someone who hates to write any more than they have to. As a former English teacher, I'm familiar with the type."

"I tend to agree, but for simpler reasons. This was produced on a computer and printed by ink jet."

"How can you tell?"

"No bumps."

"I see, but is that conclusive? I mean countless people use computers these days," Abby said.

"True, but few experiment with different fonts. Most adults cling to Times New Roman or Courier. This typewriter font is designed to be a crude reproduction of ancient typewritten script. My guess is that the writer is a fan of those Film Noir style movies with their old-time detectives and mysterious notes. This may be nothing more than a tasteless game of 'Let's Pretend.'"

"So you don't think there's anything to worry about? It's just a prank?"

"It could be just a prank, but I'm not willing to bet Mac's life on it—are you?"

"Absolutely not. What do you suggest?"

"I suggest we never take Mac off the leash until this mess gets cleared up. We'll both need to be careful about where he goes and when. Okay?"

"Anything. Nevertheless, don't you think you should tell Hank about the note? It might mean something to him that's not readily apparent to us."

"And have him land right in the middle of me for stirring up more trouble? No thank you. We'll be wary and watchful."

"If you say so." She looked dubious.

"Abby, thank you for chasing them off. I really appreciate it." Darcy scooped Mac from her lap and kissed Abby's cheek. "I'm going to bed now and sleep the sleep of the righteous. Good night."

"Goodbye Mac." Abby waved at him like you would wave at a small child, just finger waggling.

"Now don't you worry about this," Darcy said.

"Alright," she said, but she didn't sound convinced.

Darcy went upstairs and fell into bed as soon as she got her clothes off and her T-shirt on. She tossed and turned for a while trying to shut down her brain. She kept repeating a phrase her mother had taught her, "Sufficient unto the day are the troubles thereof." Finally she calmed her troubled mind and if she didn't sleep the sleep of the righteous, it was at least the sleep of the dead.

She woke up the next morning to Mac licking her face. Judging by how wet she was, he had been at it for a while.

"Yuck Mac." Darcy plucked him from her chest and dropped him to the floor. He ran to the door and started scratching to get out.

"Just a minute." She hollered at him as she tried to squeeze back into her jeans from last night that had been lying in a heap on the floor. She didn't bother to tuck in the faded Chris LeDoux t-shirt she'd slept in and scuffled into her flip-flops by the door.

"Oh no you don't young man, not without your leash. How many times have I told you not to talk to strangers? This is what you get." Darcy lectured him as she snapped his leash in place and opened the door.

Mac tried to dash ahead, but Darcy wouldn't let him. They

wrestled with each other down the stairs and out the door. Instead of turning toward the park, Darcy went the opposite way. It was creepy to think about, but whoever wrote that note knew Mac was her dog and that she often walked him in the park.

By the time, Mac had "done his business" as her mother used to call it, they'd walked a good six blocks toward downtown. Darcy fidgeted because she wasn't exactly dressed for public appearances.

Heading back, she heard a horn honk behind her. Reflexively jerking Mac's leash close, she hauled him up in her arms before she turned around. It was Hank.

"Hi. You're up bright and early," he hollered at her through the open passenger side window. "Want to go get some breakfast somewhere?"

"I'm not dressed for the world yet." Darcy smiled at him, and kept walking, but he cruised slowly alongside.

"Why don't we take Mac home, get him some water, and I'll take you for a down and dirty, cheap, and filling, diner breakfast?"

She was tempted. She loved diner food. It was simple—eggs, toast, or flapjacks with some kind of meat—served with gallons of coffee, and the bonus was they rarely gave a damn what you looked like.

"Eh, why not?"

"A gracious response." He grinned at her. "Hop in. I'll take you home."

"Thanks," she climbed into his Ford pickup. "Nice," she commented as she slammed the door.

"Not the newest model, but I like it."

Mac stepped off her lap and sat between them for the short ride home. As soon as Hank pulled up in front of the Algonquin, Darcy jumped out and carried Mac to Abby's. She was damned if she'd leave him alone.

One thing she liked about her hometown was you could get almost anywhere in 15 minutes, which was about how long it took them to get to the Ace Diner.

Hank sat smiling at Darcy across the red checked vinyl tablecloth.

"What?" She looked at the front of her T-shirt to make sure she hadn't dribbled water down her front.

"I've got some news you might be interested in." He took the toothpick from his mouth and put it in his front pocket.

Darcy narrowed her eyes at him skeptically. "What kind of news?"

"It's about Sam Carson. I assume you're still curious about him."

"Of course I am. Aren't you?"

"Probably not as much as you, but yeah he's listed as a 'person of interest' in Bridget Emerson's death. This doesn't have anything to do with that though."

"Oh, is this about him assaulting Randy Johnson?" she asked before she thought.

"Damn, girl. Do you have a mole at the police station?"

"Better. I have connections at the park. All I know is that he was arrested, but I don't know anything beyond that." She waited.

He thought for a minute and relented. "Well it's public record. He was arraigned and let out on bail."

"So he can compete." She stabbed at her cooling eggs.

"Unless the Committee bans him, yeah." Hank hooked his hand around the thick, white, diner mug and took a swig of coffee. He looked speculatively at her over the rim.

"I already asked, but they said they can't ban him." Darcy must have sounded as disgusted as she felt.

"If it helps, his face looked mauled by the time we got to him." Hank smiled at her.

"Yeah. Randy has a lot of friends," Darcy said dismissively, and a new thought hit her. "How long was he in jail?"

"I think he was arrested early Saturday afternoon and released on bail by late evening, 9 or 10. Why?"

"Uhm, nothing. Simply curious," she said, chomping into her toast. Making a mental note to check the time with Abby, but she was fairly sure Carson wouldn't have been out of jail in time to threaten Mac. Now she was really stumped.

The breakfast conversation shifted to how Darcy had chosen journalism and why he had wanted to be a cop.

"My dad always said I was nosy, so journalism seemed like a natural fit. I like to believe I'm just naturally curious," Darcy told him. "So why did you choose to be a policeman?"

"That would be Detective, a title I earned by the way. My mom always said I was too bossy for my boots. She lamented that my job hadn't helped that particular character flaw. I like to believe I went into police work to help people, but sometimes it just comes down to being bossy."

Two things surprised her, Hank Nelson was funny, and he had a sexy smile. Both discoveries were disconcerting. Darcy didn't want to feel attracted to him, dismissing the whole notion. She had a drought in her love life, but she wasn't totally desperate.

Were you born and raised here? I can't believe I wouldn't have run into you somewhere. Where did you train?

When she finally took a breath, he answered. "I was born and raised in Denver. My dad and grandpa had been cops so I thought of it as the family business. I got an associate degree in criminal justice at Messa Community college, and then trained at the Denver Police Academy."

"Did you start to work in Denver right out of the Academy?"

"Yes, for several years. I earned my Detective badge there and then my cousin who lived here suggested I might like to move here. I came up and checked it out and the rest, as they say . . ."

"Yeah. History. Another thing. Why do you keep chewing on that damn toothpick?"

Hank laughed in spite of himself. Of all the things he thought she might ask this wasn't even on the list.

"I used to smoke. It got in my way and it affected my job, so I gave it up. I use the toothpick as a crutch. Does it bother you?"

"No. I was just curious."

"Ah. Now we're back to your addiction.

They both laughed. It was easy to be with him, Darcy thought, except when she got in his way.

It was almost noon before she got back to her apartment. Abby confirmed she and Mac had gone to the park about 7:30 last night. The police hadn't released Carson by then.

Darcy didn't have time to worry about it though. She needed to unpack her boxes and settle in. She had started at the station almost as soon as she got into town. And she absolutely had to do some laundry. Later, eating some peanut butter out of the jar, she watched her clothes whirl around in the ancient washer and dryer in the basement. Mac snuggled into the pile of towels waiting to be washed.

"Who else would care about my snooping around?" she asked Mac. He looked at her with such trust. She felt awful that she might have done something to put him in danger. "Don't worry, boy. I'll figure it out. I promise." Mac rested his head on his paws as if that settled everything.

Laundry finished, and some unpacking done, and dressed for the day, Darcy dropped Mac off at Abby's and headed out to the CRD grounds. She cheated and parked by the South end of the arena. She wanted to visit Chute 9 to watch the roping and steer wrestling.

Up the steps, she found a spot by the rail which overlooked the roping chutes and gave a bird's-eye view of the timed events.

The Tie Down event was already in progress. There were several good "catches" where the calf was roped and tied in good times. Pretty impressive at this level of competition. Next up was steer wrestling or bulldogging.

Darcy let her eye wander and spotted Sam Carson, waiting for his go. He was easy to find. No one was anywhere near him. Even from up here she could see the bruises under his eye and alongside his jaw. Darcy hadn't liked him before when she thought he was a chauvinist jerk, but after he beat up Randy, Darcy thought he deserved whatever came his way.

She watched Carson maneuver his horse back into the starting gate. The steer was in place, the hazer was in place on the other side ready to keep the steer running straight so Carson could jump and wrestle the animal to the ground.

The steer shot through the barrier. Carson's and the hazer's horses bolted after the steer. Carson kept riding, but the hazer swung his horse wide to the right and watched as the steer veered off into the wide arena making it impossible for Carson to catch the steer. Carson wheeled his horse around, looked at the hazer accusingly for a heartbeat, and rode out of the arena.

There is an unwritten Cowboy Code and Carson had broken one of its rules—never pick on someone smaller than you. Worse than that, never pick on someone who is respected and well liked like Randy Johnson. Carson had made a pot full of enemies. Whatever the court did to him would be minor compared to what his fellow cowboys would do to him.

Darcy guessed Romero was right. Rough cowboy justice had prevailed. The world of rodeo was small. Carson would do better to go home for the rest of the season. No one was going to let him forget even after his wounds healed.

Climbing down the steps and walking toward the midway, she watched Carson remove the saddle from his horse. Darcy saw the back of a young woman standing next to Carson, but she was too far away to see her clearly, a flash of green jeans and a brightly patterned western shirt. Both Carson and the woman wandered farther away, and Darcy was afraid to try to get any closer.

She'd wanted to see Carson compete. He got his ride, but not the time. Darcy got in her car, went home, and finished unpacking her meager belongings. She felt good. Mac was napping in his finally unpacked bed. Getting some ginger ale from the fridge, she decided to check in with Zach since she didn't have an assignment for today. She had his cell on speed dial and he answered quickly.

"Horton," was his terse answer.

"Hi, it's Darcy. You got anything for me?"

"You mean like old clothes or money for a cup of coffee?"

"Don't try funny," Darcy teased. "You don't have a talent for it."

"Like you would know." he shot back.

"Bye."

"Darcy. I do have an assignment for you. I want you to do a feature on the Behind the Chutes Tour they do in the morning. Meet with Carol Timm at the Western Museum by the *No Looking Back* statue. You'll need to be there by 6:30 tomorrow morning."

"Are you nuts? Remember me? I'm the person you had to call

every morning in college, so I wouldn't miss my ten o'clock class. I've never done mornings."

"Well, you're doing one tomorrow. Hey. Here's a thought. Why don't you stay up all night?"

"Hey. Here's a thought. Why don't you get stuffed?"

"Yeah, yeah. Netters will meet you there. It's some kind of early, special, tour for a contingent from Japan. They're nuts for the Old West in Japan. You know you could do a thing on east meets west. That'd be an interesting hook."

"The only hook I'm interested in at the moment is . . ."

"I get the idea. The upside is once you edit the piece, you'll be free for the rest of the day. How 'bout that?"

"Better than a sharp stick in the eye . . . but only by a titch."

"That's my girl. I'll see you tomorrow morning."

The phone went dead. She looked at her watch and it was only 3 o'clock. She counted on her fingers when she would have to go to bed to get any sleep and be up by 5:30 in the morning which was the absolute outside she could push it.

If she showered tonight and laid everything, out—yee gods. She would have to go to bed by 8. Darcy grabbed her phone and speed dialed Liz's cell.

"Western Insurance and Liability, Liz Baker speaking."

"Liz, what're you doing?"

"Not much. I had to finish some details on some claims."

"What are you doing working on Sunday?" Darcy reached into a box of stale Cheerios and began to crunch.

"Not in my ear."

"Oh. Sorry." Darcy stashed the box away. "Speaking of claims, is Doc Emerson still going to sue CRD because of his daughter's death?"

"I don't know. You'd think CRD couldn't be held responsible, but you know lawyers. They'll probably try to push a negligence claim on the carnival owner and CRD as a co-respondent. I hope I'm wrong."

"Well, that'll keep Tom Hayes and Nate Myrick up at night. What would you think of going down to the Pizza Palace downtown and splitting a cheese and pepperoni?"

"Sounds great. I'll come get you about 6, okay?"

"Could you make it 5? I've got an early assignment tomorrow."

"Not a problem. Be there at 5. Bye."

By the time Darcy took a fast shower and got Mac tucked in with Abby, it was almost 5. She carefully laid out her clothes for the next day and turned down her bed. She set her radio alarm for 5:30 am and plugged it in on the other side of the room so she'd have to get out of bed to shut it off. Darcy smiled. She was as prepared as she could be.

The evening with Liz turned out to be hugely entertaining. Liz was one of those people who kept track of everyone who graduated with them. If Liz didn't know where they were and what they were doing, she could find out for you. They gobbled up the pizza and trashed a few friends. The usual.

Darcy was finally starting to feel normal for a change.

CHAPTER 9

THE ALARM ON HER CLOCK RADIO honked like a bunch of geese heading south. Groggy, it took her a while to place the sound.

She threw back the covers and lunged to turn off the annoying noise. Unfortunately, she got her foot tangled in the sheets and flopped out of bed onto the floor. She scrambled to extract herself and ended up crawling to the far side of the room. Slamming her hand down on the off button, she barely caught the radio as it flipped off the tiny bedside table. This was not an auspicious beginning.

She was glad she had taken a shower last night. By the time she did a token make-up job for the camera, and dressed in her Western best, her mood had improved. She headed out the door in search of a cup of caffeine.

Driving the empty streets on her way to the park, she vainly searched for a place that was open at six in the morning. There was nothing. She knew there were truck stops on either end of town, but that would've made her late for the tour. She grimly faced the reality that she'd have to do this shoot sans stimulant.

Darcy pulled into the parking lot facing the front of the Western Museum. The tour was easy to find. A gathering of about a dozen Japanese tourists in Cheyenne, Wyoming would be hard to miss, even at a decent hour of the morning.

"Not much traffic this time of day," Netters said as he ambled over to her in a long-legged shamble, she was starting to find endearing.

"As usual, an amazing grasp of the obvious," Darcy said and nodded in the direction of a knot of camera-toting tourists. "Do they speak English?"

"Some, but they have a tour guide with them who translates for them."

"Okay. Point him out." Darcy scanned the group.

"Her. It's that woman on the left who looks like she's still in college. Name's Midori Tanaka."

"Thanks," Darcy said over her shoulder. She was in a rush. The sooner she filed this story, the sooner she could burrow back into her bed.

Darcy strode toward the group.

"Miss Timm?" Midori Tanaka, a bright-eyed young woman with glossy black hair walked over to her and offered her hand.

"I'm Darcy Moreland from the local television station to do a story on your group. I hope you don't mind the intrusion."

"Not at all," she said smiling prettily, and turned to her little group and explained. There were a couple of questions, which translated roughly to, "Are we going to be on TV? And will we get to see it?"

Darcy told Midori that with luck it would air before the tour left town. When Midori translated her answer, they were as excited as a bunch of school kids.

Looking behind her, she watched Netters doing some set shots of the front of the museum, panning toward the gathering. The men and women were milling around a small bronze statue of a windblown pioneer woman standing by a wagon wheel.

Some were reading the attached poem about the woman saying goodbye to all that she knew. Others were looking out across the parking lot behind the East Stands, obviously intrigued by a distant view of Cheyenne Junction, a re-creation of a small town in the old West.

Striding past them was undoubtedly the leader of this excursion, Carol Timm. Slim hipped and medium height, the auburn-haired beauty glanced back over her shoulder as she passed by.

Netters shifted his attention to shoot her jeans-covered butt as she made her way across the small parking lot toward the group.

"Knock it off, Netters." Darcy nudged at him. He grinned and shrugged.

Following quick introductions all around, Ms. Timm began to shepherd her charges toward the north side of the museum along a concrete path. She opened a small gate, and they all filed through while she mounted a beautiful dappled gray horse.

Once they cleared the gate, Netters aimed the camera at Darcy in a tight close up.

"Back off, will ya?" Darcy snapped at him.

"Touchy this morning?"

"I should warn you. I haven't had any coffee yet and I've been known to be unpleasant to manic in the morning without it."

"Good to know." Netters pulled back, and she began her introductory spiel.

"It is barely dawn here at the Cheyenne Rodeo Days Western Museum and we are getting ready to take a special Behind the Chutes Tour. These tours are offered for the public around ten and eleven each day. This one was scheduled at an early hour for an unusual group from Kyoto, Japan."

She did the "cut taping" gesture and Netters stopped shooting. They were jostling along the rutted back prairie heading for the holding pens south of the Rodeo Office.

"Midori," Darcy called out and sped up to her. "When we stop for a moment, I'd like to ask you a few questions if you don't mind."

Midori smiled and nodded but kept up a steady translation of the information Carol Timm was giving about the rodeo stock and how they are gathered and sorted. Darcy was amazed by her multi-tasking skill.

Netters shot more video of Carol Timm's trim backside as she rode ahead.

"That had better be usable," Darcy whispered fiercely in his direction. He didn't even lower the camera, but his toothy grin spoke volumes.

Following Ms. Timm they entered the North gate and took a

sharp left going through an underground tunnel to emerge behind the East stands. The holding pens held several bulls milling around him. They would be used for the afternoon rodeo.

The tourists eagerly photographed the animals but were warned to stay back from the gates and not irritate the animals. Several people in the group were holding handkerchiefs over their noses. Darcy smiled at Netters. The smell back by the loading pins was pretty ripe.

"These two spaces are called the ready area for the cowboys to get their equipment ready and get themselves loosened up." Carol said.

The tourists waited patiently for Midori to translate and followed Carol into the first ready area under the stands. Darcy caught up with Midori again and they shot an insert with her.

"I am speaking with Midori Tanaka, the tour group leader. Ms. Tanaka, how did you get attached to this group?"

"I am employed by Rising Sun Travel agency out of Los Angeles. We specialize in tours from Japan."

"I understand the Wild West holds a particular appeal for tourists from Japan. Is that true?"

"Yes, it is, though I don't really know how to explain it. We are always astonished at how fast these Western tours fill."

Darcy signaled to cut and thanked Midori for her comments.

"Why don't we go up to the first level on East Stands?" Darcy said to Netters when they left the tourists and the ready area. "We could shoot both into the holding area for the bulls and get a shot of the group behind the loading chutes. What do you think?"

"Couldn't be more thrilled," he said and motioned her on.

They climbed to the second level and got set up for a medium close-up of her with her back to the rail above the holding pens.

"Here the tour will view the stock that is being held for today's rodeo. The horses and steers are kept in the north pens and the bulls are right below us." She said into the mic.

Netters shifted the shot from her close-up to a pan shot that strafed the holding pens from left to right. Darcy continued the narrative.

"The tour will wind its way under the stands to behind the chutes. It is a view of the arena that is traditionally off limits to all but a handful of people when the rodeo is on. You couldn't get any closer to the action unless you were competing."

"Shit."

Darcy blinked in shock and looked at Netters. He was aiming his camera over the edge of the railing at the holding pen for the rough stock. She leaned over the railing and peered down. At first glance, all she saw was about a half dozen bulls either milling about or standing by the rails then she saw a jarring blot of red in contrast to the brown dirt.

"What do you think it is? Can you see more through the zoom?"

"I think it's a body," Netters said softly and passed the camera over to her.

It took a moment for her to adjust the camera to her eye, and to force her hands to stop shaking, but then she saw it. A crumpled body sprawled in the middle of the bullpen. Darcy moved the camera minutely back and forth and saw a cowboy hat flopped over the face, a red plaid shirt, faded jeans and well-worn boots.

Darcy slammed the camera into Netters's pigeon chest and tore down the stairs.

"We have to see if he's alright. Come on."

By the time they had reached the pen, they faced another problem. Bulls from twenty feet in the air look gentle, slow moving, and small. Bulls on ground level snorting snot and hooking their horns back and forth were beyond intimidating.

"How're we going to get him out of there?" Darcy said as she dodged back and forth to get a better glimpse of the body. She couldn't see any movement.

"Don't snarl at me." Netters aimed his camera and started shooting.

"How callous can you get? The guy is injured or worse, and you shoot video."

"I think better with a camera in my hand." He lowered it to glower at her. "And for your information, I'm not trained in either medicine or bull wrangling, are you?"

"No but, we have to do something." Darcy practically yelled at him.

He removed his cell from a holster on his hip and tossed it.

"Dial 911," he snapped at her and kept shooting video. "Or call your buddy Hank. He won't even be fazed you've found another body, Calamity."

"Stop calling me that." Darcy was fumbling to dial the emergency number, but her hand shook, and she kept poking the two. She finally just told Siri to do it.

"And to be painfully accurate, you're the one who found both bodies. It's simply been my misfortune to be with you at the time," she said.

The emergency operator picked up and told Darcy an ambulance was being dispatched to the scene, then deluged her with questions designed to encourage an average citizen never to call 911 in an emergency. By the time Darcy hung up, she was sure the emergency operator knew more about her than most of the people she worked with.

"Can you see any movement in there?" She asked stuffing Netters's phone into his holster.

"No, except for the bulls. At least none of them have stepped on him that I can tell." He handed her the camera to look through.

Darcy saw some longish sandy blonde hair under the skewed hat, but the cowboy was facing away from them, so she couldn't see his face.

"I'd had better call someone who can get these bulls out of here. I could call Maggie . . ." She looked at her watch. It was only 6:45 in the morning. Maggie would probably be okay with Darcy calling her, but she couldn't authorize someone to come out here and move stock. "I'd better call Romero. If the stock contractor has to be notified, the Rodeo Chairman would be the guy to do it."

She pulled out a small notebook from her back pocket, grateful that Romero had given her his home phone number. She dug into her backpack for her own phone and clicked in the number.

As she waited for Romero to answer, she saw Midori and Carol with their flock of tourists peering at Netters and her from the pass through. Darcy franticly waved them back.

"Stay here," Carol ordered Midori and her charges. She nudged her horse back through the tourists like Moses through the Red Sea.

"What are you doing?" she asked Netters who was still shooting video. Carol's tone fairly shouted, "Don't mess with the animals," but for now, she was erring on the side of politeness to the press.

Netters looked up at her. "Body…" He gestured with his camera.

Carol looked startled and stood in her stirrups to get a better look. She sat back in her saddle with a plop.

"Who is it?"

"Don't know," Netters answered. "Are you okay?"

Carol looked vampire-drained-white, but she waved her hand dismissively. "Fine. We need to call someone."

"Calamity over there is calling Gary Romero."

Darcy would've taken issue with the nickname, except Romero finally answered his phone. He didn't even sound sleepy.

"Romero?"

"Yeah. Who's this?"

"Darcy Moreland. Say listen, we're out at the holding pens behind the East Stands and, there's a body among the bulls and …"

"A what?"

"A body of some cowboy," She could hear herself rushing to get the whole story out. "We can't tell if he's still alive because the bulls are milling all around. What do we do to get the bulls out of there? The ambulance has been called and …"

"Don't do anything. I'm on my way." He said firmly and hung up on her.

"He's on his way."

"What'd he say to do?" Carol asked.

"He said to do nothing. You might want to finish the tour with those folks before the ambulance arrives."

Darcy waved at Midori as if everything were fine.

"Oh—oh hell yes. Let me get them through the chutes and back to the museum." Carol turned her horse back toward the pass through.

"Meet me at the *Buckin'A* about four o'clock today and I'll tell you all the gory details," Netters called after her.

She looked back and smiled tentatively. "Okay. I guess." She prodded the group back out through the bucking chutes and into the arena.

"You're despicable." Darcy said and dropped onto a bale of hay nearby.

"Why?" he followed her over. "Because I used this unfortunate accident to tempt a hot girl into meeting me?"

"Yes, exactly."

"I admit it seems cold-blooded . . ."

"Of course it's cold-blooded. You'd use the death of your Grandma to throw a party."

"Probably, but we'd call it a wake." He smiled at her.

She opened her mouth to argue, but a laugh popped out instead. "Ya got me there. Your family Irish too?"

"Yup. My Grandma, who is still alive by the way, always said, 'The luck of the Irish has nothing to do with luck. It has to do with intelligence and opportunity.' I'd like to think she'd approve of my intelligently grasping an opportunity."

"Well you've got the Blarney part down, anyway." Darcy crossed her arms. She wasn't angry. She was edgy, and she always got cranky when she was edgy. The cowboy hadn't stirred.

Darcy heard the sirens as the ambulance entered the park and swung around the north side of the arena and on to the track. They'd pulled up by the pens, when Romero jumped out of his official CRD bright red Dodge Ram pickup and ran over to Darcy and Netters.

"Where is he?"

Darcy pointed, and Romero edged nearer the pen. He swatted the guacamole-covered butt of one of the bulls standing in the way. The bull lurched, more insulted than angry, but he moved.

Romero squatted low, closer to the cowboy. "Son, can you hear me? Don't try to get up, move your leg so we know you can hear us."

They all waited, almost holding their breath, but nothing happened.

Darcy wasn't too surprised. She'd been watching that cowboy carefully since she and Netters found him. He hadn't so much as twitched. It didn't look good.

"How're we supposed to get him outa there?" one of the paramedics asked Romero.

Romero stood, still staring at the cowboy. "I've got a couple of volunteers coming. They'll get the bulls into another pen, and it'll be safe to go in." He swung on Darcy. "What the hell happened?"

"Hey. Take it easy. We just found the guy. We didn't push him off the railing or anything." Darcy snapped back.

No one said anything for about three heartbeats, then they all looked up. An unmistakable red blotch was smeared along a three-foot trail on the railing above.

Romero was the first to move. He lunged up the metal steps, skipping every-other-one. Netters was close behind, and Darcy was last to reach the upper level.

The first thing to hit her was the smell, a rusty, coppery tang that signaled blood and lots of it. She looked at Netters and Romero. Both men were staring down at a puddle of congealing blood and a vicious looking knife with about an eight-inch blade.

"We'd better not touch anything," Romero said. "You did call the police, didn't you?"

"Uhm . . . yeah," Darcy said. "I told them about the body. I don't remember if I asked for the police. I—I don't remember . . ." she trailed off. She could not take her eyes off the blood. There was so much of it, like a red-brown pond. Darcy shuddered.

The next thing she knew, Romero had wrapped his arms around her and turned her body away from the gruesome scene. Darcy leaned heavily into his chest and reveled in the warmth. She was suddenly incredibly cold. His large, warm palm was stroking her back gently up and down and she forced her mind to focus on the soothing rhythm.

Startled by the sounds of more sirens, they all moved to the railing and looked down. The three of them watched the ebb and flow below with the same dispassionate stare they might have used to gaze at an ant farm.

Three men, two on foot and one mounted, were doing an efficient job of herding the bulls out of the pen and back down toward the barns.

"Thanks guys." Romero shouted down at the volunteers in the pen. "I'll try to let you know when this area is freed up. Until then, we'll have to move the bulls from the back pens for the show."

"Can do." the mounted cowboy shouted back.

Two Police cruisers parked haphazardly in the yard, lights flashing.

Hank Nelson's big black truck pulled in and he slammed out. He reached the edge of the pen before his door chunked closed.

Hank glanced at the body, then up at Romero, Netters and Darcy. He stared pointedly at Romero's arm resting across Darcy's shoulders. She squared her shoulders and lifted her chin.

"Problem?" Romero asked her quietly, a small grin playing around his lips.

"No," Darcy said looking at down at Hank in the yard below. "No problem." Hank was still watching them.

"Maybe we ought to go down and talk to them," Netters suggested.

"Good idea." she rotated out from under Romero's arm and headed down the steps.

She strode up to Hank.

"Did they call you from the station?"

"No. I heard it on the scanner and your name as the contact person. Thought you might need some help."

"I appreciate your concern, but Netters and I just found the body. Is there any chance he's still alive?"

The ME had finished his preliminary investigation. Two policemen were marking and collecting anything that might be related to the crime scene.

They both watched as the paramedics wrestled the body into a heavy black vinyl bag. She'd seen enough police shows to know they didn't do that if the victim was still alive.

"Doesn't look like it. No."

"There's a puddle of blood and a knife up there." Darcy pointed to the second level by the rusty looking smear on the railing.

"I assume you were all smart enough to not touch anything?"

He raised his eyebrow questioning her actions? Darcy knew that he was just doing his job. She wanted him to trust that she would know what not to do in a crime scene.

"We didn't touch a thing. Just went up to investigate because of the—well, you know,"

"Blood?" he supplied. She winced but nodded.

"I'll have them cordon off the area and tell the Medical Examiner and CSI unit." Hank said to Romero. "I don't know how long it'll be off limits, but it's fairly likely we'll have it open by noon, in time for the rodeo. I'll keep you posted."

"Thanks. I'd appreciate that." Romero watched as police unwound yellow tape around the pens.

Hank told the police to cordon off the scene upstairs too then turned to Romero. "For now I have a few questions,"

"Sure. However, I can be of assistance," Romero answered.

The two men wandered off like old fraternity brothers toward the relative quiet of the ready area. Darcy trailed behind them.

Her theory was, she found the body, she called 911, and she should be included in the investigation.

"When was the rough stock brought in for the rodeo in the morning?" Hank was asking as she jostled alongside.

Romero sat heavily on a small bench inside the chain-link fence and leaned back. Hank faced him, resting his booted foot on a hay bale nearby, while Darcy straddled the bench midway between them. Both men ignored her.

"We have the volunteers switch them out about 5 a.m. I can check the board and find out who was taking that shift this morning if you want."

"That would be a big help. Is it likely that there were any other people around at that time in the morning?"

"This is always a restless place. We also move the steers and calves up by chute 9 for slack. There're usually only the three volunteers from my committee assigned to move stock along with guys who work for the stock contractors, but there are also cowboys coming in off the road and moving on all night and into the morning."

"That doesn't even factor in the guys from the security committee or anyone who had too much to drink the night before. We try to roust everybody out and clear the park, but we might miss one or two. I'll ask around."

"Thanks." Hank swiveled his hips slightly and faced Darcy. "Now Ms. Moreland, what can you tell me?"

She was startled. She would have sworn neither man knew she was there. She looked beyond Hank and saw Netters lounging by the gate opening.

"Well, Netters and I were doing a story on the Behind the Chutes tour. There was a Japanese group who—Uhm—well I guess that's not important . . ."

"It might be. Who was giving the tour?"

"Carol Timm from the Western Museum," she said, and he wrote it down.

"Go on," he prodded.

"We went up a level to get a shot of the tour as they went from the holding pens, through to the bucking chutes. Netters was shooting a boom shot from the railing when he—he saw the body." Darcy looked up at Netters and Hank followed her gaze.

"Come on in, Mr. Netters." Hank smiled at him like the hostess at a garden party.

Netters wandered in and sat next to Romero.

"So, what first caught your attention.?"

"I was doing a generic setup shot, and I saw something red in the holding pen. I used the zoom to get a clearer picture. One of the bulls shifted and I could see the body."

"Then what happened?" Hank asked.

"Darcy and I ran down the stairs and . . ."

"And I called 911," she finished for him. "And I called Romero because we didn't know how to move the bulls out of the way."

Hank's eyes flicked to Romero who nodded imperceptibly. Hank looked back at her.

"And then what?"

"We tried to talk to the cowboy, to see if he was still alive, but he never moved, and we noticed the . . ."

"We went up and found the knife," Romero supplied.

"By then you'd arrived here?" Hank asked trying to get a feel for the chronological order of events.

"I was already up, and I don't live that far away. Just on Iron Mountain Road."

One of the investigators interrupted. He held out a black leather wallet with a silver concho decoration.

"Found this on the victim." He handed it to Hank. Hank flipped it open to look at the driver's license tucked behind a scarred and foggy plastic window. He had to hold it up to the light to read it.

"Who is he?" she asked.

"Samuel A. Carlson from Greeley."

"Oh shit." popped out of Darcy's mouth before she could slam her jaw shut.

CHAPTER 10

Hank Nelson's piercing blue eyes swiveled to Darcy, making her feel twitchy. He took the toothpick out of his mouth.

"Do you have a problem, Ms. Darcy?"

"No problem. I mean, I thought since he was Bridget Emerson's boyfriend . . ."

"You think there's a connection?" He tilted his head to the side as if the idea hadn't occurred to him.

"Don't you?"

"Generally, I try to let the evidence tell me what's going on." He responded.

"You never pay attention to instinct or act on hunches?" Darcy put her hands on her hips.

"I mean it's better to gather as much evidence as possible before coming up with theories. It usually works better that way."

"I'm as interested in the evidence as you are, "Darcy said.

"It's been my experience that the press generally doesn't much care about facts if they interfere with a good story."

She took a deep breath. *No point in poking at a rattler who was already annoyed.* "I'm sure you've had a few bad experiences with reporters in the past, but it's unfair to assume that all of us play fast and loose with the truth. I happen to have a good reputation for using both accurate facts and reliable intuition. It's a combination that's worked well for me."

"I like to use forensic science, careful observation, and focused interviews." He smiled at her. "Now if you don't mind, I'll get on with it."

Darcy watched him walk out through the gate and stop to talk to two of the officers She wondered why he was being so formal with her. He acted like their friendly breakfast had never happened. *Could he be jealous of Gary Romero?* Hank did look at her funny when he saw her with him. She dismissed the thought instantly. Hank was definitely not the jealous type particularly when they didn't even have a relationship. Maybe it was trying not to mix business with personal feeling? She would have to watch that too.

She studied the men with Hank. One officer looked like he was beginning his career and the other looked old enough to be ending his. She followed Hank out and hovered close enough to overhear their conversation.

"We've bagged this."

The young Opie look-alike officer held up plastic evidence bag that contained the bloody knife. He held it gingerly with a gloved hand between two fingers as if it were alive.

"I don't think we'll get much off of it. It looks like a standard Ka-Bar hunting knife, eight-inch blade. Maybe there are some prints on it."

"Anything else?" Hank asked.

"Not much. The Medical Examiner is still making notes. There were some footprints in the blood at the scene though." The older officer nodded in the direction of the upper stands.

"Complete or partials?"

"Just partials. Looks like a boot though. It's either a man with small feet or a woman with large feet. I need to take some pictures while the blood's still damp and run it at the lab. We might be able to reconstruct a whole print and learn more."

"Okay. Keep me informed." Hank handed back the bagged knife.

Hank jotted down some notes in his small spiral topped notebook. He snapped it shut and stuffed it into his back pocket.

Darcy walked up to him. "Do I get an official statement? Or should I just make up one?" She flashed him a smile.

He looked surprised and then laughed. He folded his tanned, muscular arms across his chest. "Just out of curiosity, what would you say if you made it up?"

Darcy loved a challenge, and she liked this guy when he didn't take himself too seriously.

"I'd probably say something like: 'Detective Nelson of the Cheyenne Police Department said they have no idea what happened.' How's that?"

"You know you really should dial down your sass," he said.

"Sass is one of my many talents." She stuck her hands in her back pockets.

"I can just imagine." His glance wandered below her neck briefly.

"Well . . .?" Darcy raised her eyebrows.

"What? The official statement is that we are investigating a murder on the grounds of CRD Park. So far, we have no suspects."

"Wait. Wait. Netters." She shouted behind her and Netters ran out of the ready area.

"What?" Netters answered, sounding annoyed.

"Detective Nelson is going to give us an official statement," Darcy told him.

"Now hold on there." Hank interrupted. "I never said anything about doing it on camera."

"Well that's my medium, so please?" She was not above wheedling if it got her the story.

He smiled a bit ruefully. "A polite request from the press? This is a red-letter day. Okay, but make it fast."

"Absolutely. Netters, can we shoot it with the bull pens behind us?"

"Sure thing," Netters swung around as they shifted to stand by the holding pens.

Darcy turned on her microphone. "I'd rather have a bottle in front of me than a frontal lobotomy. Dorothy Parker" she said into the mic.

"Got it," Netters confirmed that her level was okay.

"I'm standing with Detective Hank Nelson from the Cheyenne Police Department. We're at CRD Park where the body of a young cowboy was discovered early this morning. Detective Nelson,"

Darcy smiled at him.

"I know it is still early in the investigation, but can you tell us anything?"

She held the mic under his mouth.

"At approximately 6:45 a.m., we responded to a 911 call. We found the victim in the rough stock pens behind the east side stands. So far, we don't have much to go on. If anyone has any information, I'd urge them to contact the Cheyenne Police Department."

"Thank you, Detective. We'll continue to follow this story. This is Darcy Moreland reporting for KCWY News from CRD Park."

She made the cut gesture and Netters lowered his camera "Thanks, Hank."

"You're welcome. Wasn't too far from your made-up statement after all."

"It sounds much better coming from you. When will his name be released?"

"We'll try to notify the next of kin as soon as possible. I'd feel better if they came and identified the body before we go public. I'm guessing about twenty-four hours."

"Okay. Let me know, will you?"

"Sure."

"While you're here . . ."

"Yes?" He cocked his eyebrow in that supercilious way she hated.

"Have you made any more progress with Bridget's murder?"

"Nothing I'm willing to share with you yet."

"How about the guy who was with her on the Ferris wheel?" Netters came over and took the mic from her, but she hardly noticed.

"Nothing nailed down. We're still interviewing Bridget's friends. No luck."

"Okay. Well, thanks again."

"Well thanks for not telling all you know."

"Thanks for giving me credit for some professionalism."

"I just did." He shook his head. "That was a short honeymoon. Have a nice morning, Ms. Moreland." He sauntered away and didn't look back.

"Well, damn." Darcy watched him leave. She didn't know why that man looked good to her. So he had a cute butt. So what?

"Trouble with your new buddy?" Netters said.

She spun on him and must have jacked her jaw because Netters held his hands up in surrender mode.

"Easy, Calamity. I'm on your side. Besides, I have something to show you."

"What?"

Netters walked up next to her and hit the replay on the camera. At first, she didn't understand what she was looking at, but behind the center shot of Hank and her making nice-nice in front of the camera, was one of the investigating officers squatting on the ground anxiously trying to catch the Medical Examiner's eye.

The Medical Examiner came over, hunkered down, picked up a couple of lumps from the dust, and bagged them. That was when the clip ended.

"What was that, or do I want to know?"

"I don't know," Netters said as he rewound the clip, "But if I were an enterprising young journalist, I'd sashay over and ask. Worst that can happen is they say, 'No comment.'"

"Good point." Darcy was already moving.

She had no intention of climbing over the fence and compromising the crime scene, but it was easy to lean on the rail and talk to the young officer who had bagged the knife standing nearby.

The young policeman looked even more like Opie than before. His freckles stood out on his too pale face and his hair spiked because he kept running his hand through it.

"You okay?" Darcy was concerned.

He glanced over at her and gave a wobbly smile.

"I'm okay. This is my first murder is all."

"Nasty one to cut your teeth on, judging by your face."

"A stabbing would've been bad enough," he said and ran his hand through his hair again, "but this guy was slit like a trout and castrated. I've never seen anything like it."

"Cummings!" the Medical Examiner shouted at him. "Shut the hell up."

The Medical Examiner swung on her. "Lady, this is off the record. You broadcast anything about the cause or details of his death before I've released my findings and I'll drop-kick you to Nebraska. Got that?" He glowered at her and simultaneously shoved poor befuddled Cummings away from her.

"Yup got it," she replied. She tried to sound cheerfully obliging, but truth was she wanted to retch. She rested her head against the cool metal of the railing. Darcy had never been so glad to have an empty stomach in her life.

"Hey, Calamity, you look like you've been stomped on," Netters said as he slid up next to her. "You want some water?" He held out a small bottle of generic spring water.

She took it gratefully and unscrewed the cap. "The guy was castrated."

"I heard. Drink up while we walk back to the museum. Zach'll want us back at the station ASAP." Netters put his hand on her back and gently guided her away from the pens.

Darcy wondered at Netters's unruffled composure but was grateful for. It put the starch back in her spine.

"My God. What kind of animal does that to another human being?" she asked as they kicked up puffs of dust walking toward their cars in the parking lot.

"I don't know, but I hope to God I never run in to him. That's for damn sure."

"You sure it's a man?"

"Mostly."

"Why? Don't you think a woman's capable of that level of brutality?" She glanced over at him under the brim of her hat.

"I've known a lot of women who castrate men on a regular basis, metaphorically that is. But in this world, the fact that it takes a lot of strength to slash someone open like that makes me think it was a man." They had reached the parking lot.

"I'll see you back at the station." Darcy got in her car and turned the AC on high even though it was still cool outside. She wiped the clammy sweat from her forehead with the back of her sleeve.

Sam Carson was dead. Mutilated and killed. Darcy couldn't shake the feeling that Sam and Bridget's death were connected somehow. But how? Was he the same person to blame for both murders? Focusing on the questions helped steady her.

By the time she got to the station, she felt more in control. At least she didn't feel so lightheaded.

By the look on Zach's face when Darcy walked in, Netters had beaten her there.

"Darcy. Are you okay? Netters told me what happened."

"I'm fine—fine," she said too emphatically to ring true, even to her own ears.

Giving Zach a friendly hug, Darcy said, "Thanks for caring. It was a shock, but I think I'm over the worst of it now. Is Netters setting up the video in the editing room?"

"He said he was going to see if he could string out enough of the Japanese tour story to make it viable. If not, we'll scrap it and focus exclusively on the murder."

"Did Netters tell you that the cause of death and dismemberment have to stay off the record until the Medical Examiner files his report?"

"He told me, but he also said you got Nelson on camera. Good job. He hates to go on camera."

Darcy grinned. "Never underestimate the power of a' pretty-please', like my Grandma always told me."

The next few hours whizzed by. She focused on patching the tour story together and writing some lead-in information for the murder story. She steadfastly refused to let her mind wander to that dark and scary place in the back of her mind where a brutal, bloody, murder is committed, and life is held so cheap.

By noon, she was ready for a break. She called Abby to see if she was free and offered to bring home some sandwiches.

Darcy made it home in record time. The sandwich shop wasn't overly busy, and she wasn't overly picky. She took the front porch steps two at a time.

Abby opened her door almost instantly. Darcy handed her the sandwich bag.

Mac, with his scruffy face and Raisinette eyes, always made her smile, but today she was grateful for the pure ordinariness of it. His perky little ears wiggled, and his tail wagged in enthusiastic welcome. She scooped him off the floor and nuzzled his darkly furred neck.

"You're a good boy," she crooned at him and followed Abby to the kitchen.

"That tour looks like it knocked the stuffing out of you," Abby said as she unwrapped the turkey and Swiss on rye.

"You have no idea. I'll tell you all about it after we eat."

Abby's eyebrows shot up in surprise, but she contented herself in laying out the plates, chips, and iced tea.

They sat across from each other at the table.

"Your ham and cheese okay?" Darcy asked, thankful to fill the silence with something mundane.

"Utterly okay. I love the rye bread they bake."

Darcy tore off a bit of cheese and fed it to Mac who was sprawled at her feet. She didn't normally feed Mac "people" food, but today she wanted to keep him close. If she had to bribe him, so be it.

Her ethical standards were really taking a beating today. First, she'd "pretty-pleased" Hank to get his statement and now she was breaking her own rule about not feeding Mac what she ate. Amazing what the shock of finding two murder victims in the space of four days will do to your sense of moral rectitude.

"What is bothering you?" Abby finished off her chips.

"My lack of moral fiber," Darcy said.

Picking up her glass of iced tea she took a large gulp, then began to fill Abby in on her morning.

"Bridget Emerson's boyfriend, Sam Carlson, was stabbed to death, castrated and left in the rough-stock pens. When she'd finished, Abby sat there stunned.

Darcy cleared the plates and rinsed them off in the sink while Abby still sat and sipped her tea. She didn't say anything until Darcy returned.

"My heavens!" Abby said. "Do you suppose there's some connection between the two murders?"

"Yes, but I'll be damned if I can figure out what it is."

"That, um, castration?" Abby asked. "I was thinking that that kind of attack is alarmingly personal, don't you think?"

"I think it's real personal. I don't think you could get more personal. What's your point?"

"I was thinking. Do you know if he was murdered first, then castrated or castrated then murdered?"

"No, I don't, but why? Oh, I get it. It might make a difference about what motivated it."

"Exactly." Abby said.

"It's so savage. Do you suppose he was playing around with another guy's wife or something? He certainly liked the ladies." Darcy picked Mac up and scratched him behind the ears. He settled his little furry self into a contented ball in her lap.

"I would guess it's something like that. A crime of passion as they say."

They were both silent, lost in their own thoughts. Mac rolled over baring his belly for some attention.

Darcy chuckled. "You know, Mac. Sometimes you're a real pest." She scratched his belly anyway.

"Here's a thought," Abby said.

"Huh?"

"What if this was punishment from someone in the rodeo? Someone who was angry at him for something? Graphic message I'd say."

"Hmmm. Good point. I wonder if he had any defensive wounds. If so, I'm not likely to get anything from Hank or the Medical Examiner until they ready to release the details. Maybe I should go back out to the park and poke around." Darcy stood and placed Mac on the floor.

"If you do, be careful. That murderer could be running around killing people randomly, you know." Abby wrinkled her forehead in concern.

"I know. I'll be back in about an hour."

Abby and Mac followed her to the door.

"Wish me luck," Darcy said as she left. She wasn't feeling as casual as she tried to sound.

By the time she'd cleared security on the west entrance, Darcy looked at the clock in her dash. 1:30. The Grand Entry would be finished. The Riders would have almost completed their synchronized riding display at the beginning of the rodeo. She wandered over to the west end of the track by the barns and waited for the girls to ride over.

She didn't have long to wait. Riding in a ragged bunch, they dismounted and passed their horses over to some handlers who kept them at the ready for the next run.

Darcy picked out a girl with long chestnut hair, who was off her horse adjusting her cinch. Darcy sidled up next to her.

"Hi, I am Darcy Moreland from KCWY. Can I talk to you a second?"

The girl looked around as if unconvinced Darcy were speaking to her. "Sure. I guess so."

"What's your name?"

"Cindy Burke."

"Cindy, how long have you been a Rider?"

Darcy operated on the theory that it's easier to get people to talk if you begin by asking simple non-threatening questions.

"This is my second year."

"It sure takes a lot of time, doesn't it?"

"Yeah," she smiled at Darcy for the first time. "But I love it. The travel's fun and the girls all get so close."

"I'll bet. You must have been upset about Bridget Emerson's death." She watched Cindy's eyes cloud over with suspicion. Darcy thought if she could push just a little, Cindy might help.

"It was a shock," she said as if she could be noncommittal and still be in the neighborhood of truth.

"It's okay, Cindy. I'm not looking for dirt. I just need to find out some information."

"Why?" She stopped fiddling with her saddle and looked Darcy defiantly in the eye.

"Why?" Darcy repeated the question. "Because I knew her too, Cindy." Darcy started tentatively, then couldn't stop herself from spewing her frustration. "Because I knew Bridget and her dad, and even her mom before she died four years ago." Darcy's eyes filled, and she clamped her jaw tighter, but the words kept gushing out.

"Because I used to babysit her, and she used to follow me around all the time, like an annoying little sister. Because I was there when she fell from the Ferris wheel. Because this morning I found her boyfriend's body in the rough stock pen. He'd been murdered. And because I know her death and his are connected somehow."

"Oh-my-God." Cindy covered her mouth with her hand and her eyes went round with shock.

Darcy felt a momentary guilty twinge at telling Cindy about the murdered cowboy, but since she wasn't using it in a story officially, and she was sure the rumor mill was grinding away all over the park, she shook it off.

"Who was murdered?" Cindy looked momentarily confused.

Darcy narrowed her eyes. "Who did you think I meant?"

"I don't know." Cindy turned back to her saddle and tightened a cinch that was tight enough. "Bridget had a few guys who were interested in her."

"Who did you think I meant?" Darcy persisted. She didn't know why, but she thought it could be important.

"Jason Ford was pretty much a regular. He goes to Central High with us. He's had a thing for Bridget since we were in junior high."

"But she didn't feel the same way about him." She said this as a dead certainty. She'd had a boy like Jason in her past too.

"Not really." Cindy turned back and looked at Darcy. "I mean, they were friends and stuff, but she only went with him if there wasn't anyone else." An appalled expression flitted across her face as if she couldn't believe what she'd said.

"Don't get me wrong. Bridget loved Jason in her own way, just . . ."

"Just not the way Jason wanted her to?"

"I guess so. I'd better go."

Cindy mounted up, but Darcy stood close to her horse's flank, so she couldn't move. She was relying on the Riders' innate good manners.

"One more thing, Cindy. How did Jason react to the news of Bridget's death?"

"Well how do you think? He was upset. I gotta go."

"Thanks for your help." Darcy stepped back, and Cindy kicked her horse forward.

Darcy watched the Riders reshuffle their horses into an order known only to them and their director. They sat patiently waiting for their cue to reenter the arena.

She felt a tingle on the back of her neck, the kind you get when someone's watching you. She spun around and let go of the breath she didn't even known she had been holding.

Stacie Rogers walked up to her and smiled.

"Hi. You doing a story on the Riders?" Stacie looked past Darcy and nodded to the mounted girls.

"Not exactly. I'm trying to find out some information."

"About what?" Stacie walked over to the fence and hoisted herself up on the top rail.

"About Bridget."

Stacie gripped the rail she was sitting on so hard her knuckles turned white. "What do you want to know?"

"Well, Cindy Burke said that Jason Ford had a crush on Bridget for a long time."

"So what?"

Darcy shifted so him she was facing Stacie. "Well someone else Bridget had been dating has been murdered and . . ."

"What?" Stacie dropped from the fence to her feet. Her face went pale. "Who?"

Stacie looked like she was going to pass out. Darcy grabbed her shoulders to keep her steady and propped her up with the fence at her back.

"I'm sorry, honey. I didn't mean to blurt that out that way. Are you okay?" Darcy kept steadying hands on Stacie's shoulders.

"Yeah—Sure" she said, but Darcy was not convinced.

"What happened?" Stacie asked softly.

"Are you sure you want to know?" Darcy guided her slowly to a hay bale by the watering trough and made her sit down.

"Yes, I'm sure. What happened?"

"A young cowboy was found stabbed to death this morning." Darcy stood over her with hands jammed in her jean pockets.

"Where?" Stacie asked almost in a whisper.

"In the rough stock pens behind east stands. I saw him when we were filming a special on the Behind the Chutes tour about 6:30 this morning. I called the police."

"Are you sure he's dead? Maybe he passed out from loss of blood . . ."

"No, honey. I know it's a shock to have another murder in a short space of time . . ."

"What do you mean another murder?"

Oh, hell. She'd put her foot in it this time. "I assumed you knew the police suspect Bridget was also murdered."

Stacie stood up abruptly. "What the hell is the matter with you?" she screamed at Darcy. "Go away and leave me alone." She ran off.

Darcy understood she would always become inextricably linked in Stacie's mind with tragedy. Fresh tears trickled down her cheeks before she even knew she was crying. She swiped them away with the back of her hand and wiped the dampness on the butt of her jeans.

CHAPTER 11

Before going home, she thought she'd check with the other bulldogers and hazers. She walked slowly to chute nine. The dust she kept kicking up hung suspended in the air. She looked up at the bright blue sky and a smattering of puffy white clouds. She was so intent on enjoying the perfect summer day, she almost ran into one of the hazers, getting his rig ready.

"Oh I'm so sorry," she said as she backed up a couple of steps.

"I'm not." The cowboy's smiled looking her up and down.

Darcy shot out her hand. "I'm Darcy Moreland from the KCWY TV. I was wondering if I could ask you a few questions."

"Why sure. What do you want to know?" He took her hand and shook it. "My name is Jack Clark. Pleased to meet you." He touched the brim of his hat and smiled. Darcy smiled back.

"You might want to take that back once I tell you what I'm looking into."

"Ma'am if you're still looking into that poor girl's death, I'm afraid I can't help you. I wasn't even on the park what happened."

"Actually, I'm wondering if you can give me any information about Sam Carson."

Jack pause so long it became uncomfortable for both of them. Jack fiddled with his saddle pulling the tie downs tighter. Darcy waited.

"Ma'am I don't know why you would want to know anything about that guy. He's a notorious womanizer and an all-around loser."

Darcy laughed. "No you've misunderstood. I'm not interested in Sam like that. I want to know if he aggravated anyone in particular around here."

Jack's hazel eyes grew darker. "You mean besides Randy?"

"Yeah. Was there anyone who really hated him? Anyone he ticked off?"

"Naw. He's pretty much scum, but most of us just leave him alone. He gives cowboys a bad name."

"I watched his last run when his hazer veered off, and he got no time. What did he say when he rode back in?"

"He bitched some, but that was normal for him. We all just ignored him."

"So he didn't try and take a swing at the guy?"

"Ma'am, in case you didn't notice we're all pretty big guys back here. Carson wouldn't have the stones to pick a fight with any of us. He is a coward first and foremost."

Interesting turn of phrase, Darcy thought. "Well, thank you for your time."

Jack touched his brim once more. "No problem."

Darcy walked back to her car. She still had no answers. If all the cowboys thought he was as useless as Jack did, it wasn't likely that anyone would go to the trouble of killing him. Who would have the passion to attack Carson so brutally?

Driving home, Darcy wondered about Jason Ford. Could he have been so jealous that he'd kill Carson? Why? It made no sense. Bridget was already dead. Unless Ford blamed Carson for her death.

Could a teenaged boy be consumed with such anger, jealousy, and despair? Could he be driven to kill? Of course, he could. Prisons were full of boys in the throes of hormones and angst who committed unspeakable atrocities. That didn't even include crimes committed under the influence of drugs and/or alcohol.

Caught in a traffic snarl, Darcy dialed the number for the police department. Her call was shuttled to Hanks's extension at her request, but he didn't pick up. She ended up with a clipped message after a "Beep."

"Honest to Pete, Hank. This is the twenty-first century. Why don't you have call forwarding or something?" she began to record her message.

". . . Well, never mind that. I found out there's a guy who hung around Bridget named Jason Ford. He might be a suspect in the Carson thing. Call me. 555-2307. Bye."

Traffic was moving again. Darcy tossed her phone back on the seat beside her. She wondered how often Hank checked his voice mail, but it was the best she could do.

Deciding to swing by the grocery store and pick up some staples—eggs, milk, dog food—she pulled into the almost vacant parking lot, one of the main benefits of shopping while the rodeo was still going.

In and out with four bags in forty-five minutes, pleased with herself. She went charging up the front steps of the Algonquin and almost ran into Mrs. Carlucci who lived next door to her on the second floor.

"Oh. I'm so sorry." Darcy juggled her bags.

"That's okay, dear. I don't move out of the way as fast as I used to." She smiled at Darcy and continued to work her way down the steps with a white-knuckled, death, grip on the railing. She precisely placed both feet on each step before proceeding to the next.

Having reached the sidewalk, Mrs. Carlucci turned, waved at Darcy cheerfully, and toddled off down the street. Having older people around made her feel somehow grand-mothered and safe. After this morning that was a decidedly welcome feeling.

She stopped at Abby's and collected Mac, inviting Abby to come upstairs for her specialty omelet dinner. Abby started to refuse, but Darcy insisted and dangled the hint that she had new information to share like an earthworm in front of a trout. Abby bit.

"Come on up in a few minutes," she said on the way out the door.

In her apartment, Darcy began to unpack the boxes of kitchen paraphernalia. She didn't have much, but what she had was good quality, a testimony to her parents who got her the basics for her first apartment in Kansas.

Feeling damned domestic chopping up the smoked ham, vine-ripened tomatoes, onions, and mushrooms, she'd jacked up her stereo so loud she almost didn't hear her phone ring over Toby Keith's *Red Solo Cup*.

By the time she'd wiped her hands on the seat of her jeans, turned the stereo down and dug her phone from the bottom of her purse, it had stopped ringing.

"Damn it." she hollered and stomped her bare foot in frustration.

Mac rolled over on his rug, indifferent to her annoyance.

She looked closer to see a voice message was waiting. Darcy had expected a call back from Hank. She went through the drill to access her message.

"Lady, you don't take hints very well," the raspy, deep voice on the phone said. "Keep your nose out of things that're none of your damn business. Didja think I was kidding about takin' your stupid dog? I wasn't. Keep it up and he's dead."

The message stopped abruptly, and Darcy stared at the small phone in her hand as if might blow up. She checked the recently called list, but number was blocked. She tossed it onto the sofa.

"How in the hell did he get my cell number?" Darcy spun around in a circle feeling vulnerable. Grabbing Mac, holding him close, she tried to control her shaking.

The phone rang again, and she jumped. Mac leapt out of her arms as she leaned over to pick up her phone.

"Hel . . . Hello." Darcy stuttered, terrified she would hear that voice again.

"You been running?"

"Oh Hank. Thank God it's you."

"What's that supposed to mean?"

"I got another threat on the phone . . ."

"What do you mean, another threat?" His sharp tone had the effect of cold water thrown in her face. "Don't you remember the note that told me to stop meddling, or they'd take Mac? Well, this guy just called my cell phone and threatened me again. How could he get my number?"

There was a slight pause on the other end. "Calm down. I'll be right over," he said and hung up.

Friendly chitchat evidently concluded; Darcy left the phone

on the table. As silly as it sounded, knowing Hank was coming over made her feel better. So much for sixty-some-odd-years of Feminism.

Abby arrived moments before Hank, so Darcy only had to tell the details about Jason Ford's crush on Bridget and the new phone threat once. Darcy got agitated all over again.

"Who do you suppose it is?" Abby clamped a tall bottle of Pinot Grigio wine between her knees and tried to thread the corkscrew into the top.

"Some nutcase. Here, give me that." Hank relieved Abby of the bottle and took it into Darcy's tiny kitchen. "He's probably not even involved with the deaths. Just being a bully 'cause you're high profile." Hank popped the cork easily and went looking for glasses in the cupboards.

"But Hank," Darcy trailed behind. "How does he know I'm still asking questions?"

Hank shot her one of those "You've got to be kidding me" looks, took two glasses down, and began to pour.

"Okay—okay. So that doesn't take a genius, but what about my cell number? How did he get my cell number?"

"I don't know," he handed her a glass and scooted past her to give Abby some wine. "Does Zach have your number?"

"Of course, but I doubt if he gives it out to anyone."

"Give me a list of the people who have your number. It can't be too long. You've only been back a short time. Unless, of course, you posted your number in the bathroom at the Lariat."

He smiled at her as if that might really be a possibility.

"Oh hell. I can't remember . . ." She began to dither. She flopped down on the sofa next to Abby.

"Try." Hank dropped his small spiral notebook and a pencil in her lap.

She tried to list the people in her mind who had her cell number. Liz, Zach, her mom and dad, Abby.

"You have my number," Darcy looked up at Hank. "Should I put you on the list?"

"Yeah. I've got your number," Hank chuckled slightly at his own joke, "but I wouldn't waste time suspecting me. I generally prefer to issue my threats in person."

"You know, you're not helping," Darcy said as she jotted down Bill Netters's name next to Stacie Rogers and Gary Romero.

"There. I think that's all of them," she said as she handed the notebook back to him. "I honestly don't think that list is going to help."

"Let me worry about that. Trouble with cell phone numbers is lots of people don't see any harm in giving them out to anyone who asks for it."

"I am not that careless. Hank, it is my job to have people contact me with information," she said.

"Not even necessarily you, this Liz person for instance, might have been asked what your number was by someone who said they were interested in you. It'd be understandable if she—"

"Liz is not that careless either."

"Well, someone on this list gave your number out, probably innocently enough. The guy who called is trying to scare you off."

Darcy took a swig of wine. "That keen deduction must be an example of why you're a detective, detective."

"Sarcasm is the weapon of someone who is otherwise unarmed," Hank said to Abby as if Darcy were not in the room.

"Clever. Who'd you steal that from?" Darcy asked.

"Actually, it's original. I run into a lot of sarcasm in my job," Hank smiled at her.

"Ask those people if they gave your number to anyone." Hank gestured to the notebook. "If they did, let me know."

Darcy tore the sheet out of his notebook and handed it back. "What're you going to do?" she asked.

"Investigate two murders." He started to leave, but Darcy grabbed his arm.

"You mean a threatened dog-napping takes low priority on the police agenda?"

Hank faced her and lowered his voice to that soothing register men use when they are trying to placate. He ran his hands from the tops of her shoulders to her elbows.

"Be reasonable, Darcy. I know it's unnerving to get threats like this, but it's probably some deranged guy who gets off on scaring people from a distance."

"Well it's working." Darcy shrugged away.

His hands dropped away, but he looked intensely into her eyes. "Pay attention to your surroundings." He glanced at Abby, who nodded in acknowledgment. "And call me if you notice anything suspicious." He opened her door.

"Oh, and Darcy . . ."

"Yeah?"

"Don't go poking around this Jason Ford character. He could be dangerous." Hank closed the door before Darcy could argue.

She went to whisk the eggs for the omelet. "He acts like he's the only one who gets to ask questions as part of his job."

"Darcy, he's probably right to warn you off," Abby said as she propped herself against the kitchen counter. "Things are getting treacherous, particularly if these deaths are connected."

Darcy turned and faced her. "Are you scared, Abby?"

"Heaven's no." she answered. "I taught high school for over thirty years. Nothing scares me. But . . ."

"But . . .?" Darcy prompted.

"But there've been two murders, and I think it would be prudent to be vigilant."

"Oh, I plan on being vigilant all right. I'm going to get downright dopey with vigilance." Darcy tried to laugh, but it rang hollow.

She served up the simple omelet and Abby sat with her companionably at her tiny bistro table.

"Don't you have anything more interesting to do in the middle of Rodeo Days?" Abby asked.

"No. I'd just as soon stay home tonight. Bridget's funeral is tomorrow at ten and I don't feel in a partying mood. I wouldn't say no to some company. Do you want to play a game of *Scrabble*?"

Darcy picked up the dishes and stacked them in the sink for later and hung the dishtowel on the oven door handle.

"Well, okay. But I play a better game of poker than *Scrabble*, truth to tell."

Darcy laughed. "Product, no doubt, of your misspent youth."

"No doubt," Abby agreed.

They spent the rest of the evening playing five-card stud with toothpick bets, and Abby trounced her soundly. They were both fuzzy when Abby left around ten o'clock.

By the time Darcy took Mac out on a short and cautious walk and settled into bed, it was almost eleven. She lay there, trying to read some paperback novel she'd picked up at the store, but couldn't focus.

She finally closed the book and pondered the slightly bubbling plaster from some small, ancient, water leak from the apartment above, while her mind swirled.

It didn't seem possible that Bridget Emerson's funeral was tomorrow. She had been a sweet kid, and she wasn't even eighteen. She was pregnant when she died and that made her murder unspeakable in a way Darcy couldn't wrap her heart around.

She wasn't sure how Sam Carson's murder fit into this mess, but she was sure it did. And who kept threatening her? Would that person be at Bridget's funeral tomorrow?

That's creepy.

Darcy punched her pillow again, trying to find a cool spot, and turned off her light.

She must have thrashed around through most of the night because she awoke more tired than when she had gone to bed.

Mac could always raise her spirits even in the morning. Darcy walked him to the park and sat on a bench with the latte and paper she'd picked up on the way, keeping a tight grip on his leash. Mac uncharacteristically cooperated and sat next to her quietly.

Flipping to the inside third page, she saw Bridget Emerson's picture in the Obituary section. It must have been her high school senior picture. It had that posed, placid look young people always wore for those kinds of pictures. Darcy peered at it, trying to see a remnant of that freckle-faced tomboy she used to know.

Reading the short blurb on Bridget's life, didn't give much information. Senior at Central High School, CRD Riders three years . . .

She felt a sympathetic spasm for Bridget's father. Doc must be destroyed. Darcy closed her eyes and remembered Doc's craggy, tanned face. The lines would be etched even deeper now, she thought. Bad enough to have to bury your wife, but to have to bury your only child as well—to know she'd been murdered.

She finished off her coffee and untangled Mac's leash. They walked home slowly. Mac, always responsive to her moods, was subdued, and Darcy was grateful.

She called Zach to tell him she would come in after the funeral. She would only stay for the funeral. Even she drew the line at scrounging for news among the wreckage of Doc Emerson's loss.

Donning her most conservative white top and black wrap-around skirt, she scraped her honey blond hair back in a pony-tail and studied herself in the mirror. She looked unremarkable, exactly the impression she was going for. She had told her mom and dad she would meet them at the church.

It was close to ten when she took Mac downstairs to Abby's. He was scampering while they waited for Abby to answer the door. Tired of her somber mood and ready for someone more fun, Darcy thought.

Abby swung the door open and Mac rushed in.

"Make yourself at home, buddy." Darcy shouted out after him.

"He's fine. Leave him," Abby said.

"Are you sure you don't mind watching him? I used to leave him alone all the time in Kansas, but with these threats . . ." Darcy let the rest hang.

"You go on ahead. Mac and I'll be all right."

"I have to go to the station after the funeral, so I'm not sure how long I'll be. I'll give you a call, okay?"

"Fine," Abby said. "You take care and don't worry about us. Mac and I will keep each other company."

Darcy breathed an internal sigh of relief, waved goodbye and rushed into the foyer, already running late.

A LARGE CROWD HAD GATHERED at St. Mary's Catholic Cathedral if the number of cars parked in the two lots was any indication. Several black town cars and a hearse blocked the front of the church.

Darcy climbed the front steps, merging with others as they made their way into the cool interior of the large, gothic Catholic Church.

Darcy's family attended this church when she was growing up and it felt familiar and comforting in a strange way. She glanced down the center aisle and saw her parents sitting on the left-hand side. She hurried to join them.

Dropping to a half genuflect-on-the-run, Darcy slipped into the pew next to her mom. Donna Moreland shot her daughter a slightly disapproving glance for her incomplete genuflection. You'd think the Pope was in town.

"Darcy Marie, you should genuflect instead of dip." her mother began to hiss in her ear.

"Shush, Mom. Church." Darcy whispered back. Ed Moreland smiled benignly and reached over to squeeze Darcy's hand.

Darcy knelt down and said a prayer for the young girl who so needlessly lost her life, then sat once more and awaited the arrival of Bridget's family.

The huge organ in the loft at the back of the church was playing softly. Massive bouquets spilled over the steps going up at the front and bordered the altar.

Soon a procession of darkly clad people entered through the main doors. It was an odd mixture of generations, young and old all looking solemn and stunned. Leading the way was a tall broad-shouldered man, flanked by a man and woman about his age who propped him up by his elbows. Frank Emerson was conspicuously leaning on the man next to him, and as they passed Darcy heard a low keening sob escape from him that raised the hair on the back of her neck and made tears spring to her own eyes.

The priest processed formally up the middle aisle, and the pall-bearers followed, placing the coffin in front of the altar. The coffin was white and covered with a white embroidered cloth to remind the congregation of Bridget's baptism, and symbolically referencing her entry into another more perfect exitance. Another sob escaped Doc Emerson and the woman sitting by him patted his back ineffectually.

The priest began the funeral service and Darcy was conscious that her attention wandered in and out. Once the Mass of Christian burial was completed, several people got up to speak about Bridget. One was a girl who'd been a CRD Riders with her, and a young man who was a cousin talked about how full of life and mischief she'd been.

By now snuffles echoed all around the church. There's nothing as heart-rending as the funeral for a child. Darcy noticed some teenagers clumped together randomly. They were either stoically silent with the weight of mortality bearing down on them or clinging in soggy little groups of tears and sniffles.

She caught sight of Stacie Rogers sitting in the middle of a group of about five or six kids. They're all so painfully young, Darcy thought. It must be overwhelming to bury a friend like this.

Throughout the ceremony, Frank Emerson sobbed loudly. Darcy had never seen a man so undone before and it was painful to watch.

The service ground to a halt and the congregation stood in respectful silence while the funeral workers rolled the white, gold-trimmed casket out of the church.

Darcy wondered at the use of white. Unless a baby was being buried, usually the family opted for a different color. Surely Doc Emerson had been told she had been pregnant when she died. Must be different being buried in white as opposed to being married in white. All those societal trappings were meaningless now.

Bridget's father followed, tears streaming down his face, his eyes glassy and vague.

"Do you want to go to the internment with us?" Darcy's father asked as they exited the church.

"No. I have to get back to the station. It was decent of Zach to understand why I had to come to the funeral."

"Frank's a good friend," her dad said, quietly. "We went to high school together. Even served on the same Rodeo Days' committee until he finished his veterinarian degree. He's one of the best vets in the state and CRD was always glad to have him work the show. Damn shame. Seems like more sadness than one man ought to have."

Darcy looked at her father and saw a hint of moisture around his eyes. She reached up and kissed his cheek. "Please, give him my love, dad."

"Bye, Mom." She kissed her too and gave her an encouraging hug before they parted ways.

Darcy tried to shake the residual sorrow from her mood, but it would take time.

She went home and changed into her jeans and western shirt. She didn't stop to tell Abby about the funeral. It was too raw yet for her to talk about anyway, except in general terms. Grief demanded silence at times, and this was one of those times.

She drove to the station, and thankfully, her puffy eyes, and determined face discouraged anyone from talking to her as she wound her way to the back of the studio. She slipped into her closet of an office, looked at the pile of disparate papers scattered on her desktop, and clicked on her computer.

She buried herself in the minutiae of sorting memos and checking e-mails. Darcy remembered a fragment of an Emily Dickinson poem about a bustle in the house the morning after death. Something about sweeping up the heart and putting it away. Dealing with the ordinary to forget the enormity of it all. That's what she felt like she was doing.

Darcy didn't know how long she sat immersed in the inconsequential, but when she looked up again, it was to find Zach sitting in the only other chair in the little space she called her own.

Her heart flipped. "How long have you been here?"

"Not long. You were so engrossed I was afraid I'd scare you if I said something." He handed her a Styrofoam cup filled with the brown swill that passed for coffee at the station.

"Thanks. I could use some unadulterated caffeine."

"How was it?" Zach asked cautiously.

"Awful. I sat with my parents. Her dad is in bad shape, Zach. I've never seen a grown man unravel like that before. I couldn't bring myself to go to the internment or the reception."

"Yeah, I heard he was taking it badly, 'course I don't know how you wouldn't, but still."

"It was hard to watch. Doc was always a quietly competent man." Darcy shuddered involuntarily at the memory of Emerson's uncontrollable sobbing.

"In a related matter," Darcy said. "I talked to a Rider yesterday who said Jason Ford had a major crush on Bridget. I thought it might be worth a gentle prod to see if he could be connected to Carson's death. What do you think?"

"Did you talk to the police?" Zach plopped his feet on the edge of her desk.

"Yeah, if Hank Nelson qualifies. Why?"

"Because I don't want you getting in the way of their investigation, that's why. Can you talk to the boy without getting in Nelson's way?"

"Probably." Darcy wasn't at all sure, but she would try.

Zach's boots thudded to the floor as he loomed over her. "Darcy."

"Okay. I promise I'll be subtle." She raised her hand in the air. "He won't even see it coming. I know a mutual friend of his named Stacie. Maybe she could introduce me to him. It would seem friendlier that way."

"I know this is personal for you but be careful. Why don't you try to get in touch with Doc Emerson this afternoon? Go take a long lunch, then see if you can catch him after the reception."

"Sometimes this job feels downright ghoulish."

"Sometimes this job *is* downright ghoulish, but it's what we do."

"Thanks, Zach." Darcy got up and hugged him. Having an old friend become your boss was another reason she was glad to be home.

CHAPTER 12

DARCY SORTED THROUGH THE REST OF HER NOTES, putting them into piles to deal with later and finished her coffee. She decided to call Abby and see if she wanted to go somewhere for lunch.

Leaning back in her squeaky old chair, she speed-dialed Abby's cell. It rang several times and Darcy heard a frighteningly familiar voice.

"Keep that mutt settled down if you don't want me to dump him out on the road."

Darcy recognized the gravelly voice of her intimidating phone caller. Then she heard Abby's voice.

"I'll try, but he's scared. So am I if it comes to that. You really had no right to kidnap us."

Darcy went cold but didn't dare say anything in case it gave away her connection to Abby's phone. Terrified, Darcy ran out in the hall and frantically flagged Zach down. He came at a dead run.

"What?" Zach took one look at Darcy's white face and the cell phone she was clutching in her fist.

She shushed him with a wave while she held her palm across the mouthpiece of the phone.

"I think Abby and Mac have been kidnapped. I can hear the guy who called and threatened me . . .," she whispered and pushed the phone into Zach's hands.

He listened for a minute and mouthed, "Call the police."

Darcy ran to a vacant desk and tried to remember Hank's number. She was drawing a blank. Why did the brain shut down tight when you needed it the most? Finally, she pounded the 911 keys and waited anxiously for an answer.

When the emergency operator droned "What is your emergency?" Darcy explained that Abby McNeil had been kidnapped, and she needed to speak to Detective Nelson immediately. The operator tried to give her his number. "Patch me through, damn it."

The rattled operator told her to hold.

Not my finest hour, Darcy thought.

As she waited for Hank to pick up, she thought of that awful joke about being put on hold when you called the suicide prevention hotline. Contrary to some reports, dark humor was not always your best friend in a crisis.

"This is Detective Nelson," she heard Hank's warm voice on the other end, and she felt her heartbeat settle to a semi-rapid thud.

"Hank. Oh, thank God! This is Darcy. Someone's kidnapped Abby and Mac! We've got to find them."

"Slow down, Darcy. Where are you?"

"I'm at the station. I called Abby on my cell, and I heard some guy talking—"

"Try not to lose the connection. I'll be right there." The line went dead.

Zach was still listening on her phone, but his face looked grave. Her heart began to hammer against her chest again. Zach put the phone on speaker and then placed it on the desk next to a small pocket recorder, and they hovered on either side.

"The least you can do is take this bag off my head, young man." Darcy heard Abby say. She was trying to tell them about her kidnapper.

"Be quiet, old lady. If you hadn't kept a death grip on that damn dog, you wouldn't be in this mess. You should've let go of the leash when you could have."

"Well I didn't. So where does that leave us? Why don't you let us go? I didn't see anything and couldn't identify you or your girlfriend if I had to."

"Shit. How does she know . . .?"

They heard a female's muffled voice so soft they had to strain to hear.

"I can smell your perfume, dear. Young men do not use that scent. It's all right, extremely popular perfume. Many young women use it. It's a nice fragrance." Abby was being her most grandmotherly. Darcy hoped they were buying it.

Silence.

"This leash is cutting into my wrists. Could you at least loosen it?"

Silence.

"I presume it's just the two of you. I don't have a sense of anyone being back here with Mac and me."

"Lady. I told you to shut up." It was the male again, and he sounded tense.

"Oh God. What are we going to do?" They could hear the female's voice rasp. "We were only going to grab the dog, not the old lady. I'm sure people-napping is worse than dog-napping." She sounded like she was one spark short of hysteria.

"Shut up, will ya? We didn't have any choice," her companion snapped at her.

Silence followed and Darcy was deathly afraid they had lost the signal, then they heard Abby's voice again.

"Are you taking us out to the country? I think I smell dust. Did I tell you I have allergies?"

"Are you sure she can't see through that pillowcase?" the female voice challenged.

"Yeah, I'm sure. All she can see is light and shadow."

Darcy and Zach heard sneezes, and wheezes. Abby was putting on quite a show.

"I—I don't have my medicine—ahhhchoo!"

"Stop talking and you won't inhale so much dust." the male responded coldly.

"I hear gravel. We're on a gravel country road. I know it. Ahhhhchoo! I could tell we changed roads fifteen minutes after we turned left. Ahhhhchooo!"

Mac began to bark in response to Abby's sneezing.

"Shut that damn dog up, lady. I may not kill you, but I got no problem shooting that scrawny dog."

The fake sneezing stopped. "Do—do you have a gun, young man?"

Darcy heard Abby's terror.

"'Course I do. Right here," he bragged. "And I know how to use it, so shut up and keep that dog quiet."

"I thought you said you wouldn't harm me." Abby continued tentatively.

"I wouldn't mind wounding you if you don't keep quiet." came the gruff reply.

"Oh, well." They heard Abby sigh and silence continued except for a low-level hum Darcy assumed was the engine.

Zach and Darcy continued to listen, not daring to breathe for fear the kidnappers would hear noises from her cell. Darcy was terrified they would drive so far out the signal would drop.

Darcy saw Hank rush in through the double glass doors followed closely by a uniformed officer. He listened for a moment and then motioned for them to move into the more deserted area of Zach's office. Hank signaled to Zach to keep listening. Zach nodded his understanding. Hank and Darcy left the room, closing the door quietly behind them. Darcy was watching Zach intently through the window of his office, afraid that if she blinked, she would lose all connection to Abby and Mac.

"What the hell happened?" Hank ground out as soon as the door closed.

"I don't know." She almost wailed in her panic and frustration. "I was calling Abby to see if she wanted to have lunch—and—and . . ." a sob escaped from the back of her throat.

Hank held her by the shoulders and made her look at him. "Focus, Darcy."

"Okay. Okay. Anyway, I heard her pick up, but then she didn't answer when I said her name. I listened and heard this guy talking to her. Oh God, Hank. They've tied her up with Mac's leash and they've pulled a pillowcase over her head. He said he has a gun."

Hank moved her over to sit in a nearby chair and he hunkered down next to her.

"I know you're scared, but I need you to try to think as clearly as you can. What details has Abby been able to give you so far?"

"Uhm . . ." She gulped in air and tried to calm herself down. "There are two of them. A male and a female. Abby said she smelled dust after about fifteen minutes of driving, but you know how time can be so relative. Oh yeah. She said they turned left, but left from where?"

"Calm down. They were most likely taken from Celebration Park. Isn't that usually where they go to walk?"

"Um hum." She could not make the back of her throat loosen.

"My guess is they drove west on Lincolnway. Get out of town fastest that way. Probably jogged over to Missile Drive to take Happy Jack Road, less traffic and less chance anyone would see Abby with a pillowcase over her."

"That makes sense," Darcy agreed.

Hank pulled out his cell, and in moments was having a conversation.

"I have a kidnapping in progress. Older lady and a dog. I need a BOLO out on a car. Do we know anything about the vehicle they're in?" he asked her.

Darcy shook her head and drifted back to stare at Zach through the window. Zach looked back grimly at her and shrugged. There must not be much conversation going on.

". . . a pair of suspects, one male, and one female, an older lady with a pillowcase pulled over her head and a small Terrier type dog, brown and yellow coat. I think they're heading west on Happy Jack Road, so you'll need to contact the Sherriff's Department."

"We're connected to the victim through her cell phone, but we could lose that fast. See if you can get the provider to compare the signal strength and approximate their location with triangulation. What's her carrier and number, Darcy?"

"Verizon, 555-7724," she answered automatically. "Can they do that?"

Hank nodded. "Yeah. So far, she's been able to keep her cell on. Get back to me." He ended the call and clipped his phone back on his belt.

"What? What'd they say?"

"Most cells are equipped with a GPS system that allows us to track her phone signal. Two problems."

"Oh God." She felt her stomach turn over.

"Take it easy."

Hank was trying to calm her down but perversely, he was ticking her off.

"Take it easy yourself." she snapped.

"You want to know this stuff, or would you rather melt into a panic attack? Your choice." Hank narrowed his ice-blue eyes at her.

"Sorry. Sorry. Tell me." She clutched her hands in front of her, trying to make them stop shaking.

"Okay, here's the deal. We can track her signal if she keeps the phone on and doesn't go in a tunnel or something, so it's critical that she not hang up."

Darcy darted over to the window of Zach's office again. He was listening intently. He nodded reassuringly, but his expression was bleak.

Hank had followed her over and was looking at Zach over her shoulder. Darcy felt his warmth at her back and turned to face him. Instead of stepping back, Hank shifted forward. Not a step exactly, just a leaning in. He placed his hands on her shoulders and she looked up into his now softer eyes. Darcy caught her breath.

"The problem is that satellite coverage is spotty and unpredictable in more rural areas." Hank continued to whisper as if unaware of her inappropriate pulse spike.

Darcy pushed Hank into the hallway. "But we can track her?"

"Yes, but not consistently and not in real time. There's likely to be a lag."

"Well, let's go." Darcy pulled his arm, not a good move on her part. He was like a solid brick wall.

"Darcy, you're not going anywhere. You're going to stay put and let us handle this. Is that clear?"

Her jaw tightened and her spine stiffened.

"And before you go obstinate all over my ass," he smiled at her, "you need to remember that the main goal here is to keep Abby and Mac safe and get them home."

"Yes, but—"

"To do that, we need to have trained personnel who know how to handle emergency situations. The last thing they need is to trip over civilians when they're trying to rescue someone."

"I know, but I promise I'll stay out of the way. This is all my fault. If I hadn't been pushy, and stubborn—"

"Darcy, this is not your fault. This may come as a huge surprise to you, but people can go psychotic even without your help. This might be a good time however, to tell me about the restraining order you had taken out on a Christopher Richter in Kansas City."

Darcy's face turned an ashen gray. "How do you know about that?"

"I told you I looked you up. I have access to more information than some people, now talk. Who is he and why did you slap a restraining order on him?"

Darcy gulped and sighed. "He worked at the station with me. At first, I thought he just had a crush on me, but he kept showing up everywhere I went. If I went to get coffee, he'd be there in line behind me. I'd go to a pub with some friends and he'd just show up. It was kind of creepy." Darcy crossed her arms defensively.

"I tried to talk to him and explained that I was engaged to another man, but it didn't seem to make a difference to him. He'd send me flowers and pushed cards under my door. Kevin, my fiancée at the time, tried to talk to him about leaving me alone, but it just made Chris more belligerent. That's when I took out a restraining order on him."

"I assume he didn't take that well."

"You could say that."

"I did say that. I need you to stop giving me one-line answers and tell me the details. Could this guy have kidnapped Abby and your dog to get even?"

"No." Darcy snapped out her answer. "At least I don't think so."

"I need you to be sure, Darcy. Was he controlling, violent, or just a jerk?"

Darcy sighed and glanced at Zach who flashed her the "thumbs up" from his office.

"Okay. Chris was the sportscaster at the station I worked for in Kansas City. He began giving me unsolicited advice on my career. Everything from how I wore my hair to what stories I should do. At first, I thought he wanted to help me because he was crushing on me. I gave him a speech about how it was me, not him, with the problem and reminded him I was already engaged to another man."

Darcy glanced up from her lap and tried to gauge Hank's reaction to her story.

"Go on. Tell me the rest of it." Hank's eyes narrowed but she could tell he was straining to appear calm.

"Another incident happened. He broke into my apartment. He trashed a bunch of photos and dumped some drawers but didn't take anything and technically he was still 200 yards away from me."

"As per the restraining order?"

"He couldn't believe I refused to break off my engagement. He started calling me all the time, following me around at the station, parking in front of my apartment. I was afraid of what he'd do if he got angry again, so I took out a restraining order on him. Then, I quit my job and called Zach. I didn't want to be stuck in Kansas with Chris after Kevin left for Tampa Bay."

Hank took her icy fists in his warm hands. "Would he do something like this to get back at you?"

"Who? Chris? No. Basically Chris was a bully. He liked to control people, but I was leaving, so it was no fun anymore. Darcy shuddered and closed her eyes tight. When she opened them, she shook her head slowly. "To tell the truth, I don't think I meant enough to Chris for him to follow me here. I think when he heard I'd broken my engagement to Kevin, he stopped bugging me. Maybe he was just wanted something he knew he couldn't have. Kevin left for Tampa, and I made the decision to come home, I told the station manager about his behavior before I left. Trust me,

Chris's career means more to him than anything else. I haven't had one call from him since I left."

"Okay, but I'm checking his whereabouts just to be safe. Do you have any other ideas?"

"Someone doesn't want me digging into Bridget and Sam's murders is all I can figure. All of the warnings stipulated I needed to stop investigating. I haven't been back in town long enough to make real enemies yet."

Hank chuckled at that and stood. "I'm going to the station to coordinate with the Sheriff's Department from there. Give me your word you'll let me handle this and I'll give you my word that I'll call you as soon as we learn anything. Okay?"

"Okay," Darcy said. "But . . ."

"I'm leaving Officer Thompson with you to help monitor the call. The sooner I go, the sooner I can tell you what's going on. Hell, you'll probably find out before me if you keep that line open. Gotta go." He leaned over, kissed her hard and quick on the mouth and left.

Darcy watched him leave. While one part of her brain was still in shock from the kiss, the other part was frantic with worry. She got how people became unhinged in a crisis.

Slipping into the glass-paneled office, she pulled a chair next to Zach. He smiled at her and re-positioned the phone on the desk so she could listen too.

"How far out are you going to take us?"

Darcy recognized Abby's voice. Silence again. She was trying to give them as much information as she could, but her captors weren't being exceptionally helpful.

Zach and Darcy listened to the hum and rattle of the engine. From the sound, they could tell they were still traveling down a gravel road. Every once in a while, they would hear the chunk of rock as it bounced up the underside of the wheel well.

"Hey. Whatcha guys doing?" Bryce Atkins barged into Zach's office. Zach quickly covered the mouthpiece of the phone and mouthed for him to shut up.

He came toward them and Darcy froze.

Zach grabbed Bryce by the arm and covered his mouth, no mean feat since he kept trying to talk, and gave him the bum's rush out the door and halfway down the hall.

Darcy pressed closer to the phone on the desk, terrified that Bryce might have alerted the kidnappers about the open phone line, but it was still quiet. She whispered a small "thank-you" prayer in her head.

Zach came in and took a huge marker from his desk drawer and grabbed a piece of typing paper. He scrawled: DO NOT OPEN THIS DOOR FOR ANY REASON. KEEP THIS AREA CLEAR AND QUIET. Then initialed it. He taped the missive up on his window and resumed his seat next to Darcy.

Darcy smiled her thanks, and he nodded. It horrified her that a little bit of plastic and wires and was her only link to Abby and Mac. She stood and began to pace, trying to outrun her guilt she supposed. Out of the corner of her eye, she saw Zach waving at her. She raced over to listen.

"Where are we? Why have we stopped?"

Was it her imagination or was Abby terrified? Darcy tried to tamp down her own panic.

They heard the metallic screech of a door opening. Darcy heard Mac barking and had to cover her mouth to keep from crying out.

"Get out." The male was close by.

"Ouch. Be careful young man. I can't use my hands. It throws off my balance. I'm moving as fast as I can."

"I got the dog," said the female. She was shouting to be heard over Mac's frantic barking.

"Where are we?"

"Move."

"Ooof. Stop pushing me."

There were rustling noises, and Darcy assumed Abby had palmed the phone before she was jerked out.

"I'll kill him." Darcy mouthed to Zach. He put his arm around her shoulders and gave her a "buck up" squeeze.

"We'll leave you some water and let that Darcy lady know where you are when she promises to back off. Is that clear? If she doesn't follow our friendly advice, they'll never find you." The man untied her hands. "Keep the pillowcase on until you hear us leave or you're both dead. Is that clear?"

"I think it's despicable of you to terrorize an old lady and a little dog."

Darcy heard the righteous indignation in Abby's voice, and while she couldn't blame her, she was petrified that Abby would push them too far. Darcy wasn't sure what these people were capable of, but it was a sure bet that they were harried and desperate.

"Shut up, old lady. Get in there."

Silence.

The phone had gone dead.

CHAPTER 13

"Easy, Darcy. Hank may have a lock on them from the last known ping. Don't assume the worst."

"I've—I've got to call Hank."

"Here." Zach handed her the phone from his desk and took charge of her cell.

"Good thinking."

Darcy looked up the general office number for the police and tapped it in. It took a lifetime before the operator answered and two lifetimes before she heard Hank on the other end.

"We lost her," she said as soon as Hank said his name. "We have to do something!"

"We've got two cars out watching the identified area, but we want to be careful not to alarm them. We're not sure what they're capable of."

"Oh, Hank . . ."

"Those deputies know what they're doing. They'll move in concentric circles, but there isn't much cover out there, and they don't want to alert the kidnappers that they're close. I don't think they really want to hurt anyone. It's a gut feeling, but I have good instincts about this sort of thing."

"Now you believe in instinct? I hope you're right."

"Me too. Tell you what, I'll come and wait with you if you want. The sheriff department will contact me as soon as they find anything."

"Thanks, Hank. I'd appreciate that." Darcy hung up and repeated Hank's offer to wait with her to Zach.

"You can use that office by the back stairwell if you want." Zach said. "We store paper in there, but it'll be quiet. Almost no one goes back there, not even Bozo Bryce."

Darcy laughed. "Thanks, Zach. Send Hank back when he gets here okay?"

"Sure thing, and Darcy . . ."

She turned back in at the door. "Yes?"

"To be safe, take the sign," Zach grinned at her.

"Good call." She pulled the warning sign off the window and headed toward the back of the building.

Darcy found the place easily and after she taped the warning sign on the door. She snapped on one of the small banks of overhead fluorescent lights.

There were boxes full of reams of paper stacked against the wall. She wrestled a couple boxes down from higher stacks and plopped down on one. She held her cell in her palm and willed it to ring.

Nothing.

She knew logically that this wasn't her fault, but emotionally she felt guilty. She reviewed everything in her memory from the time she had arrived in Cheyenne.

Moving into the Algonquin and running into Abby first thing had taken a lot of the sting out of having to move home. Darcy felt a hot tear slip down her cheek and brushed it away. She dug in the depths of her Prada-Look-Alike purse and found a scrunched-up ball of tissue that was otherwise unused.

She concentrated on unscrunching the mess to produce at least one blow-worthy tissue. Finally, successful, she blew her drippy nose enthusiastically.

When she heard the door of the office click, she looked up startled.

"Is this a private pity-party or can anyone join?" Hank asked in a whisper. He closed the door behind him.

Darcy threw her arms around his neck and hugged him close.

He wrapped his warm arms around her and chuckled. "Quite a greeting."

"How did you get here so fast?" Darcy eased back, but she kept her palms pressed against his chest. "It's okay to talk. We lost her signal."

"I'm a cop remember?" He smiled down at her. She felt her stomach flutter and she stepped away self-consciously.

"Don't tell me you used your lights and sirens for little ol'e me."

"You almost never need to do that here. You do get good parking spaces though."

"Oh well, that's all right then." She laughed then turned serious. "Any more news?"

"Nope. They're continuing the surveillance. They should find something soon, Darcy. Don't worry." He sat on the box opposite her and took her cold hands into his larger, warmer ones.

"Find something . . ." she began to sputter. "What the hell does that mean? Parts?"

She tried to jump up, but he held her hands tightly and shifted so that his knees bracketed hers as he faced her.

"You don't do waiting well, do you?" It wasn't really a question, so Darcy didn't answer him. Hank smiled at her.

"I meant they'd find Abby and Mac soon and get them back unharmed."

"Sorry. I don't mean to take this out on you," she said.

"That's okay. I know you're stressed." He stood, went behind her, and began to rub the tight muscles in her neck and shoulders.

It felt good. Finally, she tipped her head back.

"Does this come under the heading of the 'Serve' part of the 'Protect and Serve' motto on your car door?"

He leaned forward and whispered in her ear, "Nope. That's public, this is private." Darcy shivered.

He continued to knead her neck and Darcy felt a small sizzle run up her nerve endings and a warm flush ooze up her neck onto her cheeks.

There were no windows in this little cocoon, and it was tempting to believe they could hide away from the sordid world full of murder and meanness. She closed her eyes and let herself melt under his hands.

Darcy jumped when Hank's phone rang. No happy little tune for this guy. His phone actually rang, like an old-fashioned telephone.

"I like the classics," he said with a wink at her shocked expression. "Sometimes I change it out with a siren."

"Detective Nelson." He said, then waited. "Great! I'll be right there. Fifteen at the outside. He sighed as if from deep in his boots. "Oh, and Thompson, thanks."

He snapped his phone off. The grooves in his forehead softened and for the first time Darcy recognized that he'd been as distressed about Abby's abduction as she was.

"They found them. Evidently they stashed them out in Ames Monument."

"Ames Monument? That old stone pyramid in the middle of nowhere where we used to have keggers? That Ames Monument?"

"Why, Ms. Moreland. You have a wicked past I didn't know anything about." He stood and held the door for her.

Darcy punched his arm as she passed by. "And where were you raised, Detective Nelson? In a monastery?"

"Not even close," he said as his hand slipped from the small of her back to the curve of her butt and back again. "We'll talk later," he whispered in her ear as he maneuvered Darcy through the hallway.

"I'm going with you."

"This is official business, Darcy. I'll bring them both right to the police station, and you can meet us there."

"Not on your life! It's my fault they were put in danger. I'm coming with you."

Hank took one look at the stubborn set of her jaw decided they were wasting time. "Okay, but you do what I tell you to do. No questions."

"Let's just go!"

They stopped by Zach's office and told him the good news.

"I'm going to go with Hank to pick Abby and Mac up," Darcy told him.

"Take whatever time you need. Why don't you call me in the morning?"

"Thanks, Zach, for everything." Darcy gave him a quick hug and a kiss on the cheek, and they continued out the front door.

"I'm not as friendly with my boss as you are with yours," Hank said as he opened the car door for her.

"Old bud from college. How 'bout yours?" Darcy said.

"Wrong sex," he answered as he got in on his side.

"Jealous?" Darcy leaned toward him and teased.

"If pushed." He put the key in and turned the engine over.

"He's married with two little boys who look just like him, only short." Darcy laughed.

"It's nice to have old friends," he said as he dropped the truck in gear and pulled out of the lot.

It took a little over 20 minutes to get to the monument. There were several police and sheriff cars parked at odd angles. Darcy strained to see if she could find Abby and Mac.

Hank's pickup barely pulled in, before Darcy jumped out and ran into the middle of the milling group. It was a good thing Hank was right behind her because the sheriff was just beginning to question her presence there. Hank grabbed her hand and pulled her behind him. He flashed his badge.

"Where are they?" Darcy said as she stepped around Hank.

"This is Darcy Moreland, a friend of Ms. McNeil's and the owner of the dog. She's understandably a little upset. Are they still here?"

"Yes, sir. We've just begun the process the scene and take Ms. McNeil's first statement. You'll find them just inside."

"Thank you, officer." Hank turned to Darcy. "It's usually poor form to jump out of a moving truck, just so you know."

Hank went first, ducking his large frame to fit the small opening. Darcy followed close behind. The interior was lighter than Darcy had remembered it being. Of course, she was usually there at night.

Abby was sitting on a rock with as much dignity as she would sit in someone's parlor. Except that she was still rubbing her wrists where she had been bound, she looked perfect to Darcy.

Mac bounced toward Darcy. He was dancing around as if he was crazy-wild to tell her all about his adventure. She lifted him up and buried her nose in his fur. The tears came. She was beyond relieved to see them unhurt.

She knelt beside Abby, brushing her tears away with the back of her hand. "Oh Abby! I am so sorry. This is all my fault. If I hadn't been so pushy and persistent, they would have never taken you. Can you ever forgive me?"

"Don't be silly. You're only doing your job. It's okay now, dear. We're all safe and sound."

"Are you sure you're okay? My God, Abby. If anything would've happened to you, or to Mac . . ."

"We're fine, dear. Now sit down and catch your breath. These nice young officers want to take my statement and to check me over for evidence."

"What do you mean evidence?" Darcy jerked her head between Hank and Abby.

"I've given them the water bottle the kidnappers left for me to dust for prints, and now they want to take some nail scrapings."

"Nail scrapings? What are you talking about?"

"While I was being hauled out to the country, I carefully scratched at the seat of the vehicle. Sometimes Darcy, they can tell what make or model a car is by the slightest threads. I don't binge-watch C.S.I. for nothing you know."

"Ms. McNeill, if you'll please follow detective Connors, we'll take you into town to get you processed and home as quickly as possible," said a young, uniformed policewoman.

"I think I'll take Ms. Moreland and her dog home if someone can drive Ms. McNeill back when she's through," Hank said as he draped his arm round her shoulders and began to lead her out.

Darcy spun away. "No. I want to wait for Abby."

"Don't bother dear. I'll be fine and Mac I'm sure would like a treat and a cuddle from you. You go right along, and I'll be home in what a jiffy."

"Okay, if you're sure." Darcy had an irrational fear that she needed to be with them now 24/7 to keep them safe, but she guessed if Abby were with the police, they would protect her enough for now.

Darcy kept a tight grip on Mac who wiggled in her arms wanting to be set down.

"Hold still you animated dust mop," she told him. "I'll let you down when we're home and not before."

"You really think he understands what you're saying?" Hank held the truck door open for her.

"Every word," she said, and she meant it.

The drive home went quickly. Hank and Darcy climbed the outer and inner steps at the Algonquin without conversation. She unlocked her door and finally dropped Mac to the floor.

He scampered around, sniffing at everything like he had been gone for two years. He finally snuggled into his doggy bed and dropped off to sleep.

"Well he seems happy to be home. Can you have a beer or something?" She went to the fridge.

"Sure. I'm off the clock now." Hank sat in the middle of her sofa and stretched his legs out in front of him. "Would you mind if I took my boots off for a while?"

"Not at all. There's a bootjack by the chair there," Darcy answered as she popped the tops of a couple of cans of Bud Lites.

"I was hoping for a more personal approach." He smiled up at her as she handed him his beer.

"Were you really?" she said. "Okay, I guess I can oblige my 'Hero of the Moment,' but don't get used to it."

She put her beer down and straddled his legs with her back to him. Bending down she put her hands under the heel of his right boot and pulled. She felt Hank plant his other foot on her butt and she twisted around to send him a cheeky grin. He pushed, she pulled, and the boot slid off. They repeated the process on the other foot. Darcy stacked his boots to the side and plopped down next to him on the sofa.

"Now how 'bout mine?" She grabbed her beer and took a gulp.

"Okay." Hank lifted both of her legs to rest on his lap and made short work of pulling off each of her tomato-red boots.

"Hey. No fair. I wanted the show."

Hank laughed but ignored her protest. He pulled her legs across his lap until her butt snugged next to his thigh. Plucking his beer from the table, he took a deep swig.

"We need to talk," he said finally.

"Okay."

"I've made arrangements to keep you and Abby under surveillance until we're sure we've eliminated the threat."

"What?" Darcy dropped her legs from his lap and would have stood except he grabbed her legs again and dumped them back into their previous position.

"Sit still. This isn't a commentary on your ability or your intelligence."

She opened her mouth to argue, but he leaned into her and covered her lips with his. By the time he let her go, she almost couldn't remember what she'd been irritated about. Almost.

"Ex—plain," she managed to moan out the two syllables. A part of her slow-functioning brain was now lucid enough to figure out she wasn't dealing with a man who played fair.

"Okay," he sipped his beer, stalling, and choosing his words. "You and Mac have been threatened because of your investigation into the murders, right?"

"So?" she agreed. The fog was receding.

"And Abby was taken because she wouldn't let Mac be taken alone, right?"

"Could we get to the point?" Darcy folded her arms across her chest.

"Okaaay. You're bait since you insist on the down and dirty rendition." Hank took another deep gulp of his beer, shook the can to make sure it was empty and tossed it the distance into the kitchen trash can. "And that's three." He punched his arms in the air.

"Bait? You want to use Abby and me as bait to catch a murderer?"

"If it works that way, it would be great."

"For whom?"

"Well, for everyone." He smiled at her.

"Now wait a damn minute." Darcy leaned forward to get up.

Hank reached around to the back of her neck and gave it a squeeze and a jerk to keep her in place. "Easy there, Sparky. No need to go off like a potato gun."

Darcy forced herself to relax, but she wasn't happy about it. Hank's hand drifted from her neck to her back, rubbing a soothing path up and down her spine. She hated to quibble.

"To be honest, I'm not thrilled about it either. Unfortunately, I think the killer has targeted you, and by extension now Abby, to try to intimidate."

"But why? It isn't as if I can do them any damage. I'm just a reporter for heaven's sake."

"Maybe they assume you're keeping the investigation stirred up." Hank pulled her into his chest, wrapping his arm around her shoulders.

"There are some members of the citizenry who believe the police don't investigate extensively unless the glare of the press forces them to. Maybe your killer is one of these."

"He's not my killer." Darcy snuggled even deeper.

Hank hugged her, responding to her burrowing. "He is now. We're assuming the man who kidnapped Abby and Mac is either the murderer or works for him, and that the girl is some kind of accomplice."

Darcy pushed up to look at him. "But are the two murders connected?"

"Don't know yet. Might not be." He pulled her back into his arms. "The point is that I would've ordered placing you and Abby under surveillance for your own protection anyway, but if it leads us to an arrest, it's a bonus."

"Well you'd better tell whoever is doing this 'surveillance' to stay out of my way. I don't want to be tripping over anyone while I'm trying to do my job."

"I intend to take over the onerous task of keeping you safe if that's okay with you." He kissed her again.

Darcy could smell the soft pine scent of his cologne and sense the heat of him against her face. Her last cogent thought.

What followed was pure, raw response. She shifted her hips across his lap and pulled him closer. Hell. She would have climbed under his skin if she'd thought she could.

His hand dropped down from the curve of her back and rested on her butt. Darcy squirmed closer, itchy. Hank kept building that itch letting his hand stroke from her butt up her side to underneath her breast and back down, ratcheting up the heat. Moving, twisting, grasping.

How long that took was a blur full of hot, pulsing, sensations. Until it wasn't. Darcy pushed Hank away and sat up.

Hank looked startled. "What's the matter?"

"I think I lost my moral compass for a minute," Darcy swung her feet around, and dangled them off the edge of the sofa, so she sat beside Hank. Hank sat up then and ran is hand through his hair.

"Did I misread the situation?" he asked cautiously. "I thought this was mutual."

"It's not you . . ."

"If I had a nickel for every time . . ."

Darcy gave him a small punch on his attractively muscled arm. "Be serious."

"Do I have a choice?"

Darcy turned sideways so she could look at his face. "I'm not that kind of girl. I know that sounds prudish and Victorian adjacent, but I take sex very seriously. I like you, Hank, and I am really grateful for all your help, but we really don't know that much about each other." She began rebuttoning her shirt.

"I know I totally approve of your choice of underwear." He dipped his finger under the frothy pink lace, that covered her breast.

Darcy slapped his hand away. "I am serious, Hank. I want sex to be a natural extension of a relationship, not just a knee-jerk reaction to a rush of adrenaline."

He stood over her. "Is that what you think this was? Adrenaline? Stress sex?"

"What?"

Hank pulled her up to stand in front of him, between the V of his knees. "Stress sex. It's sex that happens after trauma, an almost accident, an almost fight. It's a way to use up all the adrenaline your system dumped on you. Some guys punch a wall. I like this better." He leaned forward and nuzzled her neck.

Darcy pushed him away. "You mean this is just a safety valve for your raging hormones?"

"Our raging hormones," he smiled at her. "I think you participated. Yup. I'm sure of it." He looked pointedly at a small red bite mark on his shoulder.

"I think that was part of it. I find you incredibly attractive, Hank. Surely you noticed." Darcy looked down at him. "But I want to get to know you more before we . . ." She looked away, unaccountably shy, then back down at Hank.

"If you were looking for moonlight and magnolia blossoms, you need to work on your signals. I could have sworn I saw 'Take Me Now!' flash in your eyes. Was I wrong?"

"No," she squirmed figuratively and literally. "But you make it sound impersonal, and it wasn't. It was urgent, but it wasn't like wolfing down a hot dog."

He smiled large and the lines by his eyes crinkled. "Mm-mm. Too bad. I liked that image."

CHAPTER 14

Darcy picked up his shirt and threw it at him. "All the romance of taking a leak after too many beers."

"There are some similarities." He said, considering the comparison.

Neither of them had finished buttoning their shirts. He pulled her into his lap and kissed her softly as he held her.

"I wish you'd take me seriously. We work too closely to get ourselves entangled, though I am genuinely tempted."

"Why thank you, darling. I feel downright flattered." He leaned close, nipping her earlobe, and running his soft, raspy tongue down the side of her neck.

Darcy grinned. She didn't want to find Hank funny—but she did, and the more he nuzzled her neck the warmer her feelings grew. She twisted her head around and kissed him deep, slow, and wet. Never let it be said that Darcy Moreland couldn't give as good as she got.

Darcy padded toward the kitchen. Hank followed. They raided the refrigerator, sharing some leftover pizza, sitting cross-legged on her threadbare living room carpet. Darcy was feeding Hank a slice of pepperoni when there was a knock on the door.

Hank jumped up and almost tripped over Mac who had rushed to the door, yapping. Hank signaled for her to be quiet, then peered through the spy hole.

"It's just Abby." he said as he swung the door open wide.

"What do you mean 'just Abby'?" Abby said as she bustled through through the door.

Mac jumped and danced around Abby's feet until Darcy reached down and picked him up.

"I think he meant you weren't dangerous," Darcy folded Abby in a welcoming hug.

"Don't be too sure about that." Abby said as she passed them noting their disheveled clothes and plopped onto the sofa. "Picnic?" she asked surveying the pizza.

Darcy slicked her damp palms down her jeans. "Yeah. You want some?"

"I wouldn't say no to a ginger ale. I don't want to be critical, Hank, but the coffee at that station is beyond nasty. It tastes like someone's old socks."

"That's our secret ingredient," Hank said as he struggled to button his shirt and went to get her the ginger ale.

Abby looked at Darcy and arched one expressive brow with a silent question. Darcy smiled and shrugged and buttoned up her shirt.

"Did you want a glass?" Hank asked from the kitchen.

"No. No, a can will be fine."

"So, did they find anything on you that will help?" Darcy asked as she sat next to Abby.

"Well they found a partial print on the water bottle, but I don't think it was helpful. The red thread from the car seat might be more conclusive. Thank heavens for my snaggely nail I never had a chance to file." She held up her left hand.

"Can they tell what kind of car it came from?"

"Well they hadn't nailed that down by the time I left, but I hope they will, eventually."

"Um, Hank was saying that we're both going to be under surveillance for a while until they catch the killer." Darcy felt terrible that she had complicated Abby's life.

Abby's eyes widened, and she grinned. "What exactly does that entail? Do I get a guard like a secret service guy?"

"Kind of," Hank smiled at her, amused at her excitement. "Officer Taylor will be watching you during the day and I've scheduled drive-by patrols during the evening. She'll try to be as unobtrusive as possible." Hank sat on the overstuffed arm of the sofa behind Darcy.

"Oh, I don't mind." Abby's eyes sparkled with excitement.

"Abby," Darcy cleared her throat, trying to form the words. "They want to use us as bait to catch the killer if they can. You should pretend everything is back to normal. You can't give Officer Taylor away."

"Oh. Okay. I can do that. Is the poor woman going to try to follow us both?" She looked up at Hank.

"Uh, no. Hank is going to follow me around."

"Of course he is," Abby said, patting Darcy's thigh and beaming at them both.

"Well I won't be able to follow you all the time, Darcy. I do have an investigation to continue, you know." Hank placed his hand on her shoulders protectively.

"That's okay," Darcy said and leaned back into his chest. "Good way to get to know my local police. It could be fun."

"This is serious, Darcy." Hank pushed away and turned her slightly, so he could look her in the eye. "I don't want you or Abby taking any unnecessary chances, regardless of who is watching you."

"Why don't you hermetically seal us into our apartments?" She swiveled to face him full on.

"Don't think I wouldn't love to." Hank leaned in toward her.

"Now, kiddos." Abby intervened. "Let's not forget what's important here. There have been two murders and I was kidnapped, and the police have just a few leads, sooo . . ."

"You're right, Abby." Darcy said. "Okay, Hank. We both promise to be cautious. Don't we Abby?"

"Absolutely." Abby stood up. "I hate to eat and run, but I've had about as much fun as I can stand today. I think I'll go back down to my apartment, re-heat some leftover meatloaf, take a bath, and go to bed early. Good night both of you."

Abby wandered toward the door and Mac trotted at her heels.

"Oh no, young man." Darcy said as she scooped him up. "You're staying home tonight with me. Get a good night's sleep, Abby."

"Thank you, dear. You too." Abby smiled and opened the door.

"Abby. I'm so sorry about today." Darcy noticed Abby's eyes were weary and her face still looked tense. She gave her a hug and said. "You know I would never knowingly put you in danger."

"I know that, Darcy. Don't you worry. Everything turned out okay and maybe we furthered the investigation."

After Abby left, Darcy felt disheartened. Her friend had just returned after a harrowing experience, and her dog was eating cold pepperoni pizza out of a box on the floor. She was a poor excuse for a human being.

"Well, I think I'll call it a night too." She stood snatching Mac up like a shield.

"Probably a good plan," Hank said and pulled his boots back on. "How early do you think you'll leave in the morning?"

"I thought I would call Zach when I woke up and check if he has an assignment for me. I never know from day to day where I'm going."

"Me neither. Call me tomorrow morning as soon as you know what you're doing." He moved toward the door.

"Okay," Darcy said as she followed him.

He lifted her chin with his knuckle and kissed her. Mac squirmed between them, but it was a minor distraction.

"And Darcy . . ."

"Yeah?"

"Don't go anywhere until I tell you it's okay."

"Okay. And thanks for being there for me today."

Hank looked at her and glanced significantly at the sofa. "Anytime. And I do mean anytime."

"Go home." Darcy shoved out the door.

"See you tomorrow."

"Yeah, yeah. Go."

He laughed and left. Darcy rested her back against the closed door for a moment. She set Mac down and went to run a tub. A nice warm, bubbly soak was what she needed. She picked up the living room while the old claw-footed tub filled and perfumed the small apartment with Jasmine fragrant steam.

"This has certainly been an action-packed day," she said. "Don't you go having any more adventures. Do you hear me, Mr. Guinness McCann?" Darcy peered down at him as she passed. He looked up and wagged his stubby little tail.

She got in the tub and slid down to rest the back of her neck on the cool rounded rim.

Her mind swirled through the day like a slide show. She didn't dwell on any single mental picture, just immersed herself in the parade of images.

Bridget's funeral. Going back to the station and calling Abby. Darcy closed her eyes when she remembered the terror of listening to the kidnappers: the hours of waiting, the rescue, the return— almost having sex.

Oh—My—God. She slunk into the water soaking her hair and popped out again.

What were you thinking? Her brain screamed at her. She dunked into the water once more. Darcy emerged, shook the water off, and smiled to herself. Obviously, her brain had nothing to do with it.

By the time she and Mac were curled up in bed, she was drowsy. It would be nice to sleep a dreamless sleep tonight, but Darcy doubted that was possible.

She fluffed the pillows and scrunched down in bed. Mac snuggled next to her, resting his furry head next to hers on the pillow.

"I would hate to lose you, boy." She scratched the back of his neck and he licked her cheek.

Things were back in place in her world, at least for now.

THE NEXT MORNING, DARCY STRETCHED WITH A GROAN and listened to the satisfying pop of her lower back. She had slept long and hard and was still unsure whether she wanted to get up. Mac, jostled her out of a perfectly lovely dream, jumped nimbly to the ground, spun in a circle, and looked up expectantly.

"Okay. Okay, you nag." Darcy growled down at him. "Let me

get some clothes on." She seized some sweatpants from the corner, slipped them on and stepped into her flip-flops.

"Well, come on, fur-ball." She snatched the leash from the closet doorknob, headed for the front room, sure that Mac would follow.

Snapping the leash on Mac's collar, she patted him on the head, and they trundled out the door. Lists for the day were already arranging themselves into marching formation in Darcy's mind.

This was "Cheyenne Day," which always fell on the first Wednesday of the last two weeks in July during Rodeo Days. and she had promised Liz she'd try to meet her somewhere. First thing on her list was to call Zach and find out if that was even possible.

The events of yesterday seemed unbelievable on this clear summer morning, but she snapped into focus by the presence of a ramshackle car, dented covered with splotches of gray primer and parked in front of her apartment building. She was sure it didn't belong in her neighborhood. Darcy looked in but could see no one.

As she and Mac crossed the street and headed for the park, she caught sight of Hank's black Ford pickup as it stopped.

Darcy and Mac trotted up to the side of the truck.

"Hi, stranger," she said as she leaned into the open window.

Hank tipped her chin up and kissed her. His eyes were a softer blue in the morning light, Darcy noted.

"Mm-mm. Not as good as a latte with double cream, but good." She licked her lips. "Really good."

"I brought breakfast," Hank held up a white bakery bag. "Scones and coffee."

"You remembered! I may jump your bones right here." Darcy grabbed for the bag, but Hank pulled it out of her reach. "I'll meet you over at that table under the tree." He didn't wait for her answer.

Darcy watched him pull into the parking area by the playground and saunter to the table. She leaned down and unsnapped Mac's leash. "Sic him, boy." she ordered, pointing in Hank's direction.

Mac dashed toward Hank but to Darcy's disgust, sold out for a chunk of scone that Hank offered.

"You traitor, you." she accused Mac, then turned on Hank. "It's unfair to bribe my dog."

"C'mere," Hank pulled her hips snug between his legs and let his hands drift down the curve of her butt.

Darcy fought not to smile, but she couldn't help it. She hated that Hank could turn her insides into goo with just a look. He felt so good. She braced her hands on his shoulders, leaned down, and kissed him. He smelled of citrus, soap, and coffee.

"Hey. You had coffee without me."

"You weren't up, and I was."

"How do you know I wasn't up?"

"We're watching your building," he said simply and began to nuzzle her neck.

Darcy pushed away. "Are you supposed to be doing that when you're on duty?"

Hank hauled her back. "I'm on my own time right now." He nibbled her ear lobe. "When I'm on the clock, I won't be this nice. I'll tell you what to do and expect you to do it."

"In your dreams, cowboy." Darcy stepped away from the cradle of his thighs and helped herself to a container of coffee. She lifted the lid and smiled, inordinately pleased that he had remembered how she took it. She sat down.

Hank tossed the bakery bag across to her. "I'm serious, Darcy. You need to be careful please. I am asking you to consider what I am saying."

"I'm serious too. I can't do my job and trip over you or anyone else."

Hank said. "We'll try to stay out of your way, but whoever kidnapped Mac and Abby is still out there. We don't know if they're connected to the murders, but we want to make it impossible for them to take you."

"I appreciate that, Hank. I do. But I've been thinking about this. Whoever took Abby and Mac don't seem so dangerous in retrospect. Abby thought they were young."

"You don't think young people can be dangerous?"

"No. I didn't mean that." She fed Mac some more of her scone and softened when she watched her furry buddy sitting by her feet. "I just think they aren't as dangerous as we first believed."

"Based on?"

"Because they aren't good at this, are they?"

"Lack of skill doesn't mean less dangerous; it just means sloppy." Hank leaned in and popped a hunk of scone in her mouth, daring her to argue. "And sloppy can get you killed as quickly as skilled."

"Well," Darcy resumed after she swallowed, "I want to go on record and say that I'll try to be cautious, but I have a job to do. Zach's been understanding, but friend or no friend, he hired me to be a reporter."

He looked at her without comment.

"What?" she said. "No order from headquarters?" She sipped her coffee but looked at him and smiled.

He shook his head. "I guess if that's the best you can do."

"Whew. That's a relief." Darcy sighed dramatically. "I was afraid we were going to have another 'disagreement.'"

"Yeah, well, don't give up the notion." Hank popped the lid off his paper cup and drained the remainder of his coffee before continued. "Here's the way it is, Darcy. We'll keep that wreck parked in front of your apartment 24/7. It may or may not be occupied. It's mostly there as a distraction, but don't count on anyone coming to your rescue from there. We're shorthanded as it is this week."

"Gottcha. wrecked car, no cop." She snapped off a mock salute.

Hank sighed.

Darcy watched Hank's impassive face. He wasn't reacting like she thought he would. She was hoping to get a rise out of him this morning, or at least a laugh, but he was all business.

"Oh, lighten up, Nelson. I came from the big city and know the drill; be aware of your surroundings; don't make eye contact with strangers; always carry your keys notched between your figures to use as a weapon; and, oh yeah, always go for the groin. How'd I do?" She raised her soft brown eyes to his.

"Which? Parroting off the rules, or going for the groin?"

She laughed. "Both I guess."

"Someone will do a periodic check on you. More often than not that'll be me if I can. It would be helpful if you'd share your schedule with me."

"Are you kidding me? Half the time I don't even know what my schedule's going to be."

"Just try to keep me informed, okay?"

"Sure, I'll try."

"Good. Next, if you even think something's wonky . . ."

"Wonky? Is that professional cop talk?" She braced her elbows on the table and rested her chin in her palms.

"Darcy." Hank warned.

"Okay. Okay." She reached down and lifted Mac to her lap. He responded by licking her face companionably.

"If you even think something looks wrong or feels strange, make a scene. Scream, run, do whatever you need to do to attract attention. Odds are that will scare anyone away. If nothing else, it'll surprise him and buy us time. Understand?"

"Yes, sir."

"Darcy don't joke about this. In case you haven't been keeping score, so far, we've had two murders, one kidnapping and we're only halfway through the week."

"You're right. I'm sorry. I'm not taking it lightly. Misplaced humor is just the way I cope with stress." She nuzzled Mac's neck.

Hank watched her for a minute. "Call anytime you need to."

"Oh, Hank. This is sooo sudden." Darcy gushed.

Something dark and dangerous flashed from Hank's eyes.

"Okay. Okay. I'll try to follow all the rules and be a perfect little, um, what exactly am I?"

"A royal pain in the ass." Hank said with some heat.

CHAPTER 15

Hank got in his pickup and drove off.

"Well Mac, I think I pissed him off. What do you think?"

She glanced at her watch. Fifteen past eight. "Let's see if Zach is out and about yet."

She watched Mac as he sniffed around the grass. If he wandered too far, she snapped her fingers and called him back. She picked up the phone to call the office.

"KCWY, how may I direct your call?"

"Wendy? Hi, Darcy. May I speak to Zach?"

"Sure. Hang on. Oh, and Darcy?"

"Yes?"

"Sorry about your dog. I'm glad you got him back. How's your neighbor doing?"

"Mac and Abby are doing fine, thank heavens. Does everyone at the station know about it?"

"It's been the main topic of conversation around here since you left. By tomorrow, the whole town will know," Wendy said. "I think Bryce is doing a short news flash thingy on the noon show since we don't have film, and everything ended okay."

"Wonderful." Darcy muttered as Wendy dropped her on hold.

"Horton here."

"That's a goofy way to answer the phone, Zach. It reminds me of *Horton Hears a Who*. Wasn't that a Dr. Seuss book?"

"Good morning, Ms. Moreland. Did you call to harass me, or do you want something else?"

"Checking in, boss. Mac and I have had our breakfast and were wondering what assignments you have for us today."

"I've got nothing for you, but I'd like Mac to cover the Challenge Rodeo at twelve."

"Funny. Do I get a videographer?"

"Netters will meet you out there."

"You got it, boss. When I'm done with that, can I take the afternoon off for Cheyenne Day? I'd like to meet my friend at the Railroad pub if you don't need me."

"Sure. We have the night show and midway covered for tonight. Have fun. Your friend wouldn't happen to be Hank Nelson, would it?"

"No. I'm meeting Liz Baker as if it's any of your business."

"Your high school pal?"

"Yup."

"Be careful, Darcy. I don't have any on-air people to replace you."

"Gee, bud. You're all heart. Why don't you and Kelly meet us later? Call to find out where we are."

"Okay. We might."

"See you later." She snapped her phone off and bundled Mac into her arms on her way out of the park.

As she was climbing the porch steps, Abby was coming out the front door.

"Well look at you." Darcy stared at her.

"I bought this outfit at the Chi Chi Corral last year on sale. Isn't it wonderful?" She spun in a circle.

Abby was dressed in a 1950's style western yellow shirt with snaps, a blue skirt dripping with colorful yellow and red rickrack, and black boots brightly stitched with a turquoise eagle on the front.

"Damn, Abby. You look like Dale Evans."

"How do you know about Dale Evans? She was way before your time."

"I'm Ed Moreland's daughter that's how. Anything and

everything cowboy. I think I even had some PJ's with her on them."
Darcy said. "Where are you going?"

"Pancake breakfast. I'm picking up my friend Ruth. Wanna come?"

"No. No, I've got an assignment to cover the Challenge Rodeo at noon and then I'm meeting Liz at the Railroad pub to celebrate Cheyenne Day. You remember. When all us worker bees get a chance to take the afternoon off."

"Oh, but then Mac will be alone."

"Abby. For heaven's sake. He'll be all right. He's probably looking forward to catching up on some naptime. Things have been high octane since we've come home."

Abby looked at her and scratched Mac behind the ears. "Well if you say so." She didn't sound convinced.

"If you'd feel better, go ahead and take him out when you want. I'd like to promise I'll get him on my way to bed tonight, but Liz and I haven't had any time to catch up."

"You go have a good time, dear. Mac and I will settle in. Won't we, boy?"

"Okay. Suit yourself. Have fun."

"You too. You've earned it."

Darcy carried Mac up to her apartment because it was easier than watching him try to maneuver the stairs.

It it was an indulgence to take an hour to shower and dress. Darcy took her time. She enjoyed the luxury of slathering up with some shower gel she had received on her 25th birthday last March The inside of the shower smelled tropical-rain-forest wonderful.

She got out, toweled off, and dusted down with some powder from the same gift basket. She got into her underwear and grabbed the Cheyenne Day's Media Guide before sprawling across her bed.

The guide listed all the events taking place for the whole two weeks of Rodeo Days. Darcy turned to the page with the first Wednesday of the two week celebration. The guide gave some bare bones information about the Challenge Rodeo. It was good to review the events scheduled. She remembered helping with The

Challenge Rodeo when she came home during the summer when she was in college.

It didn't sound like it had changed much since then. Sixty kids with medical or mental challenges were chosen to compete. The kids got help from rodeo VIP's, the clowns, and the CRD Riders. Darcy remembered it as a lot of fun.

Lying back on the bed, she wiggled into some black Jeans, and slowly buttoned the fly. Darcy breathed experimentally, relieved the last button held instead of shooting across the room.

No more Taco Johns, she swore to herself, forever-and-ever-amen.

She paired the jeans with a pink-striped western style shirt, some lightweight socks, then slipped off the bed to tackle her favorite bright red boots.

Boots were always difficult. It didn't help when she sat on the floor to try to tug them on, Mac thought she was playing a game.

"Stop it, you mongrel mop head." She swatted in his general direction in while he dodged out of the way and barked at her. He dived at her from the other side. By now, she was rolling on her back with her fingers caught in the boot loops tugging on the boot and wobbling like a Weeble. She loved the toy but had never aspired to be one.

One boot on, and the process began again. Pull, wobble, Mac attacked, barked, then the phone rang.

"For heaven's sake." She had the second boot halfway on, so she hobbled to the phone.

"Hello." She practically growled into the receiver.

"Bad time?" Liz asked.

"Oh, sorry, Liz. No I was having problems getting these damn boots on and Mac keeps dive-bombing me." Darcy listened to her friend chuckle on the other end. "Yuck it up! Listen, I have a story to file about the Challenge Rodeo at noon today, but I can meet you in the pub around one thirty. Get a table in the corner if you can and order me a beer Okay? See you soon."

"Okay. Hope your boot thing gets resolved." Liz hung up.

Darcy stayed seated on the side of the bed to pull the last boot on. Mac peered up at her disgusted she had stopped the game.

"Give me a break. I've got to work to keep you in kibble." She checked his water and food bowls and with a stern look said, "Now be a good boy. Abby will come get you soon."

Darcy emerged in her red and black colored cowboy gear, with her press pass around her neck and her new straw cowboy hat pulled firmly down on her forehead. Only Dudes tilted a hat on the back of their head. She wished she felt happier. She glanced briefly at the decoy car parked out front. She was tempted to look inside to see if anyone was there but didn't want to call attention to it. She walked to her car a little farther up the street.

On her way to the rodeo arena, she dutifully left a voice mail for Hank about her assignment and her plans to meet Liz later.

Pulling in through park security was getting to be old hat. She slipped right into a parking place by Public Relation Committee, locked her car, and scanned the immediate perimeter. It felt strange to have to be cautious in her own hometown.

She spotted Netters sitting on a small stretch of split rail fence chomping on a corndog.

"Hi, Calamity," he greeted her. "Think we'll find another body today?"

"Funny, Netters. Damned hilarious."

"I thought it was. Want one?" He held out a grease-spattered paper with two more corndogs nestled in the palm of his hand.

"Uh, no thanks. I'm supposed to meet a friend later for lunch."

"Your call, but they're good. What's the plan for the shoot?" he asked as he smeared the tip of his corndog with a blob of yellow mustard.

"I thought we ought to see if we can contact one of the people who run the Challenge Rodeo and shoot an intro with them before the kids are taken out into the arena."

"Okay by me." Netters smiled at her and slipped off the fence railing. "Where do you want to go?" He plucked his camera and case from the gravel at his feet.

"Let's go down to the arena. My guess is someone there can point out who's in charge." She veered to the right and scanned the information in the media guide again as she walked.

The regular rodeo didn't begin until one, so they had an hour to run the kids through the events. People were already crowding into the stands: mothers, fathers, aunts, uncles, cousins. Some kids brought their own cheering squad.

Darcy watched the organized chaos. Brightly painted rodeo clowns in cut-off overalls and high-topped tennis shoes were kidding around with the small herd of kids waiting to begin.

"And this," Randy Johnson, the barrel man, flourished a large red bandana he'd yanked from his back pocket. "This is what we use to mop up all the blood."

He swooped in front of the kids and held it out for the kids to see. Most in the front row backed up in horror. "Keith. Tell 'em how much blood the cowboys lose."

"Buckets." Keith Simon, also a rodeo clown, responded with exaggerated gestures. The children giggled, reassured the clowns were joking.

"Get some intro shots of that, will you, Netters?" Darcy pointed to the kids.

"Sure." He glided into position, kneeling in front of the kids to frame them in the shot. He did it so seamlessly, most of the kids weren't even aware he was there.

Darcy glanced around and spotted a brightly dressed woman about her mother's age giving directions for setting up the "Barrel Bronc," a barrel suspended by ropes to a free standing frame to simulate a bucking horse or bull ride. Darcy walked over to her and stuck out her hand.

"Hi. Darcy Moreland from KCWY. Are you Tina Gervais?" Darcy consulted her guide.

"Yes, I am." She smiled a perfect smile and her green eyes sparkled with welcome. "I'm so glad you're here. The kids get a kick out of being treated like big-time celebrities."

"I know. I used to help my dad and mom when they were volunteers. Ed and Donna Moreland?"

"Oh, my gosh. I wouldn't have recognized you, Darcy. I'm sorry I didn't make the connection."

"I was wondering if I could film a short interview with you

about the kids and the rodeo."

"Sure thing. Give me a minute to tell Jim what I'm doing."

Darcy watched her walk over and talked to Jim Darnell, a former chairman who helped run the event.

Darcy signaled to Netters she wanted to set up in the relative shade of the concrete pad in front of the main grandstand. He followed her over and began framing his shot. Once Tina rejoined them, they filmed the interview in less than four minutes.

"Thanks again for coming." Tina shook both Netters and Darcy's hands. "It's thrilling for the kids." She dashed off to finish preparations.

"You want to go get some action shots and then we can do a summary bit and get out of here?"

"Whatever you say, Calamity." Netters grinned at her. Darcy scowled at him.

She sat on one of the folding chairs on the pad and tried to compose what she wanted to say to finish off the story. She was so engrossed in her notes, she didn't see anyone approach until a shadow fell across her notebook.

Startled, Darcy gasped, and her hand flew to her throat in an instinctively protective gesture.

"Oh. Sorry. I didn't mean to scare you."

After Darcy recovered from her fright, she noted Cindy Burke was dressed in one of the CRD Riders outfits the girls wore for the rodeo. Darcy admired the brightly patterned violet colored shirt paired with matching pants.

"Can I talk to you for a minute?" She slipped into the chair next to Darcy and looked furtively around as if afraid someone might see her.

"Act natural and I'll pretend I'm interviewing you," Darcy suggested. Darcy flipped to a clean page in her small notebook, then looked up at the girl expectantly.

The young girl looked so relieved Darcy smiled. "First, what is your name?"

"Cindy Burke," the girl answered.

"What is it you'd like to tell me?" Darcy asked

Cindy glanced around again reassured no one was watching. "Well, we all heard what happened to your friend and your dog yesterday and . . ."

Darcy froze. "Do you know something?"

"Not exactly, but I overheard a guy from school talking to someone last night by the Buckin' A Saloon. It was dark and I couldn't make out who he was talking to, but I heard Matt go— Matt Daniels was the guy I recognized—I heard Matt go, 'That's probably the dumbest move anyone could make, kidnapping an old woman and a dog.'"

Darcy pretended to be calm, but it took all the acting experience she could muster. "What did the guy in the dark say to that?"

"He said he'd tried to talk him out of it, but—"

"Wait, a sec. Who is 'him'? Was Matt talking to the guy who stole my dog?"

"No, but he must be a friend of the guy because he was talking about how this friend was desperate and thought it was a good idea. They didn't use names, but I thought you'd want to know." Cindy smiled weakly.

"You bet I want to know. How do I find this Matt Daniels?"

"He lives in town with his folks and graduated from Central this May. He should be easy to find, just . . ." Cindy stood.

"Don't tell anyone I told you, Ms. Moreland. I still have to live here."

"You've got it, honey. And thanks." Darcy watched Cindy meld into a group of other girls dressed exactly alike and stabbed the speed dial number for Hank.

Expecting voice mail, she was surprised when he picked up.

"Darcy? Are you okay? Darcy?"

"I'm fine. Listen, I got a tip that a kid named Matt Daniels might know who took Mac and Abby. He graduated from Central High School this May and lives with his folks."

"A tip? From . . .?"

"I can't tell you. It's a third person source. An overheard conversation. Please, Hank. Can't you follow up on this?"

"I guess so. Everything else is okay though?"

"Yup." Darcy looked at the kids running, roping the fake steer head attached to a hay bale, and biffing it off the Barrel Bronc. There were excited screams and shouts. "I've got to finish filming this story at the arena and then I'm meeting my friend Liz at the Railroad Pub."

"Yeah. Okay. I got your other message. I'll look into this other first chance I get." He said.

"Thanks," she said sweetly then snapped her phone off and stuffed it deep into her pocket.

Netters had already shot a lot of video, so they did the finish and Darcy sent Netters off with the story to edit with the promise of payback later.

Darcy raced home and registered Mac was gone. She changed from her long-sleeved shirt to a bright salmon-colored tank top with a deliciously low-scooped neck and kicked off her red boots trading them for some tan strappy sandals that barely had enough leather to qualify as shoes. Wriggling her toes she admired her pink pedicure. She completed the look with some pink chandelier earrings. A quick run of her hairbrush through her honey blond mane and let it fall in soft waves over her shoulders and took care of her "hat hair" then dashed down to Abby's.

Abby answered the door instantly with Mac at her heals.

"Don't you look attractive?" Abby did a quick survey.

"Did you even look through the spy hole before you opened this door?"

"Matter of fact, yes I did. I'm not senile yet, Miss Moreland. Go away." Abby waved as if Darcy was a pesky fly.

"Sorry. I'm wound tight I guess." She stooped to scratch Mac behind the ears.

"Go . . . Unravel. We ordered an On-Demand movie, *Dirty Dancing,* from the classic collection." Abby beamed at her.

Darcy grinned back. "Okay. Have fun."

It didn't take long to drive to the pub housed in the old train station. Darcy managed to slip into a space just as a school-bus-yellow Volkswagen was pulling out.

The pub was crowded with locals dressed from drugstore-western to summer shorts and tanks. Knots of people swelled, then broke off into splinter groups, only to morph again into another configuration.

Darcy spotted Liz at a small table tucked into a back corner of the bar. There was a tall, dewy-looking pilsner glass by an empty seat. She kissed Liz's cheek as she breezed over to slip into the chair.

"This *is* heaven, right?" Darcy sipped deeply from the glass in front of her.

"I was sort of hoping for angels, but if you're willing to settle for a tall cold one, who am I to criticize?" Liz flashed her high watt smile.

"You look hot, girl," Darcy said as she surveyed Liz's sleeveless denim shirt and her tanned and toned arms resting on the stainless steel topped table. Encircling one of Liz's small wrists was a shiny silver cuff. She wore a necklace with a large turquoise cabochon framed in silver that dangled enticingly between her breasts, within her slightly unbuttoned shirt.

"Thanks. You look decidedly un-western", Liz said.

"I need a break from cowboy duds. I have to wear them all the time when I'm reporting, and I really like dressing like a civilian."

"You do it well. Maybe I'll introduce you around as my cousin from Columbus, Indiana."

"That's kind of random. Why that city?"

"It's a town actually, and I really do have a cousin from there. All you need to know is that they are inordinately proud of their architecture. It's a thing."

"Speaking of architecture they've done a great job with this place." Darcy twisted in her seat to look at the banks of large-screened TV's flickering with infinite sport coverage.

"Reminds me of a high-tech coliseum, only now you get to see the gladiators up close and personal. Uhm . . . yum. Look at him." Liz raised her glass in a mock toast to a close-up of an Italian soccer player.

"He can scatter focaccia crumbs in my bed anytime," Darcy said.

The muffled clatter of a departing train framed by the tall windows was the only reminder this had once been a well-traveled passenger stop on the Union Pacific east/west route. The San Francisco Zephyr had passed through here regularly. The arching ceilings and dark wood trim bespoke a time of leisurely, luxurious travel.

Now it clattered with the clink and babble of enthusiastic Millennials, let out at noon from their entry-level jobs to party. A grownup recess period on a playground that served beer.

"Tell me everything, Liz prompted. "How's the new job? Is Zach a nice guy to work for?"

"The best." Darcy let her eyes roam around the rapidly filling bar. "He's been amazingly supportive."

"And the cop?" Liz leaned forward and slightly skimmed her pink-glossed lips with the tip of her tongue.

"Oh. Take the hungry look off your face. You'd think we were still in junior high. We almost had stress sex if you must know," Darcy said, disgusted Liz could always make her confess.

"Almost . . .?"

"What the hell do you want? Video?"

"If ya got it."

Darcy could tell Liz felt not one twinge of shame in wanting to know all the details. Liz had grown up in a family of six girls and she was the oldest. Not a clandestine or confidential event happened in any of her sister's lives she didn't feel privy to.

"It was hot and quick, then soft and sexy, and then it stopped. That is positively the only information you're getting out of me." Darcy sipped her beer and pretended to be fascinated by the crowd.

"Wanna bet." Liz fluffed her fingers through her cap of dark curls. "The night's still young."

Darcy looked at her elfin-faced friend and silently reminded herself that this was Liz. Liz in another era would have been a gifted inquisitor. Part of her charm was she always looked harmless and pleasant. A larger, cagier part was her ability to drop questions into the conversation without undo inflection.

For instance, Liz was a shoe-a-holic and had been known to be distracted from conversation if a cute pair of shoes walked by, but then she'd look you square in the eye and ask if you liked guys who wore boxers.

Using the element of surprise, Liz could get you to tell her any-thing. Darcy made a silent vow she'd watch herself tonight.

It wasn't she didn't trust Liz. Darcy just wasn't sure herself where she and Hank fell on the relationship continuum and she didn't feel comfortable discussing it yet. It could truly be a product of stress, kind of like sweaty palms. Darcy felt a smile tease the corners of her mouth.

"What's up with you?" Darcy was determined to beat Liz at her own game, or at least wrestle her to a draw. "Any hot prospects in your life? And I think you know how I mean that."

"Sooo subtle," Liz cooed with fake naiveté. "Since you asked. I am seeing the guy I told you about before. You know, the micro-wave engineer. And before you ask, no, I have no idea what it entails except a lot of travel. I told him to meet us later at the Cowhand if he wanted."

"We're going to the Cowhand Bar? You've got to be kidding."

Darcy remember the raucous bar catered to a hard-drinking, hard-dancing clientele, with a mechanical bull Darcy was destined to end up on before the night was through if she didn't stay sober. This had disaster written all over it.

"Wouldn't you rather find a quiet place somewhere and talk? Damn, Liz. We haven't seen each other forever."

"The one word answer would be—NO. We can cozy up after Cheyenne Day. Hell, I'll even put you on my calendar, but tonight, my friend, we're going to howl at the moon."

CHAPTER 16

Darcy and Liz ordered some sweet potato fries and cheeseburgers to sop up the beer. They both wanted to pace themselves. Cheyenne Day, if done properly, was a marathon rather than a sprint. They chatted about jobs and Darcy's ex-fiancé, Kevin.

"I seriously never worried about your taste in men until you told me about Kevin. He just didn't sound like the kind of guy you'd go for." Liz reached across and stole a fry from Darcy's plate.

"Kevin was okay. We just wanted different things. I'm here to tell you, it happens fast, and it happens sticky. First, you think it's just a friendship, and then you start going everywhere together. Next thing you know, you graduate into a commitment neither one of you wants. It's all sugarcoated with 'I love you and I need you.' After that, it's all over but the mud-wrestling."

Liz shivered. "Well, thank heavens you reevaluated."

"It was mutual, which made it easier. He had his life all mapped out complete with two kids and a dog in his imagination. Besides, although he was a really nice guy, there were no fireworks. One day I just woke up and asked myself, can you live the rest of your life with no fireworks?"

"And the answer was?" Liz prompted.

"Obvious." Darcy ate more fries. "So what's going on in your life?"

Liz brought Darcy up-to-date on all the gossip she could think of for the moment and after an hour they finally got up to leave.

Darcy's phone rang, and she grinned when saw it was Hank calling. She mouthed, "Sorry" to Liz.

"Hi. If you're looking for a status report, Liz and I are at the Railroad Pub and have consumed one beer each and some cheeseburgers."

There was silence on the other end. "You think that's wise?" Hank asked.

"Probably not. I tried wise once, but it didn't agree with me." Darcy clicked her phone off.

"Darcy. You don't have to be so rude to him. He's just doing his job." Liz steered her through the dense clumps of people clogging the pub out to the parking lot.

Darcy shook her head in self-disgust. "I know. Maybe it's all that talking about Kevin. He was cloyingly overprotective."

"Yeah, I get that, But Darc, this cop guy is trying to protect you from real danger. Maybe you should cut him some slack."

"You're probably right. I'll apologize to him when we get to the Cowhand and update my itinerary."

Liz beeped her bright blue BMW open. Darcy slid in and ran her hand over the soft caramel-colored leather seats.

"Not too bad for an old one, huh?" Liz started her car and barely eased out of her parking place before someone else zoomed in to take her spot.

Darcy turned, watching the maneuver. "Just like the hole you leave if you put your fist into a bucket of water."

"Wait till you see my moves, girlfriend." Liz smoothly zipped across to the viaduct and in ten minutes, they were hunting for a place to park across from the Cowhand.

The lot was packed seven deep and too many across to count. Liz cruised the rows patiently, finally pulling into a spot so tight, she barely missed scraping the paint off a red Mazda on the right.

"I may have to get out your side," Darcy complained.

"Suck it up, sista." Liz squeezed out of the car.

They dashed across the wide street with their arms draped over each other's shoulders. They already heard the band from across the street.

When they pushed open the heavy wooden doors, the first thing that hit them was the smell of spilled beer. The Cowhand always hired a live country band for Cheyenne Day. Sometimes they were more loud than good.

Darcy took Liz's hand, and they struggled up to the bar. They sipped their beers slowly and shelled peanuts. Having a conversation in this place was out of the question.

Some drugstore cowboy with a buckle bigger than his brain, steered Liz to the dance floor, steering being the operative word.

"I thought he was trying to plow the north forty!" Liz shouted when she returned to stand at the bar.

"You looked cute out there," Darcy said.

The Cowhand was deliberately dark and loud. Like casinos in Vegas, they didn't want their patrons to be aware of the passage of time. Even on a regular night, it was full of canned music, pick up pool games, and buckets of beer, which ultimately degenerated to shots of 'Jose' or 'Jack' as the evening wore on.

It would be easier to blast someone out of the third ring of Hell than to pry them out of the Cowhand before they were ready. There were actually legends about dents made in the asphalt in front of the exit door from wedding rings slammed to the ground because of real or imagined infidelity.

Tonight, at the Cowhand was no exception. Darcy immersed herself in the rowdy fun. She even took a couple turns around the floor herself.

It did make a girl thirsty, Darcy discovered. Both girls monitored themselves. As the old saying went, this wasn't their first rodeo. At least they hadn't yet been seduced into trying the Tequila Trail Ride, a deadly mixture of several kinds of tequila layered with beer. They were sticking to nursing Bud Lites.

Liz joined her after an energetic romp to *Cotton Eyed Joe*. "My God. These boys don't get to town much, do they?" She swiped the back of her hand across her dripping forehead.

Darcy decided to try the bull before she was too far gone. She stepped into line and waited her turn. She'd tucked her five-dollar bill behind her buckle. She couldn't afford this utter insanity, but, hell, it was Cheyenne Day.

The line moved quickly. More often than not, the riders were more lubricated than they should have been. The operator let them ride gently at first, then jacked the controls. The rider would fly off and land on a vinyl covered, thick foam pad. The crowd followed the fall with catcalls and jeers,

Darcy knew it wasn't a question of if, but when, she would be bucked off. When she got to the front of the line, she fished out her money and smiled at the operator.

"Take it easy on me at first will ya? I haven't tried this for a while."

"Sure, sweetheart. Settle that cute little butt in the middle there. Don't forget to hold on tight with your knees." The guy's brown eyes twinkled at her and he flashed her a smile.

Darcy squished across the mat and threw her leg over the padded, leather covered contraption. She got a white-knuckled hold on the leather handle, waved to the guy with the chocolate eyes, and he turned on the bull.

At first, it gently rocked and dipped. Soon it began to spin, but still slowly. Darcy caught sight of Liz on the far edge of the crowd.

"Hey, girl!" Liz shouted at her.

"Yee-Haw!" Darcy shouted back as the bull jolted her to the left.

She scrambled to keep her seat, and it spun to the right and dipped, jerking her arm so hard, she almost let go. What followed was a progressively energetic ride that ended, predictably, with Darcy on her butt, trying to make her eyes focus.

Liz struggled to steady her as she got off the deeply cushioned landing area.

"You did fine. It must be like riding a bicycle. You never forget." Liz dragged her back toward the bar.

"Another Bud for my bud," Liz ordered once they got back and squeezed into a place at the bar.

"How many have you had?" Darcy asked.

"Let me pay for them, Ms. Moreland."

Darcy spun around to see who had offered, and jostled into a tall young man, dressed in a bright yellow western shirt with white piping and snap closures rather than buttons. He managed to look gawky and earnest at the same time.

"Jason Ford, ma'am. Pleased to meet you, finally." He touched the brim of his hat.

A bit surprised, she peered into his young face. "Are you even legal?"

He smiled and slapped some crumpled bills onto the soggy bar. She had yet to pick up the beer he'd paid for.

"Ya want to see my ID?"

"I'm not so old that I don't know everyone has a fake ID at one time or another. Hell, I used to have a friend who made them."

"Seriously," he handed her the wet can. "I wanted to thank you for being so nice to Stacie the other day. She's taking all of this real bad. I guess I am too. Bad enough Bridget is dead, but now the cops are questioning all her friends and stuff."

Darcy sipped on the beer, wanting to prolong the conversation. "Stacie a good friend of yours too?"

"You could say that. When you look like me, you get to be the 'good friend' or nothing." There was some slight acid in his tone.

Darcy studied at him for the first time. He looked almost like a caricature of a cowboy. He was tall and lanky with an overlarge Adam's apple that bobbed nervously in his scrawny throat almost hypnotically.

His non-descript brown/black hair stuck out in tufts from under a Tom Mix style hat. Darcy's heart began to pound in her chest.

Get hold of yourself, she told her brain frantically and tried to think of something non-confrontational to say. He couldn't be the only guy in the world to have a hat like that. For heaven's sake, there must be hundreds of them.

"I think you're being too hard on yourself, Jason."

Jason took a deep swig of his beer. "Kind of you to say that ma'am." He smiled and revealed a mouth full of slightly crooked teeth topped with a moist, protruding gum line.

"I, ah—nice hat. It looks like the real old-fashioned kind."

"Yes ma'am." He smiled down at her. "It's an old one. Belongs to my dad. He lets me borrow it now and then." He took another sip of beer and his eyes roamed over the crowd.

Darcy relaxed. Jason wasn't the Marlboro Man, but he had an unassuming charm that reassured her.

"You here with friends?"

"Actually, Stacie's over there and the rest of our crew is scattered all to hell and back. Well, again, thank you for your kindness, ma'am. You be careful now." He smiled his uneven smile and Darcy found it endearing.

"I will, but you be careful too, Jason. You and your friends could get in trouble." Yuck. Darcy cringed inwardly. She sounded like her mom.

"I will, ma'am. I'd better go round 'em up. We all rode here in my pickup. Night." He actually tipped his hat this time.

Darcy was chuckling to herself about Jason alarming her. He was a young, gangly kid when all was said and done. She sipped her beer slowly and watched Jason join Stacie and some other kids not far away. Jason was leaning in so close to Stacie their heads almost touched. Darcy watched Stacie raise her head and looked straight at her, then away quickly. Something didn't feel right. She couldn't shake the feeling.

Moments later Liz dragged up a tall young man in her wake. "Darcy, this is Greg Murphy, the guy I was telling you about."

Darcy looked up at Greg, who was handsome in a non-classical way. His nose looked like it had been broken awhile back and he had soft green eyes under slightly bushy brows. What made him attractive though, were his genuinely warm smile and the gently protective arm he had slung across Liz's shoulders. He was hooked.

"Hi, Greg. Microwave Engineering?"

"I know." He laughed at her scrunched-up face. "Sometimes I just say I'm a cook at Burger King."

Darcy's ears felt deadened after the blaring noise, but the band had stopped for a break, so they could actually hear each other.

"How'd you two meet? Oh wait. I remember. In line at the post office. Liz dropped an armload of mail and you helped her pick it up."

Liz laughed "Good save, Darcy. Sometimes I'm not sure you listen to me when I tell you stuff."

"Excuse me for second," Darcy said. "I'll be right back." She put her beer down on the closest available table and then began to wind her way toward Jason and Stacie. She took it slow stopping to talk to friends along the way. She didn't want to make it obvious. Eventually she ended up with her back to the two teens, who were engaged in a heated conversation.

"I'm telling you; she don't know a thing. I just talked to her. She couldn't of been nicer," Jason said.

"I hope you're right. I am so sorry. This is all my fault. I should have never given you that stuff of my brothers. How could I be so stupid?"

"Well it's not like you held a gun to my head to give it to her. We had no way of knowing she'd go all limp like that. It was an accident. Stop crying, Stacie. People are looking at us."

Darcy felt like she been punched in the stomach. Did she just hear those two kids confess to Bridget's murder? She had to go tell Liz she had to leave. She needed to call Hank. She barely rejoined Liz and Greg when Liz pointed toward the front doors.

"Oh, hey," Liz said. "Isn't that your friend Hank over there?"

Darcy spun around and saw Hank and two uniformed officers push through the crowd to the other side of the room.

She started to walk in his direction and skidded to a halt when she saw the officers and Hank confront Jason. She couldn't hear a word they were saying, but she watched in horror as one officer began to cuff Jason and drag him forward.

Frantically pushing and prodding, she fought her way through people standing around gawking at the small drama unfolding before them. She eventually forced her way to the small circle comprised of Hank, Jason, two officers and Stacie Rogers.

"Hank, I have to talk to you." Darcy pulled on his arm.

Hank spun around and glared at her. The officers were first

surprised then amused at her preemptive interruption. Jason and Stacie looked wary and apprehensive.

"Stay out of this, Darcy."

The second officer secured Stacie's hands behind her back as well.

"But Hank, I really need to talk to you. It's important!"

Hank and the two officers ignored her. The uniforms looked at Hank, who nodded. The officer began to drone on, Mirandizing the youngsters as they marched them from the bar.

Darcy stared at Hank and took a step back. He looked terrifyingly glacial.

"Lady, don't you ever interfere like that again."

He had said it softly, but Darcy felt like he'd punched her. By the time she had her breath back, he'd left.

Darcy chased after him.

"Hank! Hank! Wait!"

Hank turned and looked at her. Out of the corner of her eye, she could see the officers loading Jason and Stacie into separate patrol cars.

"I'm sorry. I shouldn't have meddled . . ."

"Damn right."

"They're kids, Hank. They may be stupid, but I don't think they're intentionally malicious. I talked to Stacie the night of Bridget's death and I just talked to Jason.

"Those *kids* are being arrested on suspicion of kidnapping Abby McNeil and your dog. If you hadn't behaved like a pissed-off-Princess when I called earlier, I'd have given you a heads-up."

"I was just about to call you. I overheard some of their conversation. They may be guilty of more than just kidnapping Abby and Mac."

Hank swung around and looked at her. "Like what?"

Darcy watched as the two patrol cars left the parking lot. "Are you going back to the station?"

Hank's face hardened. "Like what?"

"If you're going back to the station, I could go with you and tell you what I heard."

"Is this about getting the story, Ms. Moreland?"

"Partly, she admitted, but I am worried about them, Hank. They strike me as scared and really upset. "

"We rarely use enhanced interrogation techniques on our suspects these days, Ms. Moreland." Hank put his hand at her back and nudged her toward his pickup. "I'll give you a lift back to the station, but no special access. Is that understood?"

"Absolutely! I just have to tell Liz I'm going with you, so she won't worry. I will only be a sec."

"Make it fast," Hank said as he slid into the cab of his truck.

Darcy ran back into the bar. Scanning the crowd, she anxiously looked for Liz. There were too many tall men in too tall cowboy hats. Thanks to her unquenchable spirit of curiosity and love of drama, Liz found her first.

"My God. Darcy. What's going on?"

"Liz, I need go to the station with Hank. I'll catch up with you later and tell you what I find out if I can."

"You're not going anywhere until you tell me what's going on."

"Damn it, Liz. This is an emergency. Hank's arrested Jason Ford and Stacie Rogers for the kidnapping, but I think it's much worse than that. I'll call you as soon as I get any news. I promise."

"Okay go!"

"You're the best." Darcy sprinted toward the door almost knocking into a couple who were coming through. "Sorry. Sorry." she shouted over her shoulder. She was breathless by the time she slipped into the cab of Hank's pickup and pulled the door shut.

Hank put the truck in gear and eased it slowly out to the road. It was still early, and the night show hadn't finished at the park, so the traffic wasn't too heavy. Hank continued to drive in stony silence as he headed over the viaduct.

"So, talk," he said finally without taking his eyes off the road.

"I was just standing by the bar with Liz and Jason came up to me and offered to buy me a beer. We discussed fake IDs, and I told him to be careful. He said he wanted to buy me a drink because Stacie told him I'd been so kind when she was upset about Bridget's death."

"Is that it?" Hank steered the truck off the viaduct onto Lincolnway.

"No of course that's not it. Jason went back and stood by Stacie. I caught them both glancing at me then looking away. Teenagers aren't particularly subtle. Anyway, I worked around until I was standing close but with my back to them."

"And?"

"And I heard Jason say that I didn't know anything. He told Stacie he'd just talked to me and I couldn't have been nicer. Then Stacie said it was all her fault. She said that she should have never given Jason something she got from her brother."

"What does that mean?" Hank glanced at her.

"I'm not sure exactly, but Jason said he was responsible because he gave it to Bridget. And then Stacie started to cry. Jason said how should they have known it would make her go all limp like that, and that it was an accident."

"So, you think they gave Bridget something like a drug that Stacie supplied, and Jason administered?"

"That's what it sounded like to me. What's going to happen to them, Hank?"

"Nothing good," Hank said as he pulled into his parking space by the station.

The police station was a couple of blocks up from the center of downtown. Pushing through the front double glass doors, Darcy followed Hank into the lobby which had all the warmth of a European Youth hostel. Lots of washable surfaces and nothing to dull the sound of clicking heels as they crossed the floor.

Hank walked up to the receptionist. "This is Darcy Moreland a reporter from KCWY. I need to get her statement. I'll come out and get her when I need her." Hank turned to Darcy. "Stay put." He walked through some doors at the side of the reception desk.

Darcy sat in a low slung, vinyl-covered chair. She tried looking out the large windows that faced the street but not much was going on yet. It was still early.

She waited, not patiently, but quietly, leafing disgustedly

through a three-year-old copy of *Field and Stream*. Bored, she tossed it back on the table.

"Ms. Moreland?" the woman behind the desk beckoned her forward.

"Yes?"

"Detective Nelson said to be sure you waited for him."

Darcy could tell by the look on the receptionist's face she was convinced Darcy had attained the equivalent of a Papal Dispensation. She smiled as if in congratulations.

"My own damn fault," Darcy said mostly to herself.

"Beg pardon?" The young woman raised her perfectly plucked eyebrow at her.

"Sorry. Talking to myself." Darcy smiled and walked out the front doors. She leaned against the smooth stone surface of the building and tried to let the soft summer night air calm her nerves.

If she felt a twinge of doubt, she mercilessly repressed it. She pushed the speed-dial number for Hank and waited. She hoped he hadn't shut off his phone.

"Darcy!" Hank barked in greeting. "You'd better be in trouble and there'd better be blood."

"I've been more than cooperative through this whole mess . . ."

"I can't waste time with this conversation. I will record your statement and then I'll send you home. Is that clear?"

"But eventually I will be able to release a story, right?"

She waited for a reply, but the phone went dead. She was about to call him back when she saw him storm through the door. He glowered in her direction.

"Come on."

"I've had more gracious invitations in my life," Darcy said as she swooped past him into the lobby once again.

He came up behind her with his hand in the small of her back. "Don't push me, Darcy."

CHAPTER 17

Hank steered her into the hallway by the interview rooms. He pointed to a hard-wooden bench. "Sit here until I'm ready to take your statement. I trust you know better than to make any calls while you're waiting."

"I get it, Hank. I won't do anything to jeopardize the investigation. I promise." Darcy looked up at Hank towering over her.

"Are they both in there?" She gestured toward the door in front of her.

"No. Jason's in this room and Stacie's in the other," he pointed to the door farther down the hall. "Stacie is lawyering up, but Jason's dad said he would come down and see what the fuss was about first. Jason waived his right to remain silent, so they're questioning him now."

Hank left her there to go into what Darcy assumed was an observation room. She got up and wandered over to the room Jason was in. She could see Jason through the small, reinforced pane of glass. She stood off to the side so no one could see her looking in. Seated at a metal table across from one of the officers Jason was slumped forward holding his head in his hands. His hair stood up in spikes because he kept running his fingers through it. His father's prized hat was off to the side of the table, placed brim up.

Darcy couldn't hear anything, but she watched Jason sat up straighter, crossing and uncrossing his gangly legs, and taking a sip from the soda can in front of him. The officer continued to question him, but Jason kept shaking his head back and forth, finally dropping his head into his hands. Darcy couldn't tell whether he was crying, or just trying to think.

When Jason lifted his head, Darcy got her answer. Tears streamed down his face, and he rubbed them away with the back of his hand. Darcy could tell he was explaining, almost pleading. The crying continued, and his nose and eyes got red. The officer stood up and walked to the door. Darcy barely had time to rush back to the bench. She sat on the edge facing the lobby as if she didn't know or care what was going on in interrogation.

She sat very still and watched the officer pull out a box of tissues from the supply closet, then he reentered the interrogation room. Darcy was just thinking how nice that he gave Jason some tissues when the other officer came out once more. He walked to the interrogation room Stacie was in and knocked on the door.

Darcy watched the two officers began a soft-voiced consultation. She scooted slowly across the length of the bench to get close enough to hear.

"The kid is taking full responsibility for everything. He says the girl was only trying to help him. She gave him some kind of drug to use on the victim so she would be more responsive. They didn't expect her to fall out of the ride."

"Does the kid have a lawyer yet?"

"No, but his dad's on his way. He's 18 so we can question him without his dad here, but I don't think he realizes how much trouble he's in. Has the girl said anything?"

"Nothing of any substance. She's waiting for her dad and a lawyer, but she just keeps saying it's all her fault."

"Well at least we're not short on confessions. I'm going to leave the kid alone for a while till his dad gets here."

One of the officers went back into the room Stacie was in, while the other headed down the hallway. Darcy got up and began to pace. Hank came out of the observation room.

"Well, now what?" Darcy asked.

"We wait."

Darcy folded her arms across her chest. She didn't care if the second coming erupted in the middle of the hallway she wasn't going to budge.

"Would you like some coffee? It's likely to be a long night."

Darcy unfolded her arms startled by his offer she smiled up at Hank. "Yes, thank you."

"Don't worry. It's only a small truce. We don't have to sign any peace accords." Hank moved toward the break room down the hall, but Darcy caught up with him.

"Hank, I'm sorry I have been such a pain in the ass lately," she offered by way of making amends.

He smiled at her. "I'm getting used to it," he said over his shoulder and continued down the hall.

Darcy sat down again. She wished she could ask Jason why. Why had he frightened her with the threats and the kidnapping? From what she saw tonight, he didn't strike her as someone who would terrorize someone for the fun of it. She was well and truly baffled.

Hank returned minutes later with two small Styrofoam cups, full of steaming liquid. After the first tentative sip, Darcy was sure it wouldn't fit even the kindest definition of coffee.

"They only had powdered creamer. Hope it's okay." Hank canted his hip leaning against the wall by the bench.

"You know, you can sit by me. I don't bite." Darcy gestured to a place beside her.

Hank raised his eyebrow at that, and Darcy blushed remembering his shoulder she had nipped when they had tussled on the sofa.

"You don't have to bite to be venomous." He smiled at her when he said it, but Darcy knew he meant it.

"Okay, so I've been a little cranky,"

"Cranky? I've seen convicted felons behave better than you."

"I get it. What's going on now?"

"Stacie's father's here with a lawyer and Jason's father's here without one."

"Now what?" she looked to Hank. He had that twinkle in his eye and his lips were twitching with suppressed humor.

Darcy narrowed her eyes at him. "So help me, if you say 'wait' one more time, I'll . . ."

Hank chuckled at her. "It's straightforward. When the lawyer comes, he will will give Stacie basic instructions about what to answer and what not to, and if one of her parents have arrived, we'll resume the interrogation."

"That sort of translates into 'wait' doesn't it?" Darcy leaned back in on the bench and narrowed her eyes.

"With the promise of action in the near future. Yes. I have to get back in there. Will you be okay here?"

Darcy nodded and watched Hank going to the observation room. She set her coffee down. A female officer came through from the lobby leading a small parade. A tall, lanky man who looked like an older version of Jason, was guided into the first interrogation room. Another man who looked frazzled as if he just rolled out of bed was walking swiftly behind the officer with a lawyer type trailing behind. For the fraction of time the doors were opened Darcy could see both parents.

Jason's dad stood with his hands on his hips, "What the hell is all this about?" he shouted. Darcy could see Jason raise his tear-stained face toward his dad just before they closed the door.

Darcy shifted her attention to the other interrogation room. She could see Stacie jump up throw herself into her father's arms begin and to cry. "It's all my fault!" She began to babble to her father. Her lawyer tugged at her arm to warn her to watch her words, but she shook him off.

"Leave me alone. I'm sick of this. I want it to end now." Stacie practically screamed. Her father led her back to her chair and whispered something in her ear. Someone shut the door, so Darcy couldn't hear anything else.

She took another taste of coffee, grimaced, and headed toward the break room hoping she could doctor it up, so it was at least palatable.

The ancient coffee pot was down to about one more cup. Darcy decided to make a fresh pot. She had been a waitress when she was in college, so she knew how the apparatus worked. Instead of using the tap water from the stained sink, she rinsed out the pot then went over to the water cooler and filled the pot with the filtered water. She doubted it would make any make any perceptible difference, but it was worth a try.

She set up the coffee pot and waited for it to perk through. She was just rinsing out her cup to try the new brew when Hank came back into the break room.

"What's going on?" Darcy asked.

"They told them both about the forensic lab evidence that they collected the fingerprints, tire tracks, the threads Abby dug out." Hank poured himself a cup of fresh coffee and took a sip. "This is almost decent. Did you make this?"

"Yeah, I had to do something to fill my time. How did the kids react?" Darcy went over and sat at the Formica topped table.

Hank sat across from her pulled out his small notebook and pen. "I need to get your statement."

"I told you already. I overheard the conversation between Jason Ford and Stacie Rogers at the Cowhand Bar. Stacie said she was sorry she gave Jason something to give to Bridget. Jason told her it wasn't her fault. There was no way they could have predicted she would fall out of the Ferris wheel. That's pretty much it in a nutshell. What did they give her?"

"I can't tell you that," Hank said. "I can tell you that their testimony corroborates what you overheard."

"Can you at least tell me why they kidnapped Mac and Abby?"

"Pretty much as you figured. They were hoping you'd stop being so nosy. I could've told them it was a wasted effort."

"It makes sense now why Stacie tried to steer me away from Jason and even Sam. So a drugged, pregnant, Bridget was dragged onto a Farris Wheel and fell to her death. Is that it?"

"Basically. There are some more bells and flourishes, but that's the basic story."

"Jason was in love with Bridget, and Stacie was trying to help them out. Let me guess, Stacie was interested in Sam and offered Jason up to Bridget as a consolation prize." Darcy swirled her plastic stirrer around in her coffee.

"How did you know Stacie was interested in Sam?" Hank asked.

"It just makes sense. Sam isn't the kind of guy to stick around once he finds out he's gotten a girl in trouble, and Stacie would think that Jason would have a chance if Bridget were on the rebound and needed a friend."

"It could be Jason killed Sam to avenge his treatment of Bridget." Hank theorized.

"That's just absurd," Darcy said. "They barely killed Bridget. And that just by being clumsy and stupid."

"That's kind of like being 'a little bit pregnant' isn't it? I never heard a corpse claim he was 'barely dead.'"

"You know what I mean. Those kids are guilty of bad judgment, and cowardice, but the murder of Sam Carson was bloody and premeditated."

"How many murders have you seen?"

Darcy held her tongue, shifting her focus to her coffee. "What now?"

"Now, they'll be booked and detained tonight, and probably arraigned in the morning.

Darcy let out a deep, heavy sigh.

"It's simple when you know why, isn't it?" Darcy turned to Hank.

"Most crimes are. Human beings like to think they're complicated, but on the most basic levels, pain, fear, or love, a human being is primitive. You can dress all that up in its Sunday Best and send it off to church, but those are the realities."

"Why Hank Nelson, who knew you were a philosopher?"

Chagrined, Hank cleared his throat.

"I'm off duty now. You want to get a beer?"

"I'd love to wash the taste of this from my mouth. You bet."

"Give me a few minutes to check out. I'll meet you out front."

"Okay. I'm glad you gave me a ride here. If I had wrecked Liz's car there would've been a lot of pain and fear coupled with primitive behavior."

"Not to mention a possible DUI" Hank laughed and held the door open for her.

It didn't take long before Hank joined her, and she climbed

into the cab of his pickup. By tacit agreement, they went to a small bar off the beaten track and away from a lot of the rodeo celebration traffic.

They found a hole-in-the-wall bar off 17th and decided it looked deserted enough. The bar was empty except for a couple cuddling in the far corner.

Darcy smiled up at Hank. "Cute, huh?"

"They should get a room," he muttered to her.

Finding a quiet table, they sat, and Hank began to rub the back of his neck to release the kinks.

"Want me to do that for you?" Darcy asked.

Hank smiled at her. "I wouldn't turn it down."

"Okay. Later. We'll get a room." She waggled her eyebrows at him. He answered with a ghost of a smile. Darcy knew he must be tired.

They ordered a couple of beers from the waitress, an attractive woman in her early thirties with frizzed mousey brown hair and large hoop earrings that almost reached her shoulders.

"Not much action here tonight," Hank commented to her when she returned with the beers.

"No," she answered. "Our regulars will come back after circus leaves town." She smiled, popped her gum, and wandered back to the bar.

Hank waited until they were alone again.

"One down, one to go."

"Your math's off. It is two down, one to go. One death and one kidnapping. I must say, I'm relieved to have those questions answered." Darcy said.

"Cold comfort for the Emerson family though," Hank swigged back his beer.

"Every journey of a thousand miles begins with one step," Darcy quoted.

"Don't go getting oriental all over me unless it includes one of those walk-on-the-back massages. I could go for that."

"What do I get for services rendered?" Darcy teased. Hank smiled at her and winked suggestively.

"Before we leave the topic altogether, tell me what's most likely going to happen to Stacie and Jason."

Hank leaned back in his chair sighed and took a drink. "They'll probably be charged with involuntary manslaughter, obstruction, and kidnapping. Stacie will probably be tried as a juvenile, but Jason, since he was older and more actively involved, might be tried as an adult."

"How long will they have to . . ." Darcy stopped. She couldn't finish the thought.

"Be in prison?" Hank finished for her. "Depends on how their lawyer pleads it. I'm guessing that Stacie's lawyer will want to separate her case from Jason's. She provided the idea, the drug, and helped with the cover up. Poor Jason was stupid enough to follow her lead."

The waitress hovered nearby, but Hank waved her off. He peeled some bills from a small wad and left them on the table.

"Drink up," he said, finishing the last sip in his bottle.

Darcy raised her eyebrows and smiled. "Sometimes impatience in a man is amusing."

"Puppies are amusing. Little boys playing T-ball are amusing. I don't feel the least bit amusing. Drink it or leave it." Hank stood and waited.

"Don't rush me . . ." Darcy said, but tipped her beer empty.

As soon as her bottle returned to the table, Hank pulled out her chair. Darcy stood and flashed him a grin over her shoulder. His blue eyes had turned smoky and his lips thinned in resolve. Darcy felt a tickle of anticipation dance across her nerves.

"You have no way of knowing this," Darcy said as Hank opened the door to his truck, "but I'm not usually so . . ."

"Easy?" Hank asked and cocked his eyebrow.

"I was going to say acquiescent, malleable, seducible . . ." She slid into the passenger seat.

"Easy." Hank slammed the truck door closed, but not before Darcy heard his low chuckle.

She wanted to retaliate, but all empirical evidence was on his side. She practically dropped into his basket like a ripe peach at harvest time.

She'd never taken sex casually. Kevin called her the last virgin in captivity. She wasn't really a virgin when she met him, but she was pretty uninterested in sex. She had been with a couple of guys in college, but nothing serious. Her experiences had been clumsy, painful, and messy.

She started to think her lack of interest in sex was because she was frigid. She was discovering frigidity was not a problem for her, at least not with Hank. She was unnerved and a little embarrassed at how eager she always was to be with Hank. She always felt she was on a precipice. She had never felt so primal with another man. Maybe it was all the drama and fear, but she seemed to have zero control when she was around him.

Hank started his truck. "I don't claim to know much about your last relationship . . ."

"This is not a relationship." Darcy snapped, then cringed inside, mortified by her automatic reaction.

Hank was silent. He let his breath out slowly as if fighting for control. "Okay. We can table that hot button item for later."

"Are you going to give me details of your last relationship?" Darcy asked.

"I haven't been in a relationship for a long time."

"How long?" she pressed.

"Embarrassingly long. Can we stop this discussion?"

"Sure," Darcy said, but she couldn't control a small smile.

They drove to her apartment in silence. When Hank's truck pulled up in front of the Algonquin, Darcy rested her hand on the door handle.

"I guess I'm more tired than I thought. Maybe we'd better call it a night." Darcy swung the door open, but before she could negotiate the long drop to the street, Hank was in front of her with his hands clamped around her waist. He swung Darcy in front of him, closed the door, put his hand at the small of her back and began prodding her forward.

Darcy tried to turn around and face him, but the pressure was both gentle and insistent. "I think I need to go to bed," Darcy glanced up at the large man who had shifted to walking beside her.

"No argument there," Hank continued helping her up the front steps of the building.

"I mean alone."

"I know what you think you mean," Hank opened the front door of the building.

Darcy managed to spin around. By now, they were through the lobby and on the steps leading to the second floor and Darcy's apartment. Darcy was a couple of steps up. It gave her the advantage of being eye level with Hank.

"Hang on one minute. What happened to 'no' meaning no?" Darcy braced her hand on his chest and felt the steady beat of his heart against her palm.

Hank smiled at her. "Ya know Will Rogers used to say 'There are two ways of arguing with a woman. Neither of 'em works.'" The blue of his eyes softened once more, and the surrounding crinkles made her stomach jump. "You did say you wanted to go to bed, didn't you?"

"Nelson, you know exactly how . . ."

"Yes, I do know how . . ." Hank leaned in and nuzzled the soft skin under her ear.

Darcy didn't want to acknowledge the sizzle rushing down her spine. She pushed against Hank's chest, but he pulled her closer.

"We have two choices," he whispered. "We can continue to stand here in this dark, uncomfortable stairway . . ." Hank's mouth swooped over hers, kissing her silent when she started to interrupt. "Or we can go upstairs to your comfortable, if starkly furnished apartment, and avail ourselves of your totally adequate bed."

"We can't do this, Hank. We both know it will complicate an already complicated relationship."

Hank's next kiss was deeper and had heat. Darcy felt her bones liquefy. Her arms clinched around his neck and she began walking backward, pulling him up the stairs.

"Stop. You need to go home now. I find you attractive . . ."

"Attractive?"

"Yes, and if pressed, sexy . . ."

Hank pulled her closer. She pushed away once more.

By the time they reached her door, Darcy was breathless, and it had nothing to do with climbing the stairs.

"I am serious, Hank. Go home."

Hank blinked once, then touched the brim of his hat, and turned to leave. Darcy wasn't sure she hadn't just made the biggest mistake of her life.

CHAPTER 18

THE BRIGHT SUNLIGHT WOKE HER. She had dreamed of Hank, but when she opened her eyes, it was Mac she was cuddling. Sensing she was awake, Mac began to lick her face. She remembered she had brought Mac home after Hank left.

"Yuck! Mac stop." Not the kind of kiss she thought she was going to get.

She swung her feet off the bed and stretched, satisfied by the successive pops along her spine.

"It was the right thing to do," she said to Mac. She didn't believe it herself.

She threw on her clothes and took Mac for a walk. By the time she got home she had decided to call Hank and see if he was still talking to her.

The phone rang for a long time and Darcy was sure it was going to go to voice mail when Hank picked up.

"Nelson. What do you need?"

Darcy squeezed her eyes shut in frustration. She had really messed things up. Apparently, you didn't actually have to sleep with someone to screw up a relationship.

"Well, first I want to apologize for last night." She waited. No response. "I know I was sending really mixed messages." She rushed on. No response.

Okay official, she thought. "I was also wondering when I can release the details from last night?" She thought for a second and clarified. "I mean about Stacie and Jason?"

"Not today. I have to go out to Doc Emerson's this morning and let him know what happened. Even when you do the story, I am not sure you can name names. I'll have to check."

"I can't wait the whole day to release this, Hank. Zach will be foaming at the mouth if the print media gets it before we do, and you know they will.

"I am not going to let poor Doc learn about how his daughter was killed on the Early Show."

"Okay. Point taken. Will you at least promise to call me as soon as you tell Doc?"

There was a long pause. Darcy was fairly sure she was in no position to ask for favors.

"If you promise to go to dinner with me tonight."

"You're not mad at me?"

"Darcy, I'm not 16. I've been told no before. I would still like to see you. I think you have real potential."

"Potential for what?"

"You figure it out. I'll pick you up at 6 unless I hear differently from you. Okay?"

He hung up. Darcy caught her reflection in the window. She was smiling a big Cheshire cat smile.

She couldn't wait to tell Abby about Stacie and Jason. She also wanted to tell her about Hank. Not exactly dressed for prime time, in T-shirt and jeans, she sprinted down the stairs.

"Well, good morning." Abby smiled, and Mac pranced around her feet.

"You look wonderful," Darcy said as she bent down to pick Mac up.

"Pretty fancy, huh? I don't know why women stopped wearing hats. You'd have thought they would've come back after Princess Di."

"Turn around and let me look at you."

Abby did a model spin. "I don't know why they gave me a dress with a bustle. I have my own after all. Comes from sitting too long at a desk correcting papers."

Darcy chuckled, but she did think Abby looked wonderful. Her dress was damasked silk in a dark green color, perfect for Abby's English rose complexion. The glorious hat was trimmed in the same fabric with the addition of peacock feathers and tule. She looked picture perfect with matching gloves and a parasol.

"Did they actually give this to you from costume supply? It's just gorgeous."

"Well, technically yes. For several years now I've had them set this outfit aside. Since I'm a regular rider they don't mind the accommodation. I won't tell you how much time it took initially to put this together. Going through all the stacks, finding a hat, gloves, et al."

"You look stunning," Darcy said. "Why do you wear that gigantic ring over your gloves?"

"That's my hanky ring," Abby replied. "You're supposed to waive a hanky through the whole parade. After several years of dropping my hanky a friend taught me this trick. Using a costume jewelry ring worn over your gloves, you tuck the corner of your hanky into the ring to hold it. Haven't lost a hanky since."

"Ingenious."

"Well, I'd better dash. I'm meeting my friend for breakfast before we go. We're going to the mansion."

"Mansion?"

"Yes, dear. Carter-Nevil Mansion. While you were gone, the mansion was bought and turned into an Airbnb. Since it it's an authentic restored Victorian mansion, it does a great business. We're going for the breakfast part. And after, we're riding in the same carriage in the parade."

"Before you go, I need to tell you, they caught your kidnappers. They used the forensic evidence you provided to get a confession."

"Oh, my." Abby braced her gloved hand on her chest.

"There's more. They confessed to being partially responsible for Bridget's death. Jason fed her what they think was a roofie like drug Stacie gave him. Bridget passed out and fell out of the basket on the Ferris wheel."

"Oh dear. I've heard about those drugs. What will happen to them?" Abby reached out and scratched Mac behind the ears.

"Nothing good. There's the use of an illegal substance, involuntary manslaughter, kidnapping, and obstruction. I hope the court will take into consideration how young and stupid they are." Darcy finally put Mac down because his wriggling was distracting.

"How sad."

"Yes, it is. You have to keep this under your pretty little hat though because Hank hasn't told Bridget's father yet."

"Oh, that poor man! Well, I need to leave, or I'll be late." She waved her lace handkerchief gaily as she floated out the door.

After Abby left, she checked in with Zach who said he'd get back to her. She picked up a latte from the coffee shop down the street, and by the time she returned, all she craved was peace, quiet, and a moment to sit at her table and stare out the window.

Her phone went off just as she'd finished her coffee. She smiled at Mac rolling on his back in a puddle of sun.

"Hello, boss."

"How'd you know?" Zach sounded cranky.

"It's called Caller ID."

"Darcy. Busy here . . ."

"Okay, okay. Down to business. They've arrested the kidnappers and found they were also responsible for Bridget Emerson's death. Before you go ballistic though, I can't release any of the details until Hank Nelson gives me the go ahead."

"Ah hell. How long?"

She snapped her fingers at Mac to keep him from digging in the dirt under her potted fichus tree.

"Yeah, I know it sucks, but her dad hasn't been informed yet. It's kind of reasonable."

Darcy tilted the paper coffee cup up to slurp the drippy dregs.

"I want a follow up, Darcy. See if Doc will agree to be interviewed."

"Yes sir, boss. I'll go right over to Doc Emerson's as soon as Hank gives me the go-ahead. But truthfully, I'm going to ask Hank how Doc is first. I have no desire to add to his sorrow right now. Mind if I sit here and wait for the call?"

"Don't wait too long. Okay?"

"I'll call you when I get there to get scheduling information if he agrees to make a statement."

"Make him agree," Zach said, and hung up.

She ended the call and carried her phone into the bathroom while she took a shower. Forty minutes later, she was showered and dressed and still waiting for a call. She punched the number for Hank.

"Nelson," Hank said.

"Damn it. I am sitting here waiting."

"Sorry. We sent a man out there this morning."

"Well, you could've called a girl. How'd he take the news?"

"Not well."

"I suppose it wasn't much comfort to know it wasn't so much murder as a horrible mistake."

"Nope. I'll call you later."

"Yeah, I should go too. I'm going to drive out and see how he is and if I can get permission for a statement. I'll be back here at six." She clicked off.

She checked Mac's food and water and left.

Doctor Frank Emerson lived about fifteen miles north of town. The drive was relaxing on a summer's day, but Darcy knew it would be harrowing, and dangerous in the winter with a ground blizzard obscuring the road.

Today though, she felt extraordinary. The police had caught the kids who'd been threatening her. The cause of Bridget's death had been resolved, and all was right in her world. She felt a little guilty about that.

Although she dreaded interviewing Doc, she was strangely relieved Bridget's death was a horrible accident rather than something more sinister. Thinking about what was coming, Darcy jacked up the stereo and opened her sunroof, trying to remain mind-numb for the rest of the drive.

She slowed down to check the turn off-road and mailbox. After bouncing down a winding, washboard dirt trail for ten minutes she reached the Emerson's. The picture-perfect two-storied clapboard house she remembered from years ago sat at the road's end. It had a red roof and an inviting front porch with a railing that reached out and welcomed you.

Getting out of the car, she half expected to be met at the door. When you lived out this far, there wasn't much traffic. You could be sure if anyone pulled into your yard, they were either lost or coming to see you specifically.

She mentally braced herself to confront a still-sorrowing father. She used the heavy brass knocker vigorously, but there was no answer. Darcy tried to peek through the lace curtains covering the small windows on either side of the door, but she couldn't see anything.

Turning, she looked around the yard. The corral was empty except for a single roan mare. It was a beautiful piece of horseflesh and Darcy intuitively knew it had been Bridget's.

There was a large old-fashioned barn to the left. It had the kind of roof like a tipped-over boat complete with a lever arm and pulley for hoisting bales of hay to the loft. It looked like real barns were supposed to, she thought.

She decided to call out, so she wouldn't startle him if he was nearby.

"Doc Emerson? It's Darcy Moreland from KCWY TV, Ed Moreland's daughter," she added thinking her dad's name would give her more currency with Doc. "Doc?"

No answer. She walked slowly into the darkened coolness of the barn. It took a minute for her eyes to adjust.

There was a corner used to store saddles and tack, and another with bins holding oats for the horse. Buckets and pitchforks lined the wall as well as large shovels and rakes used to muck out the stalls took up most of the rest of the floor space.

"Doc?" she called out again.

No answer. She turned to leave when some hay sifted down from between a gap in the loft above and landed on her shirt.

"Doc?" she called out again.

She walked slowly toward the wooden ladder. Glad she'd worn her boots; she began to climb up.

Her head and shoulders barely cleared the loft floor before she heard him growl, "Git out! Leave me alone, damn it!"

Her eyes followed the sound to find Doc sitting on a hay bale in a deep, dark corner.

"Doc, don't you remember me? I'm Darcy. You know, Ed Moreland's girl. I'm so sorry for your loss. Can I come up?"

Doc peered at her through the dim light. "Did you know my Bridget?"

His voice was so sadly hopeful, it twisted Darcy's heart.

"Yes sir. Don't you remember? I used to babysit her for you and Mrs. Emerson a long time ago." Darcy stepped up one more rung. "I know she was a really special girl."

"She was that" Doc said. "She could sit a horse by herself when she was only three. Used to scare her mother half to death galloping around the corral." He laughed softly, but it sounded like a dry rattle.

"I understand she was a in Riders for three years. That's not easy when they have to try out each year." Darcy eased her butt onto the loft floor and sat with her legs dangling through the opening, afraid to move in too closely too quickly.

"The child didn't understand the concept of caution. It's why she got mixed up with that damned bulldogger. No idea how dangerous men are."

"I know I gave my father several gray hairs because of boys," Darcy smiled at him.

He looked at her, but she felt like he was looking through her. It gave her the willies.

"Ran off and met him. She let him. Let him . . ." He couldn't say the word.

"I know, sir," Darcy said softly so he wouldn't have to say it aloud.

"Damn rutting bull. Jumping good girls. Tempting 'em. Teasing 'em. My Bridget didn't know how to handle a horny little bastard like him." He lifted a bottle of Jack Daniels to his lips and drank deeply.

Darcy shivered. "Doc, why don't you come in the house and I'll make you some coffee?"

"Don't want coffee." He lifted the bottle again. "Want my Bridget back. She was the only thing stickin' me here after her mama died. The only thing I cared about. I tried to live an upright life for her sake. Well, her and her mama's. I'd hoped when the time came, I'd get to be with Katie again."

"I'm sure you will, Doc."

"Don't be stupid, girl. I'm never getting into heaven."

"Don't say that. You're a church-going man. Everybody respects you, Doc. I can't believe you wouldn't go to heaven when the time comes."

"What the hell do you know, girl?" He drank some more. Rivulets of whiskey ran down both sides of his mouth.

"My father always says you're one of the kindest men around. That's why you're such a good vet. He said animals sense a good man." Darcy pushed herself up and took a couple of steps toward the poor man.

"'And Cain said unto the Lord, my punishment is greater than I can bear.' Genesis."

Darcy stopped in her tracks. He sounded so hopeless, she felt tears well up.

"Oh, Doc. Come on down and I'll make you some breakfast." She walked over and sat on a bale across from him.

Then she saw what she hadn't seen before. Tied around his neck was a hangman's noose. Her eyes followed the rope from his neck tied to the loading arm that stretched outside the barn.

"'And if he smite him with an instrument of iron, so that he die, he is a murderer: the murderer shall surely be put to death.' Numbers." Doc quoted again. He seemed unaware Darcy had come close to him.

Darcy slipped her hand inside her pocket and palmed her phone. Holding it behind the bale of hay she was sitting on, punched in the speed dial for Hank, and dropped the phone carefully to the floor.

"Doc . . . Frank. I saw those kids. It was all a terrible, tragic mistake. Jason loved Bridget. He would've never do anything to intentionally hurt her."

"'Lust not after her beauty in thine heart.' Proverbs." He was rattling off scripture as if he were a robot.

"Yes, yes, I know it was wrong of him, but I think he cared for her." Darcy took a chance and patted his knee gently.

Doc looked at her and blinked. "Who are you again?"

"Darcy. Darcy Moreland. I'm Ed Moreland's girl." Forget the statement for TV, she thought. This man was in the throes of major despair.

"Always liked Ed. Steady man. Used to tell him he'd do to ride the river with. Old cowboy sayin.'"

"Yeah," Darcy smiled at him reassuringly. "I think I heard it somewhere before."

Doc cleared his throat and lifted the bottle.

"Doc, you know what Dad would say if he were here right now?"

"Can't say."

"He'd tell you to put the bottle away. It isn't doing you any favors."

A bark of laughter erupted from Doc's throat and surprised the pair of them.

"He most likely would, but he's still got his little girl."

Doc reached out a shaky finger and ran it down Darcy's cheek. She tried not to flinch. It felt terribly intimate.

Darcy looked at the devastated man. He had several days' growth of beard on his face. Probably hadn't shaved since Bridget's funeral. His eyes were red-rimmed and blood-shot. No doubt a combination of tears and whiskey. The more she looked at him, the more disturbed she became by the presence of the noose around his neck.

"Doc put the bottle down and let's go inside. Please?"

"See, I thought I was the revenger. You know like: 'The revenger of blood himself shall slay the murderer: when he meeteth him, he shall slay him.' That's from the book of Numbers, too. I looked them all up. All the verses on murder and killing and revenge."

"I don't understand what you're trying to tell me, Doc."

"I looked it all up, damn it. I wanted to make sure I got it right, so I'd see Katie and Bridget again. And I screwed it up, anyway."

Tears coursed down his cheek, but he didn't make a sound. It scared Darcy to the soles of her boots.

"Doc, what did you screw up?" Darcy could barely force the words from her dry throat.

Doc looked at her, solemnly studying her face as if it were the Rosetta stone and could unlock some mystery for him.

"I killed Sam Carson. I planned to. I meant to." He stated his confession as impersonally as if he were ordering a hamburger.

"You thought he'd killed Bridget and . . ."

"And an eye for an eye. Yup."

"But Doc. You were overwrought. They'll take that into consideration. People will understand the enormous grief consuming you."

"I called him and told him I had some things to give him. Told him Bridget said he'd given 'em to her. It was a lie, but the greedy little bastard had no way of knowing that. Probably hoping it was something valuable like jewelry.

"Anyway, I told him to meet me by the east stand before slack. I told him I'd meet him around six 'cause I was nursing this injured horse I needed to check on. Like I would give a damn about a horse when my baby was lying cold and dead. He was too stupid to live. Said he'd come.

"I waited for him in the stairwell. He was standing there looking down into the bullpens. I took my hunting knife out and came up behind him. I pulled his head to the side, so I could reach the artery and slit his throat in one swipe. He crumbled to the concrete floor. Then I slit his pants open, and I castrated him like you'd do any cull.

"I threw his balls into the bullpen, then I threw him. I figured it was a fitting end for a fornicator and a murderer. I was sure he'd killed Bridget because she'd told him she was pregnant. But he didn't. He didn't kill her. He ruined her, but he didn't kill her." He lifted the bottle once more.

Through the whole narration, Doc's voice had been flat, uninflected. Like someone repeating words by rote.

"Okay," she choked out. "It was heinous, but it's over and you're sorry."

"No! No!" Doc shouted. "I'm *not* sorry I killed him. That's the pitiful truth. He used my little girl. He used her like a piece of meat. I enjoyed killing him. See, that's why I won't be going to heaven to see Katie and Bridget. I enjoyed it."

He stared at Darcy and drank some more whiskey. She couldn't have looked away to save her own soul. It was the grisly sight of a man's spirit disintegrating right before her eyes.

"Why don't you talk to Father Bailey? He could grant you absolution."

"Yeah. I thought of that briefly but then I remembered you can't get absolution if you're not sorry and I ain't sorry."

"Wouldn't it be better to try to earn forgiveness by, I don't know, good works? Then you could go to heaven and see your family?" She was clutching at straws here and knew it.

God, why didn't someone come to help her? she thought. She was terrified he was spiraling deeper into the black hole of depression, and she didn't know how to stop him.

She couldn't be sure she'd punched the right number for Hank but anyone on her speed dial should be able to tell this was an emergency. She had to try to keep Doc from killing himself before someone came.

"You ever hear tell of an egg-suckin'dog?" Doc interrupted Darcy's panicked thoughts.

She smiled at him nervously. "Yeah. Wasn't it a country song way back? *Dirty Old Egg Suckin' Dog* Wasn't that it?"

"Yup. Well it's a song based on a truth. See when you got a dog who's supposed to keep the coyotes away from the hen house, you expected him to guard the chickens and their eggs. Once in a while, a dog'd start eating some eggs from the nests. Lots of time it'd take a while for the rancher to notice, but when the guy figured it out, he shot the dog. Know why?"

"Uhm . . . no."

"Because once a dog's got the taste in his mouth, you'll never break him of it. I'm like an old egg suckin' dog. I killed a man, and I liked it. I need to take myself out of this world."

"Doc don't make a decision when you're drunk and depressed.

Come down with me and we'll get you some help." She stood up, hoping he would follow suit.

He stared up at her for the longest time, set the bottle down gently, and stood too. She heaved a deep sigh of relief. But Doc wasn't taking off the noose nor moving toward the ladder. He was just standing there looking at her.

"Ya know, a long time ago, before we got so sophisticated with stuff like lethal injections, and a man had committed a crime requirin' hangin', his family and friends would come to watch.

"Sounds ghoulish, but there's a reason for it. They'd come to help him die quickly. They'd wait 'til the body dropped, and they'd grab his legs, so the added weight would kill him faster."

Doc stepped toward her and she instinctively backed up, but the backs of her legs bumped against the hay bale and she would've fallen except Doc grabbed her arms.

"I think Katie and Bridget sent you here to help me. You're my own personal angel of mercy."

Before she could react, Doc wrapped his arms around her waist and lifted her off the floor. He ran full tilt and jumped out the loft opening.

Instinctively Darcy threw her arms around his neck and wrapped her legs around his hips to keep from falling twenty feet. She didn't recognize her own scream.

She heard Doc gasp and gurgle and looked into his face.

It all happened in slow motion. She watched as his head lolled to one side and his eyes bulged as if surprised. She smelled the whiskey on his last breath mixed with the stench of the evacuation of his bladder and bowels.

She clung to him frantically while he kicked and twisted and then went still.

She heard Hank bellow her name as if from a faraway tunnel.

Darcy fainted dead away and dropped into Hank's waiting arms.

CHAPTER 19

HANK KNEW IT WOULD TAKE HIM A LONG TIME to wipe the image of Darcy hanging on to the corpse of Doc Emerson out of his memory.

Even when she dropped into his arms, and he collapsed in the dust from the weight of her fall, it took him a minute to register that she was warm, and whole, and uninjured.

She came to quickly, but then shock took over. She began to shiver, and her teeth chattered. Hank wrapped her in a blanket from the house and drove her into town to the emergency room. He called the station for someone to come pick up Doc's body.

Forty minutes later, Darcy was lightly sedated and released. Darcy's mother when called, insisted Hank bring her to their home. Darcy slept around-the-clock.

Grateful for the soothing numbness of the drugs, Darcy knew she'd have to 'cowboy up' as they say. She had to face the sheer shock of looking death in the face and the bone-deep sorrow she felt.

Zach had been wonderful. He told her he was really impressed how she had handled all the sordid stories.

"I had no idea what I was getting you into, Darcy, but you handled it like a champ. I am proud of you."

He'd told her to take however much time she needed. Her mother even made her favorite meal, beef stroganoff, and Abby brought her a basket of her much-loved scones. Hank called, but he was busy wrapping up the investigations.

She was fine, most of the time, but she dreaded the night. She knew as soon as she closed her eyes, the nightmares would start. Sometimes they were of Bridget falling at her feet. Everything moved in slow motion. More often though, she dreamed of her conversation with Doc before he jumped. Sometimes she dreamed that she had dragged him out of that hay loft, but most times she relived the horror of clinging to his dying body.

By the time Sunday rolled around, Darcy was ready to break out. She went to Mass with her folks. Later, she decided she wanted to go to the rodeo finals. Planning to stay for only a short while, she refused her father's offer of his tickets.

"I'll just watch from between the stands. My press credentials should get me that far. Stop worrying about me. I'm fine." she told them. She could tell they didn't believe her.

Like she had done countless times this past week, she parked in front of the PR office and walked to the midway and through the portal to the stands. She had no trouble finding a spot to view the rodeo.

She watched the Grand Entry of the Committee Chairmen. The CRD Riders, one rider short, galloped by as well. By the time Miss Cheyenne and her Lady in Waiting had appeared, Darcy wished she'd taken her dad up on his offer for the seat.

Her legs were getting shaky and her stomach was wobbly. She put her hand out to brace herself on the side of the stands. Feeling a strong hand grip her arm, she turned to see Hank.

"How'd you find me?" she asked.

"Your mom told me you were here. Let's get you a seat."

He led her forward and spoke softly to the volunteer who was controlling entrance to the pad. He smiled at her and let them in.

Once seated, Darcy felt a little better.

"How's the investigation going?"

"Off the record?" He smiled at her.

"Yeah. Way off."

"Well, we found some journals and notes in Doc's house.

Evidently he planned his hanging based on Tom Horn's."

"You mean the last guy hanged here in Wyoming? Doc was planning to rig the water weights and stuff?"

"No, but he studied how the gallows were set up with water containers, counterweights, ropes and pulleys. He was figuring on how short the rope would have to be and how much weight it would take to snap his neck without tearing his head clean off."

Darcy looked queasy and swallowed hard.

"He wasn't in his right mind, Darcy," Hank said softly.

"I know."

They sat silently in the warm sunshine. Darcy took joy in watching the white puffs of clouds float by in the crystalline blue sky. She took a deep breath of clear, crisp air and felt the tension in her neck and shoulders soften a bit.

The announcer began to read the names of volunteers from Cheyenne Days who had died that year. It was a long-standing tradition. Darcy recognized only a few of the names, but she bowed her head and said a small private prayer when they read Bridget and Doc's names.

By the time they began to read *The Cowboy's Prayer*, by Charles Badger Clark Jr., another tradition, she let the tears she had been holding, empty down her cheeks.

> . . . Forgive me, Lord, if sometimes I forget.
> You know about the reasons that are hid.
>
> You understand the things that gall and fret.
> You know me better than my mother did.
>
> Just keep an eye on all that's done or said
> And right me, sometimes, when I turn aside.
> And guide me on that long, dim trail ahead
> That stretches upward toward the Great Divide.

"Amen," Darcy whispered softly with Hank and the rodeo crowd. She brushed away her tears.

After the rodeo, Hank helped her move her stuff from her parent's home back to her apartment.

They stopped in to see Abby and pick up Mac. When Abby opened her door, she opened her arms and Darcy walked right into a surprisingly fervent hug.

When Abby finally released her, she held Darcy by her upper arms. Abby searched Darcy's face as if it could confirm that she was okay. Darcy knew she looked like a wreck, but even with careful makeup, she couldn't hide her lack of sleep.

"Come sit for a minute." Abby gently pulled Darcy to the sofa. Hank sat next to her holding her hand.

"The nightmares will fade eventually, and you'll be able to sleep again. You must trust in the restorative nature of our humanity. People we love die, and we think we'll never get over the shock and sadness of it, but we do. And then we feel guilty because we do, but that's the saving grace. I am much older than you and have buried my parents, my husband, and countless friends. I can't tell you the pain will go away forever. You'll think you've healed and then a song, or a scent, or a prized memory will slap you back. I can tell you that with each death you get stronger."

"I don't want to be stronger," Darcy said.

Hank squeezed her hand.

"None of us do but consider the alternatives. You can't forget, and you can't go around it. You have to go through it. It is life. Not the fun part, but somehow necessary to test us in a crucible and temper us into stronger souls." Abby bent over and kissed her cheek. "You were strong before this happened, and you'll be stronger now. I promise."

Hank helped her pack up most of Mac's stuff and they climbed the steps to her apartment, Mac trailing behind.

When Darcy unlocked the door, the comforting smell of soup fill the room. Abby had obviously set the table, made the soup simmering on the stove, and the salad that rested on the counter. She even left a bottle of Darcy's favorite Pinot Grigio in a wine cooler on the table next to a small basket with two small baguettes nestled into a red checked cloth to keep them warm.

Mac instantly curled up in a corner on his plaid blanket.

"It's good to be home." Darcy said as she snuggled under Hank's arm. "I am much blessed with you and Abby and all of my family and friends. I think I will try to concentrate on all the blessings in my life right now."

"Sounds like a good plan." Hank kissed her gently and gave her a one arm hug. He seated her on the sofa.

She snuggled deeper into Hank and she chuckled a little.

"What's so funny?" Hank asked.

"I was just thinking. All-in-all, it has been an eventful home-coming: two murders, one kidnapping and a suicide. Whatever made me think I was coming home for peace and predictability?"

"Well they say, 'home is where the heart is.'" Hank rubbed his cheek against hers, and she turned into his embrace.

After dinner they did the dishes. Darcy felt unaccountably shy, but she put her arms around Hank's waist. "Will you stay with me tonight?" she asked.

Hank bent down to kiss her in answer. His arms encircled her and pulled her close. She knew for a certainty she was home, and he was rapidly becoming her heart.

Ryan Erickson Elevate Photography

PAULLA HUNTER is a long-time resident of Cheyenne, Wyoming, the capital of the state. She lives in a historic downtown area of the city with her husband. She is a member of Rocky Mountain Fiction Writers, Sisters in Crime, and Wyoming Writers. She earned her B.A. from the University of Wyoming in English, Speech and Drama. She has a passion for history, reading, theatre, travel, and obviously writing.